The man who had rescued her pinned her to the wall.

He brushed his lips across her forehead and down her right cheek. The featherlight touch, there and gone in a few fleeting seconds, left Riley breathless.

Had she made a mistake thinking this was a good guy?

Putting a finger under her chin, he carefully tilted her head so that he could look into her eyes.

His intense gaze would have held her captive if his body hadn't. She detected a flicker of real wildness there.

Hell, had she made this guy up? Could she have banged her head that hard?

Because...

She was sure...

No. She wasn't sure at all, actually.

Riley winced when she heard the words that came out of her mouth next.

"But there's no such thing as werewolves."

The stranger's smile was like being bathed in white light.

Linda Thomas-Sundstrom writes contemporary and paranormal romance novels for Harlequin. A teacher by day and a writer by night, Linda lives in the West, juggling teaching, writing, family and caring for a big stretch of land. She swears she has a resident muse who sings so loudly, she often wears earplugs in order to get anything else done. But she has big plans to eventually get to all those ideas. Visit Linda at lindathomas-sundstrom.com or on Facebook.

Books by Linda Thomas-Sundstrom

Harlequin Nocturne

Red Wolf
Wolf Trap
Golden Vampire
Guardian of the Night
Immortal Obsession
Wolf Born
Wolf Hunter
Seduced by the Moon
Immortal Redeemed
Half Wolf
Angel Unleashed
Desert Wolf
Wolf Slayer
The Black Wolf
Code Wolf

Harlequin Desire

The Boss's Mistletoe Maneuvers

Visit the Author Profile page
at Harlequin.com for more titles.

CODE WOLF

LINDA THOMAS-SUNDSTROM

Recycling programs
for this product may
not exist in your area.

ISBN-13: 978-1-335-62967-8

Code Wolf

Printed in U.S.A.

Dear Reader,

Werewolves. Secret desires. Seattle cops who are much more than they seem and voluntarily police the streets for the monsters that prey on humans. Women, either human or Were, who catch a wolf's eye and incite passion unlike anything we can conceive of...

These things are the reason I write about werewolves, and why I love every minute of telling their stories. Add a full moon to the mix of tall, edgy, dangerous and gloriously sexy...and *look out*! We've got werewolves.

Whether genetic Lycans or newly initiated into the werewolf clan, my heroes are take-charge guys. They can be cops, detectives, rangers, district attorneys or emergency room surgeons by day, but they are all a bit beastly at night, especially during the full moon.

And yet each of my wolves possesses certain qualities that make me fall for them. High on that list are intelligence, loyalty, nobleness of heart and the desire to help others in need. They know how to keep secrets. They know what passion means, what a woman needs, and they are all looking for the perfect mate. (Linda raises her hand.)

I'm hooked on werewolves, and I hope you will be, too, after reading my latest book, *Code Wolf*.

Please do check out my website, www.lindathomas-sundstrom.com, to read more about my wolves, more about this Wolf Moons series and to keep track of what's coming up next. Connect with me on my Facebook author page, www.Facebook.com/lindathomassundstrom. Stop by and say hello. Let me know what you think of my tales. I'd love to hear from you.

Cheers—and happy reading!

Linda

To my family, those here and those gone, who always believed I had a story to tell.

Chapter 1

Detective Derek Miller howled at the moon...

And that call was answered.

He sprinted down a side street, careful to avoid the stares he'd have received if any of Seattle's human population saw him all wolfed up. Humans weren't in on the secrets of his kind, and it was best to keep things that way.

His lethal claws made driving as impossible as ignoring the moon would have been. That big, bright, full moon over his head. Thing was, the claws came in handy on nights like this, when bullets and the usual paraphernalia tied to the justice system wouldn't take down a supernatural enemy. And there were plenty of enemies like that around.

The air he breathed was pressurized and heavy with the odor of trouble. The enhanced capacities that came with being a werewolf made it all the more intense, when his preference would have been to avoid that smell altogether.

No such luck, though.

Full moons brought out the worst in everyone, no matter what species they belonged to. Who the hell knew the actual reason for that?

The moonlight that ruled Were shapes always made his job tougher—the job he was doing in order to get a jump on bad stuff before it happened. He took to the streets most nights around the moon's full phases, when the crazies came out to play, even though big moons made keeping his werewolf identity to himself in a city Seattle's size damn near unmanageable.

When the moon called, Weres obeyed.

Besides the obvious risks of being outed as an *Other*, working the night shift had its perks. He wasn't the only Seattle Were in law enforcement, and the bonus of having packmates for backup was important when another species showed up.

Not many folks would have understood about the presence of monsters, the way he and some of his friends did. And though most werewolves didn't classify themselves as monsters, humans around the world would have if they knew they weren't the only species sharing the place.

Derek was all right with that, though. He was a good detective and also the alpha of a two-dozen-strong werewolf pack that was helping to clear this city of the morbid creatures stalking it.

Running suited him.

Chasing bad guys suited him.

Tonight, he had a larger body, more muscle and longer hair, which were giveaways of his species. A slightly longer face and more feral features rounded out the look. Still, he might have been recognizable if viewed up close by someone who knew him well enough. And it was a fact that any guy running around Seattle shirtless wasn't normal even if there was a badge pinned to his belt.

Got to love those perks, though...

He used his enhanced sense of smell to break down scent particles so that he could follow the foul odor blowing in from the eastern part of the city.

That odor was bad news.

Unreleased growls rumbled in his chest like a bad case of heartburn as he inhaled.

Streets in the east were crowded with apartment buildings and lofts in renovated warehouses, where people were piled on top of each other. Singling out the source of that odor there could have been tricky, even for a werewolf. But he had no problem. There was nothing like that particular smell anywhere else. The foulness in the wind had a name, and that name was *vampire*.

He hated vampires.

Upping his game, Derek ran on legs that seldom tired. Any indication of vamp presence was cause for immediate action, and the packmate that had responded to his call would also be heading this way.

Keeping near to the shadows and squeezing between them, he skirted the public places people frequented on Friday nights, careful to avoid being seen. Detective Derek Miller was a wolf on a mission that required his full attention.

Bloodsucking parasites had become the bane of his existence for two years straight. He must have killed a hundred of them already, but for every one vamp taken down, five more popped up in its place.

Nighttime hours meant snack time for vampires. Old brick exteriors in the eastern portion of Seattle made those buildings easy to climb, and picking off people had become easier for bloodsuckers on the prowl.

Growling again, Derek hopped a curb. His boots were heavy, making stealth difficult. His size didn't help, either. Still, there was nothing to be done about that at the moment. Because his job was to protect and serve, Derek was already working on a creative reason to explain any human deaths that could possibly occur. Lately, that kind of creativity was not only imperative, but it had also become a full-time job.

Tonight's moon was going to be the equivalent of a giant dinner bell for fanged parasites. Luckily for this city's inhabitants, that full moon also gave him a leg up in dealing with them. In werewolf form, Weres were twice as strong as any human and meaner than hell when it came to trespassers with evil intentions.

He didn't like this, but he was used to the routine.

Come on, bloodsuckers. I know you're here somewhere.

The odor he had detected became noticeably stronger as he rounded a corner. In case he changed back to a more human form, the gun strapped to his belt was loaded with silver bullets, one of which could take down a vampire if the shooter had good aim.

A small dose of silver to the head or chest would send those undead bastards back to the kind of afterlife they should have been experiencing.

Of course, a sharp wooden stake would also suffice… though a proper staking would require meeting a vampire face-to-face and up close and personal. Which he'd never advise.

Following the fetid trail, Derek slipped into the narrow space between two buildings, where the atmospheric pressure he had noticed earlier got worse. He ended up in an alley that appeared to be deserted, but wasn't.

The stench he sought had competition here. Overflowing garbage receptacles lined the walls. Beer cans and paper littered the ground. Although there were no artificial lights, broken shards of glass glittered like gems in the thin streams of moonlight shining down from overhead.

Other than his breathing, there was a marked absence of sound. Yet somewhere in all that darkness, among the discarded detritus that could have masked their presence, a couple of pale-faced lunatics hid.

Her pale-faced lunatics. Minions of Seattle's vampire queen. Two of them, at least, were using this alley for their hidey-hole and probably waiting to do their Master's bidding.

Got you...

Derek took another deep breath to process the danger. The air here was rife with Otherness that only supernatural beings were attuned to. From experience, he had a good idea these vamps would be fledglings. The degree of foulness saturating the air hinted at this being the case.

There was no mistaking the metallic scent that pointed to the blood meal these vamps had recently ingested. The pair had been sloppy at the dinner table and were coated in the evidence. It was unlikely that their victim, or victims, had survived.

His next growl echoed off the mildewed walls, sounding like thunder.

I met your queen once, he would have told these abominations if he had proper vocal cords in his Were state. *I saw your grand dame near here on the night my ex-lover was almost killed.*

The thought sickened him to this day.

I know your Master's name. I've seen her face.

He had heard that vampire's name whispered during a midnight battle with her kind, and afterward had caught a glimpse of the black-haired soulless diva whose talent for drawing every bloodsucker within this city's boundaries to her side was no joke.

The fanged bitch was like a black widow spider, thriving in her lair while her creepy hordes fed off the living and created an army. *Damaris* was her name. Most divas only had one.

He owed her a good fight for personal reasons as well as professional, so Derek scanned the darkness with his claws raised, ready to do some damage.

As he waited, Derek adopted a wide stance and slowed his breathing. Seconds passed. The fangers would have to eventually acknowledge his presence, if they dared.

Derek was counting on his formidable appearance to provide an edge. His normal height of six-two stretched upward when he shifted. All that new muscle rippled with anticipation over how this might go down.

He moved his jaw, clenched his teeth. His face might have been more human than wolf, but it wasn't enough like a human to confuse the two species. It was helpful in this instance that one of Seattle's most decorated detectives looked like everyone's worst nightmare.

Come out, you filthy bastards.

Nothing moved. The vampires would be sizing him up and preparing their response. Finding and dealing with them like this was vigilante justice, but justice nevertheless. They couldn't be allowed to kill more of Seattle's citizens or break the spell that hid Were existence. For humans, the supernatural world didn't exist.

His pack and other packs like it policed the shadows, exacting payback on misbehaving monsters that preyed on the humans in this jurisdiction. The goal was to keep the peace and maintain Were secrets, and Derek had taken this goal to a whole new level after the woman he had loved left Seattle because of the influx of monsters.

There was also the fact that his ex-lover hadn't known

about his secret wolfish life and the moon that ruled his kind. But that was history.

His fault.

Long story.

The packmate he had been expecting silently slid into place behind him, barely ruffling the air. Derek didn't have to turn around to know who this was. Dale Duncan was a fearless cop and no stranger to things that went bump in the night. Officer Duncan was good to have around no matter what outline he presented to the world.

The two of them could have taken on a slew of vampires. These fledglings had to know it. Word traveled fast in underground circles.

Bathed in moonlight, he and Dale stood like sentries near the entrance to the alley. There was nowhere for these bloodsuckers to go. As newbies they'd be full of themselves and energized by their recent kill. Maybe they didn't yet know about all that ancient enemy shit between Weres and vampires, and that it continued today. Was it possible they believed vampires were the superior species?

When Derek's packmate growled menacingly, the ground shook. Near the opposite end of the alley, a tin can rolled.

"Monsters have to try to fit in now," Derek silently chastised. But the warning wouldn't have done much good if the vamps had heard it.

He added, *"Werewolves, for the most part, have evolved alongside our human counterparts and most of the time can fit in with the society surrounding us. You guys have obviously never gotten the memo."*

A slight, sudden wave of extra pressure in the darkness suggested movement. The back of Derek's neck tingled in acknowledgment of what that meant.

"Any minute now," Dale messaged.

What Derek failed to mention in all this was his anxiousness over finding himself less than half a block from the building his ex-lover had once occupied—the same building where real vamp trouble in Seattle had begun two years back. His pack had cleaned out this area after that event. Keeping the public from finding out about it had been a cleanup job worthy of the Nobel Prize.

So what the hell had happened?

Why were the vampires back?

Even the smallest twitch was a waste of energy, but Derek rolled his neck to ease some of the tension building there. Waiting made him angry. There were too many memories in and around this place.

When he heard the swish of a swipe of claws, he nodded. Dale had torn holes in his jeans, and the scent of blood filled the air. *"Smart move,"* Derek messaged. That smell might draw vampires lacking the facts about how bad furred-up werewolves tasted.

However, a positive outcome was never completely assured when dealing with fanged hordes that were almost subliminally fast on their feet and ruled by an outrageous thirst that no one alive could possibly have understood.

Derek dared a quick sideways glance to calculate the exact distance to the building he had often visited in the past in order to court and bed McKenna Randall.

Too damn close.

His nerves buzzed. His skin burned white-hot. Hell, he still missed having a talented bed partner.

"The place is cursed," Dale messaged to him.

Derek grunted in agreement.

Both of them knew what to expect here. There weren't going to be any surprises in this alley tonight, hopefully.

To catch more moonlight, Derek took a step forward. Silvery moon particles settled on his bare shoulders like a hot lover's breath, setting off a series of internal sparks that in turn started a chain reaction. All of that centered on the word *anger*. And okay, maybe also a more personal need for revenge.

Behind him, Dale was experiencing something similar and waiting for the signal to get this over with.

Tired of playing hide-and-seek, Derek gave that signal.

Chapter 2

Riley Price blinked back an almost supernatural wave of fatigue and unlocked her car without getting in. She leaned briefly against the cool metal of her silver sedan and glanced up at the moon, wondering if she should howl at that big round disc the way werewolves did in the movies.

She sighed instead.

The hours at work this week had been long and tough to get through, leaving little energy for extras no matter how fun those extras could have been. After her first days on the job, she could have used a little jolt of excitement. Listening to other people's problems day in and day out was exhausting, especially when she had a few fantasies of her own.

Wasn't that the premier joke about psychologists—that people in this kind of field went into it because of their own need for answers?

The boulevard was crowded with people coming and

going at 9:00 p.m. Shouts, laughter and revving car engines nearly drowned out the sound of the keys jangling in her hand.

And there was something else, wasn't there? Beyond those normal city noises, Riley could have sworn she heard another sound. Something that didn't quite fit in.

If she hadn't just thought about howling at the damn moon, she might have imagined that someone else had.

"It sure sounded like that," she muttered.

The back of her neck chilled. In spite of the common sense she had always been known for, she secretly wished for adventure. It was one of those personal issues she had to deal with. The desire for a little action was probably what was craved by every female who had done her schoolwork straight through and ended up in a job with no break whatsoever.

Riley Price, PhD. Helpful, empathetic, on her way to becoming successful and, these days, quite bland. Bland on the outside, at least. Deep inside her was where her more rebellious ways had always been corralled.

She turned back to the car, opened the door and slid carefully onto the seat, respecting the restriction of her black pencil skirt. But she didn't get both feet inside before that same eerie, slightly discomforting sound came again from somewhere in the distance.

A wolf's haunting howl?

"You know you have a vivid imagination," she reminded herself with a stern head shake. One strange belief too many and she, in spite of all her education in this area, would be in need of a psychiatrist's comfy couch.

How many times had she thought that she should have become a cop like her father and let out all of her pent-up energy? For cops, the world was viewed in black-and-white terms, without too many murky gray zones. As it was, her need for independence and a life of her own outside of law enforcement had dictated taking another route toward helping people. So here she was, several states away from her family in Arizona, and on her own.

One more head shake ought to do it.

"Wolves in downtown Seattle? Give me a break."

Feet in the car, key in the ignition, Riley released a slow breath and closed the door, then paused before starting the engine. Opening the door again might have been willful, but she did so anyway. She hoped to hear a repeat of that eerie sound and wished that things didn't actually have to be black and white in terms of reasonableness and reality.

She shivered at the incoming breeze of cool night air and was overtaken by a sudden onslaught of chills that weren't related to a change in the weather. Waves of ice dripped down the back of her neck to lay siege to sensitive skin beneath her baby blue sweater. She did hear that howl again, didn't she?

"I'm sure I did."

This third sound made it seem like there had been no mistake. Someone had howled. Not some*thing*, because everyone knew there were no wolves in the city and no such things as werewolves. So who, like her, was digging into the beauty and mythology of this full moon? Who, like her, had watched a few too many movies that had activated their imagination?

She could try to find out. Chase down those sounds. Meet that person. Though those ideas were intriguing, women weren't always completely safe on their own in a city the size of Seattle after dark. It wasn't that she was afraid of the statistics. Fear hadn't been part of her upbringing, and inquisitiveness was a trait that had been tightly wound into the strands of her DNA. But it wasn't wise to throw caution to the wind all at once for the sake of folly.

Somewhere out there a human being with a similar sense of fun and fantasy was having one on. Since moving to Seattle, she hadn't met anyone quite like that. Didn't that fact alone determine the need for a closer look?

Fatigue melted away. Riley was out of the car in seconds, listening hard, and issuing a whispered challenge. "Come on. Do it again. I dare you."

Cell phone in hand—she wasn't stupid, after all—she locked the car, turned toward the sidewalk and started out in three-inch heels that wouldn't let her win a race, but would get her far enough.

She hadn't experienced tingling nerves like this in some time. They drew her half a block to the east, where she'd still be within safety limits. Men and women strolled in both directions, oblivious to the finer art of adventure. None of them glanced up at the sky. Noise from the pubs and restaurants blurred her ability to hear much else.

When more chills arrived, along with a sudden awareness of being stared at, Riley slowed to glance at the man who leaned against the side of an open doorway. His face was half-hidden by the shadows of an overhead awning that spanned most of the sidewalk, and yet Riley knew he was looking at her in a predatory way. Not man-to-woman stuff. Something else. Something more.

With a tight grip on her cell phone, she passed by him, careful to avoid any kind of contact that might have been misconstrued as an invitation. She'd been fed those kinds of self-defense tips for breakfast in the Price household and knew them all by heart.

Show no weakness.

Be a predator, not someone else's prey.

Almost able to hear her dad say those words, Riley smiled, which would have been the wrong thing to do if she hadn't already put some distance between that creep

by the bar and herself. Nevertheless, she took one more
quick look over her shoulder…just before she felt the firm
grip of a hand on her arm.

Derek silently counted to five, nodded and took another step forward, hoping to taunt the vampires that were
hiding here into showing themselves. Possibly they were
going over their options for getting away, as if they actually had some.

Another step took him closer to the cans lining the
walls. The stench of rotting food was unbelievable. And
this was taking too damn long.

He kicked the closest can with the tip of his boot, providing more incentive for the fanged abominations to make
an appearance. Vampires had sensitive hearing and didn't
like noise.

He kicked the can again and it rolled sideways, spilling
what was left of its contents—unrecognizable stuff with
an unbelievable odor.

The challenge worked.

One of the vamps dropped from above the trash cans
as if it actually might have been half bat, as the old wives'
tales suggested. Its partner followed. They were a pair of
completely colorless creatures whose dirty and tattered
clothing suggested they might have recently crawled up
from the grave.

A ripple of disgust rolled over Derek.

Both of these guys were drenched in blood that was now
darkening. Tiny red rivulets of what had been some human's life force ran in tracks down the sides of their white
faces. Red-rimmed eyes peered back at him with dull, flat,
lifeless gazes. Whatever kind of voodoo had animated this
pair remained one of life's great mysteries.

Derek didn't waste any time in going after them. In this

instance, their newness to the vamp bag of tricks was in Were favor. The dark-eyed pair had speed, but he and Dale far outweighed them. When their bodies collided, the two vamp fledglings shrieked with anger, yellow fangs snapping, but couldn't escape the claws that snagged their rotted clothing.

After spinning his bloodsucker around in a circle, Derek tossed his opponent against the brick. The bloodsucker quickly rallied and was on him again in a flash with arms and legs flailing. The creep was a hell of a lot stronger than he looked.

Derek's muscles corded as he fought to send this ghastly creature back to its natural state of death. Actually, he was doing these monsters a favor, because who would have wanted to end up in such a sorry state?

He felt the breeze of snapping canines that had gotten too close to his face and he roared with displeasure. The sheer menace in that preternaturally wolfish sound temporarily stunned the vampire in his grasp.

That's it. Those teeth of yours won't harm anyone else in this city. You won't accidentally make another bloodsucker in your image, and further contribute to the pain in my ass.

Dale had maneuvered his vampire to the back of the alley, where there was an even slimmer chance for it to escape. Derek danced his flailing abomination in the same direction, whirling, ducking, lunging to the side to avoid the sucker's uncanny ability to recover.

The only way to keep those pointed teeth from making contact with his flesh was by taking a firm hold on the bastard's neck. But since vampires didn't actually breathe, a good squeeze wasn't going to suffocate the creature into submission.

The vampire's spine hit the wall with a thud that shook

the brick. The wily creature brought up its filthy bare feet and straddled Derek's body with legs made mostly of brittle bone and strings of sinew.

Fine little hairs on the back of his neck lifted as Derek shoved off the creature. With a fresh round of strength fueled by disgust, he finally got the vampire on the ground, on its back, where it fought like it had five limbs instead of four. When the sucker gurgled with anger, black blood bubbled from its lips.

"This is the end. I'm sure you'll thank me later. And really, there is no pleasure in this, and only a necessary kind of justice."

Dale, close by, tossed him a stake, which Derek caught in one hand. With one final burst of energy, he stuck that wooden stake deep into the vamp's chest, in the spot where its heart had once beat.

Go in peace, vampire.

The creature exploded as if it hadn't been actually composed of flesh and bone at all, but merely a bunch of musty pieces that had been glued together. Seconds later, a rain of nasty, odorous gray ash swirled through the area like a twister.

A second explosion rocked the area moments after that. Amid a flurry of ash that was temporarily blinding, Derek turned his head to see Dale smiling back at him.

"Mission accomplished," Derek messaged to his packmate. Or so he thought before the soft, muffled sound of a human in trouble reached him from the street beyond.

Across the filthy, ash-strewn alley's crackled asphalt, above the musty gray dust that had quickly settled to the ground, Dale's eyes again met his.

Chapter 3

Riley was no weakling, but the guy was extraordinarily strong and fast, using his other hand to spin her around. He now had her by the waist with a hand clamped over her mouth.

Despite her rocketing pulse, she got one good kick in before he pulled her into the shadows so fast, it happened between one blink of her eyes and the next. Still, she wasn't going to play dead or be reduced to a teary mess, and managed to connect with the guy's shin with a second kick. When his hand fell away from her mouth, Riley shouted for help.

The fight she put up had surprised her attacker. His hold on her waist loosened enough for her to pull back and spin sideways. They were near the entrance to an underground restaurant and yet no one had seen this happen because the asshole's timing had been impeccable.

She heard her phone hit the sidewalk and didn't have

the opportunity to retrieve it. Hands came at her again as if the guy was half octopus, and as if he had more at stake here than she did. He clasped her throat to choke off a call for help.

"Bastard!" she shouted.

A filmy blur of movement danced around her, reminiscent of a storm system moving in. The whirlwind was so strong, she flew backward, stumbled and almost lost her footing. The jolt of hitting a wall knocked her senseless. Her head snapped back. Stars danced in her vision and her stomach turned over.

That's when things really got fuzzy.

Did the ass who had manhandled her have accomplices? There were now three moving blurs of speed in the area. Mere streaks of movement. Nothing defined. And she had a concussion. Either that or these new guys were larger than any humans she had ever seen. The sounds they made were fierce, threatening, and similar to sounds animals made in the wild. Each grunt and growl added to the pressure in her skull.

It occurred to her that she had been dropped into the middle of one of those horror movies she had been thinking about. Strange sounds under a full moon reinforced the thought.

Looking up made her dizziness worse. Her knees started to buckle. Her vision narrowed as a hovering net of blackness slowly descended. Riley dug deep for more courage. She could get away while no one was looking, find the phone she had dropped and call for help.

Another arm closed around her before she had completed the plan. Although she struggled to get free, she could hardly breathe past the pain in her head, let alone rally for another attack.

Uttering a string of curses, she tried to focus her eyes

and found nothing in front of her but a wide expanse of someone's bare chest.

"Damn it."

She whispered more curses as she was lifted up and swept off her feet. The only way to stop the unusual sensation of having the ground ripped from beneath her was to close her eyes.

Another sound ricocheted inside her head, seeming to echo noises she had heard before. Though she couldn't have been colder, a new round of chills arrived when she recognized what that sound was.

With her heart rate nearing critical mass, Riley slowly opened her eyes and took a breath before having to face whatever her fate was to be.

Nothing happened immediately. Cool wind on her face soothed the icy shame of having put herself in harm's way. But she was in somebody's arms, and moving away from the street. For some reason, she didn't sense harm here, though.

Her inner defiance sparked and anger burned like a beacon.

"Put me down. Let me catch my breath."

The arms holding her loosened considerably. Riley again felt the hard support of a wall behind her as the man did as she asked and set her down.

In her vision, this guy's body continued to move as if he had the ability to fluidly alter his shape. Yet she knew that couldn't be right, and after a tense moment of silence, he spoke.

"Can you stand?"

The husky, overtly masculine voice cut through the pain behind her eyes.

"You'll be all right in a minute. We've called this in and someone will come to get you," he said.

Hell, had she just been rescued? Was that what all the commotion was about?

Shaking off the last vestiges of dizziness, Riley focused all her attention on the person who had spoken to her, grateful that someone had heard her shout for help. Her attacker had been thwarted and she was going to live, after all.

Her rescuer leaned closer to her, his bare chest wide and bronzed. Her gaze traveled slowly over that broad expanse of flesh before she worked her way upward. The thanks she had meant to offer was delayed by a question that took precedence over anything else she might have said.

"Why are you half-naked?"

"You're welcome," the shirtless man returned after a beat.

He hadn't stepped back to leave her. Instead, her rescuer seemed to be waiting to make sure she actually could stand up.

His physique was rock-solid. Since he towered over her, there was no way to see his face without again banging her head against the wall behind her. One concussion per night was all she could manage.

"I'm sorry." Riley's voice wasn't as steady as she would have liked. "Thank you for helping me."

The guy didn't respond verbally. His hard, muscled body pinned her in place for a few more seconds, as if body language had its own form of communication. Riley hadn't noticed how much she had been shivering until she felt the warmth of the man's closeness. Through the loose weave of her sweater, her rescuer's heat was welcome.

She sighed.

He leaned closer.

"Not an invitation," Riley warned, turning her head to the side.

"Didn't think it was," he replied.

His voice was gruff, as if he hadn't spoken in a while. At any other time, she probably would have been intrigued by that. Now she just wanted to go home.

He spoke again. "Will you be okay? I'm sorry, but I have to go. I'll have to leave you here."

The wail of a siren in the distance reminded Riley that this guy had mentioned something about calling in the incident. But as she contemplated that, wondering again why this Good Samaritan was roaming the city without his shirt, he disappeared.

His heat was gone and the night's coolness returned. She had no one to lean against now. It was a miracle she was still standing.

The first thing that popped into her mind as she waited for the police to arrive was a ludicrous reaction to what had happened, and meant nothing, really. Nevertheless, she pursed her lips, took a deep breath and howled softly, almost to herself.

"Ar-rrooo-ooo..."

The heat returned, quick as a flash. The man who had rescued her was there to pin her to the wall again. With a mouth that was as feverish as the rest of his body, he brushed his lips across her forehead and down her right cheek. The featherlight touch, there and gone in a few fleeting seconds, left Riley breathless.

Had she made a mistake in thinking this was a good guy?

Inching backward far enough to put a finger under her chin, he carefully tilted her head so that he could look into her eyes with a studied observation. His eyes were light, maybe blue, and surrounded by dark lashes.

Riley couldn't look away or break eye contact. The intensity in those eyes would have held her captive if his body hadn't. In his gaze she found something weirdly beautiful and at the same time troubling. She detected a flicker of real wildness there.

Had she made this guy up in some head-injury-induced coma? Could she have banged her head that hard?

Because…

She was sure…

No. She wasn't sure at all, actually. How stupid would that have been?

Riley listened to the absurdity of the words that came out of her mouth next, and winced when she was done.

"There are no such things as werewolves. You do know that?"

The smile this stranger offered her made her feel like she was being bathed in white light. She saw pearly teeth in a tanned face. The area around his eyes crinkled slightly at the corners, above chiseled features partially darkened by a five-o'clock shadow.

That's all she got, all she was allowed, before she found herself alone again with the lost cell phone he had some-how placed in her hand…and a splitting headache.

Chapter 4

Derek had to leave the woman or risk being caught by the people he took such pains to his hide true identity from on a daily basis. Dale was already sprinting in the opposite direction in human form, racing from shadow to shadow. But though Derek had also downsized to a human shape, he hated to leave before further help arrived for the woman they had rescued from harm. That part of being a werewolf sucked.

The woman had howled. Sort of. And she had mentioned werewolves. That alone would have intrigued him, even if she hadn't been so damn beautiful.

What did she know about his kind? Anything? Could it be that she was just having him on with the werewolf remark, with no real idea how close to his reality she had come? Or was she fully equipped with knowledge about his kind?

She was a fierce little thing. No wallflower when it

came to protecting herself. He'd witnessed that kick she had given to the imbecile he and Dale had left unconscious and handcuffed to a drainpipe.

She'd handled herself the best way she could without succumbing to shock. That took courage and also meant that her girl-next-door, wholesome looks were somewhat deceiving.

Small and *feisty* would have been a turn-on for a big bad wolf if he had time for such things…and if she hadn't been human. Add to that her pale oval face, big eyes and mass of shiny blond hair, and she became a real curiosity.

With so many battles to fight these days, it was best for him to ignore distractions. He hadn't indulged in anything that could have been considered a relationship since his heart had been broken, and he was still picking up the pieces of that breakup. It was also possible he had been wallowing a bit too long in its aftermath.

The only reason he had risked a shift back to human form in this woman's presence was because she hadn't been in any kind of state to have recognized what was going on at the time. Only by shifting could he have offered assurance that she was going to be okay. Her eyes had barely focused. She had been confused.

Still, and again, she had howled and mentioned werewolves.

Dale was waiting for him around the next corner, at the edge of a dimly lit parking lot. He stood in the shadows of a large sign, just any old half-dressed human to an observer's eye. Dale also was a big guy, and formidable. No one in their right mind would have moved closer for a better look, or questioned his shirtless state. Dale's posture alone would have prevented that.

"Do you know her?" Dale asked as Derek pulled up beside him.

"Never saw her before," Derek replied.

"You got sort of cozy back there."

"I just had to make sure she was all right."

Dale grinned. "Yeah. Well, you took a while to do that. And you shifted in the presence of a human."

"She was half-unconscious at the time," Derek pointed out. "And she's unusual."

"She's no Were," Dale said. "I'd have thought you had learned a lesson about human women."

Derek nodded. "Learned it loud and clear, my friend. Have no fear about that."

Dale's gaze swept over the parking lot. "It's quiet now."

Derek didn't want to jinx things by agreeing or mentioning unnecessarily that there usually were a few moments of calm before a storm. The moon had only been up for a few hours. There was more night ahead. He figured that when word got back to the vamp queen about two of her young fledglings being dusted, vamp activity would pick up. He had a special sense for that kind of thing.

"We'd better get back to it," he said.

"Right," Dale agreed with a big breath as he stepped into the moonlight and, to get Derek to laugh, pounded on his chest the way male apes did in the wild. Then he pinned another grin to his rapidly morphing features. Unlike Derek, Dale was a more frightening rendition of their werewolf species—wolfish body, wolfish face, fur follicles and all.

When the light hit Derek, he closed his eyes. With an internal rumble, the changes began. The expansion of his chest came first, followed by an icy burn in his hips and legs as the mysterious chemical reaction coded into him gave his system a bump.

In a quick lightning strike of pain, his arms and torso muscled up, stretching his skin and the bones beneath.

Light brown hair, usually only a little too long for a detective in Seattle, lengthened, as if a year had gone by with no trim. Last to alter were the parts of his face that took on another look with a brief, sharp, short-lived sting.

Weres, early in their lifetimes, had to either learn to adapt to these physical changes or die. The first shape-shift often weeded out the weak. There was no escaping or hiding from the inner explosions that set off a shape-shift. Everyone supposed this was a survival-of-the-fittest sort of biological trick. But getting used to the art of a body's physical rearrangement was a Were's mission. Being Were was a serious game of species-imposed destiny.

Dale was waiting for him to acknowledge the job of alley sweeping ahead, and Derek nodded. More vampires would come out sooner or later, and he and Dale had to be ready.

"I suppose you'd like to drop by that place and make sure the woman and her assailant were picked up?" Dale messaged wryly.

"Do you think you can read minds now?" Derek returned.

"Not all minds. Just yours."

Derek barked a laugh. It was true that he wanted to go back there. He wanted nothing more, in fact.

"Just to check on the perp," he sent to Dale.

"You go right ahead and tell yourself that," Dale messaged back.

Hell, maybe Dale really could read minds...

"It's dangerous to retrace our steps," Dale warned.

Derek shrugged his massive shoulders. *"Dangerous for whom? The idiot that tried to attack a woman on a busy street, or us?"*

"Well, you've got me there."

Dale matched Derek's confident stride across the parking lot as they turned to the east again with renewed purpose.

At the very least, Derek decided, he had to find out who that woman was, and what her remarks about werewolves meant. She would have been questioned by the officers who picked her up, so there would be paperwork filed. Her personal information would be on that paperwork.

Even better, with the attacker in custody, she'd have to be questioned further. And he knew just the right detective to help with that, even if doing so might mean treading on another detective's casework.

"Smell that?" Dale asked.

"Hell yeah," Derek returned.

They exchanged glances, growled in unison and took off in the direction of the latest ill wind.

Four cops arrived in Riley's rescuer's wake. She marshalled her strength, since she needed to make sure they took the guy who had caused all this chaos into custody.

The jerk was still unconscious and was handcuffed to a pipe near the entrance to the nearby alley. Cops were looking from her to him with unspoken questions on their faces.

"A couple of big guys came to my rescue," she said. "Looks like this was my lucky night."

"They did that? Cuffed him?" one of the officers asked, checking out the standard-issue cuffs she had seen a thousand times hanging from her father's belt loops.

"Cops?" the officer continued.

"Possibly," Riley replied. "Though they weren't in uniform."

The officer nodded. "Plainclothes guys, most likely. Are you hurt, ma'am? Are you in need of medical assistance?"

Riley thought about that. Actually, she was okay, except for the headache and the thought of having had a near brush with death.

"A ride would be nice," she said. "To my car."

"We'll have to take a statement," another officer pointed out.

Riley nodded. "I can give you that."

She knew the drill about that, too. She could talk about the attempted abduction, but she couldn't even begin to describe her rescuer in any way that wouldn't make her sound crazy. Shirtless male? Rippling muscle that didn't seem to be able to settle on his big frame? Volcanic heat? Eyes like laser beams?

Maybe since these guys assumed she'd been helped by plainclothes officers, they wouldn't ask too many questions or press her for descriptions.

Should she mention those howls she had heard?

No way. Absolutely not. In doing so, she'd be putting her reputation on the line before she even had a reputation. Besides, the strange noises she'd heard had nothing to do with what had happened here. She had merely been in the wrong place, at the wrong time.

No longer dizzy or wobbly in the knees, Riley glanced up at the sky. Though clouds were moving in, the moon was on full display. After what had happened tonight, that moon suddenly seemed kind of sinister.

A young officer—the badge on his shirt said his name was Marshall—helped her to the cruiser parked at the curb with a steadying hand on her elbow. Silent and subdued, he waited until she sat down inside before making eye contact. Then he smiled knowingly, as if they were co-conspirators and shared a secret. Riley recognized the look.

"You know who my rescuers might have been?" she asked.

The officer shrugged.

"Will you thank them again for me?"

He nodded as two more cops walked up, and then Officer Marshall backed away without looking at her again. Whether or not he knew anything, she'd have liked a way to speak with that young cop again and get a line on finding out about the men who had quite possibly saved her life.

She owed them so much more than a beer.

Tucked into the cruiser, Riley answered each question she was asked to the best of her ability and with as much detail as she thought prudent under the circumstances.

Adrenaline still pumped through her body from the fight she had put up. In spite of regaining some strength, her shivering had doubled, leaving her longing for the kind of warmth she had been temporarily offered by the nameless, shirtless man who'd come to her rescue on a cold night.

A guardian angel was the way she'd think of her rescuer from now on...except maybe for the few seconds when his lips had traveled over her face. She wasn't sure what to make of that.

Had he wanted a special kind of thank-you for helping her? Should that have left her feeling further abused and icky?

Used to looking inside events in search of deeper meaning, Riley wondered what the guy might have been searching for in such an intimate touch. It seemed to her at the time that he had been seeking a way under her skin to get a look at the real Riley Price, not the professional cover-up artist she had become. She didn't need another shrink to try to analyze that idea because the absurdity wasn't lost on her.

If she were to perform self-analysis, her interest in this rescuer had been caused by a latent sense of loneliness, of being alone in a big city, and so far from home. That, along with a healthy suspicion that she might actually have met a real live superhero tonight.

Unfortunately, as a mental health professional, she realized there was more to it than either of those things.

That man's touch had left her feeling exposed and excited, and sorry there hadn't been more excitement, all at the same time. She had wished for adventure and it had smacked her on the head a bit too hard.

One little kiss that wasn't actually a real kiss at all, from an anonymous man, and the memory of how that had felt, was keeping her pulse on warp speed.

Nope. There was no way she could mention much about her rescuer to these cops and come out unscathed. Something in her voice would give away her interest if she mentioned him out loud. The creep who had attacked her was now in custody, she was okay, and that was that.

Statement, check.

Witness form, check.

Perhaps an interview at the police station would follow in the next day or two, and life would go on.

Crowds had gathered on the sidewalk and in the street, lured by the presence of cops like insects to a bright light. Riley tried to find the officer who'd seemed to know her rescuer as the cruiser pulled away from the curb, but had lost him in the throng of spectators. She told herself it didn't really matter, anyway. Things were what they were, and all that mattered was that she was going back to her small, rented house in one piece.

Nevertheless, she peered out the back window of the cruiser and hoped for a glimpse of the broad shoulders that would now be the highlight of her dreams. And as the car wove expertly into traffic, Riley clutched the edge of the seat and gasped, thinking she just might have caught that glimpse.

Chapter 5

"*They're back, and we need to go,*" Dale messaged, vying for Derek's attention, which was riveted to the cruiser getting ready to pull away from the curb.

He and Dale were on the rooftop of the pub, peering at the scene below after taking this slight detour from their agenda, though it could be a costly detour if they didn't get moving toward any new vamp problem that turned up.

He just had to be sure *she* was safe.

Derek turned around, nodded to Dale and walked to the opposite edge of the roof, where the shadows were deeper and there was no hint of human presence. It was a shame, he decided, that the owners of these buildings didn't upgrade their lighting systems. Bloodsuckers hated lights almost as much as they hated noise, and would have been much easier to spot without all that pooling darkness.

"*Marshall will take care of her. You know that,*" Dale added, following along in Derek's wake.

"Yes."

"She's not your type anyway, Derek."

"Most assuredly not," Derek half-heartedly agreed.

But the woman had some kind of hold on him that he could not shake. Or didn't want to.

She had smelled so damn good. Her skin was like velvet. Yes, she wasn't a Were. They had nothing in common. Yada yada.

His head came up. There was a scuffling sound to his right and an unnatural wave in the shadows below where he stood. The sudden distraction broke into Derek's inner discourse on the pitfalls of human-Were relations. It seemed that Dale had been right. Bloodsuckers were gathering here.

Hell...

Derek knew there'd be no way to slow down these numbers unless they could find and deal with their queen. Without a Prime or Master, most vampires couldn't survive on their own for long. The undead didn't possess the brains and the skills to keep up their attacks. A Master was just that—the mastermind behind the nest. The core that kept a nest growing.

There might have been one sure way to find this one, but he wouldn't go that route, since it would entail bringing back the immortal Blood Knight, who had faced this queen down years before. The same f-ing immortal that had driven a Harley away from Seattle with McKenna Randall on the seat behind him.

Immortality aside, some women seemed to prefer bad boys in black leather.

"Five," he sent to Dale as he peered into the dark. *"Five more parasites down there."*

"Is that all?" Dale messaged back.

Derek looked at his partner. *"Piece of cake?"*

Dale nodded and leaped onto the brick ledge next to Derek. *"Right behind you."*

"I wonder," Derek sent back, *"why it is that I always have to go first."*

"Shinier badge," Dale said as they jumped.

They landed in the alley side by side and on their feet. Derek's announcement of their presence was a deep, guttural growl that served to halt the moving trail of shadows now hugging the building beside them. He really was tired of fighting vampires without ever seeming to stem the tide, but if he and his pack were to give up, who would take over?

Beyond the alley, several police and fire sirens wailed in earsplitting decibels that might have caused these vampires to think twice about emerging from behind the pub, if in fact they maintained thoughts about self-preservation. As it was, the swirl of moving darkness pressed on.

Derek caught one of them with his claws and dragged the bloodsucker backward. The sucker didn't have much time to protest or put up a good fight, and was reduced to a cloud of flying dust seconds later.

The vamp in front of that one paused, whirled and hissed like an angry cat through chipped fangs that no longer could have punctured human flesh. Derek tossed that one back to Dale and held his breath as the filthy, foul-smelling ash rained down.

That little deletion left three remaining vampires. If he and Dale took care of them quickly, he could get a last look at that woman before the officers took her away. One final glimpse was all he needed to settle his nerves and maybe even the question of why he wanted that last look so damn badly.

He barreled through the vamp lineup like a football lineman and turned to head them off before they reached the street. With Dale bringing up the rear, the three vamps were squeezed between them. It wasn't much of a party, and the fighting, which didn't last long, wasn't pretty. Black blood dripped from Derek's claws. Ash swirled everywhere like dark, discolored snow.

Wasting no time, Derek stepped onto the street, careful to keep to the shadows that no longer stank of vampire presence. He leaned forward to view the cruiser that was making its way into traffic. His heart was beating faster than normal and his boots were already starting to move him in that direction…until a claw snagged his belt.

Dale's message came through loud and clear. *"I wouldn't recommend taking that next step, boss. And I think you know why."*

Well…maybe he did know why.

And maybe he didn't have to like it.

Riley stared out the window of the police cruiser until her chills had subsided, but hadn't gotten anywhere in terms of finding her rescuers. When she thought she saw something, it turned out to be nothing more than a passing flash of tanned flesh seen against a dark backdrop, and could have been anyone.

She didn't speak to the two cops in the front seat. It angered her to think that she had nearly been a victim of a violent crime, and that she might have placed herself in danger by following a whim.

"Turn right, here," she finally said as the cruiser approached the parking spot where she had left her car. "This is it."

No longer feeling quite so weak or frightened, Riley opened the door and got out on steady legs. Her hands didn't shake when she brushed her hair back from her face.

"You'll be okay?" one of the officers asked.

"Yes. Thanks for your help." She fished in the pocket of her skirt for her car key. "I'll be fine."

"We'll follow you home, all the same," the cop said.

She hated to turn down an offer like that. The only problem was that she had to. The car key wasn't in her pocket. The damn thing was missing. Short of heading back to the site of the incident to look for it, the only way she was going to get home would be to either take a bus, or have these nice officers drive her. Then she'd have to break into her house because she had left her purse, which contained the rest of her keys, locked inside the car.

Riley blinked slowly to absorb all of that.

The alternative was to go to her office, where she kept spare keys. The building's night watchman would let her in to get them. Although she didn't particularly like the idea of going into that building alone after what had happened tonight, it would be all right. Plenty of people worked late, and the building was well lit and secure.

"Thanks for the offer. I need to go back to work first to pick up a few things. My office is just down the street," Riley said.

The cop that had helped her out of the patrol car nodded as he peered into her car. "No key?"

"I seem to have lost it," she admitted.

"I can help with that lock."

He had it open in less than thirty seconds with a slim-jim device, and it was difficult for Riley to hide her relief. But it still didn't help in the long run, since she couldn't start the car without that blasted key.

After retrieving her purse, Riley glanced at the cop and shrugged. "I'll be fine now." She waved a hand at the street. "There are lots of people around."

"You sure?" the cop asked.

"Positive."

He nodded again. "Please come to the precinct tomorrow for a more formal statement. And take care."

"I'll do both of those things," Riley said.

She searched the street in all directions when the patrol car drove away, knowing she had to get going, but unable to shake the feeling of being watched. *More imagination?*

Instead of wondering who had made those howling sounds that had kicked the night into high gear, she now wanted to punch that person for his or her part in nearly getting her killed.

Derek couldn't help taking a closer look at the woman whose rapid steps gave away little of what she had been through tonight. His packmate's expression was filled with sympathy, but there was only so far a Were could go in a disagreement with his alpha. And Derek had never been mistaken for stupid.

Both he and Dale were in human form again. Derek's nerves were charged from changing back and forth so many times in a single night. Shape-shifting came with a cost, and he was experiencing that cost now. Prolonged time spent as a wolfed-up version of himself not only heightened his senses for a long time afterward, but actually also left him feeling kind of beastly.

His animal instincts were working overtime at the moment and directing him to go after the woman who had looked into his eyes not more than an hour ago. He had questions about her that needed answers. For instance… how had she seemed to have gotten past the incident so quickly? She was carrying on as if nothing had happened.

She was tough, at least on the outside.

He liked that.

Who are you? I wonder.

Dale leaned against an ivy-covered wall, content for the time being to have dealt the vampires a warning blow. But in terms of the antics brought about by a full moon, the night was still young. Hell, the hunting hadn't even really begun.

"Happy now?" Dale asked, stripping most of the wryness from his tone.

"I wonder where she's going," Derek said.

"Maybe she has a hot date."

Though Derek gave Dale a long glance, Dale persisted. "A hot *human* date."

Jealousy was an ugly emotion that Derek understood all too well, having had a tough time watching his ex and her new lover together. Still, he experienced a brief pang of jealousy now for whatever lucky bastard had this woman's attention.

"We'd better check in with the pack," he said, ready to put his muscles to more good use. He couldn't just follow the woman to wherever she was going because of a wayward bit of electricity that had flared between them earlier, or because of the fact that he still felt that electrical buzz when they weren't anywhere close.

He had lost sight of her, and shrugged off the desire to follow. There were more important things to take care of in the city's shadows. Other Weres would be out and about now, and as the alpha of a Seattle pack, he was needed for his directions.

Coming from his human throat, the growl he issued sounded downright rude. Even as his boots thudded on the asphalt and he moved in the direction of the last skirmish with the vampires, he felt the tug to turn around. It had been a long time since his allegiance had wavered between duty and a woman, and he had solemnly vowed never to let that happen again.

From several steps behind him, Derek heard Dale say, "Good choice."

Chapter 6

After Riley reached her office, the thought of going outside again wasn't appealing. She had made it this far without collapsing, but wasn't sure she could keep up the farce for much longer. Although her dad had long ago taught her about the art of the good cop face, no one was around now for her to have to pretend with.

She wasn't all right. The shaking had started up again, so hard that Riley had to sit down. All the moments leading up to this one merged into a single thread of riotous emotion.

She had not made up any of this. Just because tonight's events were over didn't necessarily mean she could move forward without recriminations. She had paid dearly for her stupidity, sure, but why did she have to feel so stupid now? Why did she want to march back out there as soon as her legs were capable of carrying her and find the men who had rescued her from harm?

Hero envy was an emotion she was familiar with. In her job, she had dealt with a few cases of people who had come close to death. And though it was true that she could empathize, and invest in years of clinical-training work in order to try to help others, being affected by such a thing herself was a different ball game.

Cops had always been her heroes. Had those two guys been undercover? Maybe she'd see them tomorrow at the precinct and get a better look at them.

She rubbed her temples with cool fingers and sat back, aware of a growing ache in the spot on the back of her head where it had struck the brick. Her fingers drifted to the cheek her rescuer had touched. She remembered it all as if it had been etched on her brain.

What she couldn't do was break through the fog that blurred out several minutes of the ordeal. The moments when she had actually started to believe that the man whose lips had rested on her cheek might actually have possessed some sort of superhuman powers.

All that warm, rippling muscle...

The long hair...

His incredibly handsome face...

Riley clapped a hand over her mouth. What had she said to him in place of a proper thank-you? Had she actually mentioned werewolves? Maybe it was insanity he'd searched for in her eyes.

Well, it was over, and here she was, snug in her office, where street noise was blocked by dual-paned windows and howling wolves had no place among the credentials and diplomas framed on her wall.

She would not go back out there, that was for sure. Possibly she'd spend the night here on the couch and go home in the morning for a shower and clean clothes.

Relieved to have made up her mind, Riley stood up and walked to the window that offered her a good view of the street for half a block or more in two directions. Traffic was light at the moment. Signals on the corners flashed red, yellow and green. All of this was normal. The problem here was that she wasn't.

After shaking her head to clear her mind of the notion that if she looked hard enough and long enough she'd find her rather wolfish rescuer or others like him out there, Riley continued to search. When she closed her eyes, she could see him. She could again find the light-colored eyes that had seemed to see deep into her soul. She felt him beside her, leaning in.

With her eyes open, the only thing she experienced was the sense of her own mortality and a reminder of how closely she had managed to escape.

The glass was cool when she rested her forehead against the window. "Thank you," she said aloud to the nameless man whose face she would always remember. "And if it turns out that there are such things as werewolves, you'd be a perfect specimen. Just so you know."

She headed for the bookcase and the decanter of amber liquid she had hoped to reserve for special occasions in the future, but was necessary now.

She poured some in a glass and swirled the contents. Never having been a fan of alcohol, she held her breath as the glass touched her lips, and then felt the burn of the whiskey as it trickled down her throat.

Carrying the glass with her, she moved back to the window feeling slightly better, thinking she'd be able to handle the rest of the night like a pro. After all, she was a pro. Those framed credentials said so. And besides, everyone she had treated so far in her short time in this office had seemed comfortable on her couch. She'd make do with it tonight in lieu of going back out to the street.

Just in case things weren't as safe out there as they seemed.

His pack was a formidable bunch. Most of them were around his own ripe old age of thirty-two in human years. A few were slightly younger. The older Weres tended to hang out in areas beyond the city proper, and patrolled no less vigorously than their younger counterparts.

Having seen plenty of action already, they all helped to foster the kind of enthusiasm every Were needed for handling the things that hid in the shadows. Every good-guy Were had a place and a job. The pack was a second family to most of them. For some, it was their only home. For Derek, who had lost his family to a vampire attack in Europe fifteen years ago, the pack was a real comfort.

They met for the meeting two streets over from the precinct, in a private room in the back of a restaurant whose owners liked having cops around. Four Weres were in uniform, the rest weren't. The rule was to behave in public, get their orders and dish out their own version of justice to fanged troublemakers.

Because there had been vamp activity tonight already, the plan was to comb the streets and alleys within a quarter-mile perimeter of the incidents. Energy levels were particularly high tonight as the Weres dispersed. Even Weres under a full moon had to remain alert to the danger those vamps presented.

Dale led the charge so that Derek could stop by the precinct for a look at the interesting woman's attacker. In honor of that visit, he had put on a T-shirt and leather jacket, and thought he looked almost completely human.

Alone again, he stood on the sidewalk, beneath the overhang, silently contemplating where his senses were urging him to go…though he could have predicted where that was. In his estimation, another little detour was warranted. A quick in-and-out, and then he'd get on with the plan.

That's what Derek told himself, anyway, as he tilted his head back and called up the fragrance that seemed to have coated his lungs. Her fragrance. That woman's.

He sent his senses outward to locate the trail of that one unforgettable scent among so many others, and walked west, then east, keeping well away from the moonlight until he found what he sought. Then, grinning like he had won the lottery, Derek whispered, "Got you," and smiled.

The building he'd found was a nice one just steps off the main drag. Four stories' worth of large windows overlooked the street. There was a revolving front door. Inside, his boots echoed loudly on the black-and-white marble tiles. The only hang-up was the security guard manning a reception desk not quite twenty feet in.

Derek showed him his badge. "I'm looking for a woman."

The security guard smiled, his expression saying, *Isn't every guy in Seattle?*

Derek continued. "I believe she would have come in not more than an hour ago. Tall, slender, blonde, in a black skirt."

"May I ask what you might want with a woman of that description?" the guard asked.

"We're missing a few things on the statement she gave us tonight about an incident. I'd like to clear that up."

"And you didn't get her name?"

Derek strengthened his tone. "I'd appreciate it if you could help me with that, silence being a possible obstruction of justice, and everything."

Derek's inner wolf was bristling over being repressed

when there was a full moon. He could easily have yanked the guard over the desk and spoken to him nose-to-nose, but he refrained. The Seattle PD was trying to upgrade their image with the masses, and this guard was only doing his job.

"Name's Price," the guard finally said. "Third floor, three-ten."

Derek nodded. "Miss Price is here now?"

"The after-hours policy is that she would have had to sign in and out. She hasn't signed out."

Derek nodded again. Though his insides were throbbing and his pack was out there doing the dirty work, he told himself that he just needed one little peek at the woman in 310 in order to put his overactive imagination to rest.

"Okay to use the elevator?" he asked.

"The middle one is in operation," the guard replied, pushing a notebook and a pen toward Derek.

Derek signed in and headed for the elevator. As a rule, he didn't like small spaces and the feeling of being confined. He especially didn't like those things tonight.

So, he asked himself as the doors closed, what did he really want from this unauthorized visit? He had already memorized every detail about the woman. A second look at her wasn't going to change any of those things.

It was that remark... But he wouldn't tell her that. Bringing up the word *werewolf* would only cause her to focus on it more.

Another reason for showing up on her doorstep unannounced was to find out if she would recognize him. There was danger in such a move, and a lot at stake if she put two and two together and came up with a connection between him and the shirtless werewolf vigilante that had helped her out of a jam.

Nevertheless, Derek didn't even consider turning

around. He blamed this brazen act on the wolf that tugged on his insides in need of freedom.

When the elevator doors slid open, Derek looked around and then turned to the left. Number 310 was halfway down the hallway. Double doors. Brass plaque.

He read: Dr. Riley Price, PhD.

Price...

The name had a familiar ring to it. Then again, there were probably hundreds of people in the city with that name. *Riley* was unusual, though. He decided it suited her.

Riley Price had walked away from the attack as if it had been a minor thing when he knew better than to believe that. He had felt the quakes that rocked her and could still see the expression of fear, hurt and confusion in her eyes.

His hand stopped in midair before his knuckles actually stuck wood. He closed his eyes, able to *feel* her in there, knowing such a connection with a human was also unusual.

He knocked three times. So that he wouldn't frighten her more, he called out, "Seattle PD, Miss Price. I just need one more thing to help with this case. The security guard told me you were here. Can I have a minute? I know it's late."

Stepping closer to the door, Derek willed her to respond. To grant his request.

The strange thing was that she did.

Chapter 7

Riley hesitated before turning toward the door, annoyed by the interruption. The glass was still in her hand, though she had only managed one more sip.

There was a cop in the hallway. The front-desk guard wouldn't have let him in without showing proper identification, which meant she didn't have to worry about that. She could either respond and let him in or ignore him. He wasn't going to break down the door if she stayed where she was. Eventually, he'd go away.

Riley found herself heading to the door, hoping that this would all be over with sooner, rather than later, and then she could get on with her life.

She paused with her hand on the knob. "What's your name, Officer?"

The same deep voice that had requested a minute of her time said, "Miller. Detective Miller."

"I'm quite busy, Detective."

"I won't take up much of your time, Dr. Price."

Riley took a deep breath to settle down and opened the door. The man in the hallway appeared to be as surprised as she was when their eyes briefly met. There was something familiar about him.

"Do I know you, Detective Miller?" she asked, breaking the silence that had stretched for several seconds. "You seem familiar."

"I'm sure we've probably passed on the street. I get around on the job, as you can imagine."

That could have been true, Riley supposed. But besides the eyes, there was also something distinctive about his voice that caused her to tighten her grip on the glass in her hand.

His gaze drifted to the glass.

"For my nerves," Riley explained.

The hunk in the hallway nodded. "You've had quite a night."

Detective Miller truly was a hunk. He was tall, dark-haired, and obviously more badass than desk jockey in his worn leather jacket and fitted white T-shirt. He said, "Can I come in, or would you prefer answering questions like this?"

Her sudden interest in guys who looked as good as this detective surprised her.

This guy, at first glance, hit most of her attraction buttons. She liked the shaggy hair, his height and the shape of his face. *Action* and *adventure* were probably his middle names. But he was a cop, and she had vowed never to put herself through what her mother had suffered, never really knowing whether her husband would come home at night or be killed on the job.

With that thought firmly in mind, Riley stepped back,

opened the door wider and gestured for him to come in with a wave of the glass.

The room was dim, lit only by a lamp on her desk, and yet she easily saw every move this detective made. She was glad the dimness wouldn't allow him a closer look at the paleness of her face. Putting the desk between herself and the detective, she said, "What do you need from me?"

He hesitated for a few beats too long for her not to notice. "You're a psychiatrist?" he asked.

"Psychologist. And very new to the business."

"That's good."

"Why?"

"Maybe you can better manage what happened tonight and put it in perspective."

He again glanced at the glass she was clutching.

Detective Miller's voice was deep enough that its vibration quietly filled the room. His eyes, however, told another story, and made Riley imagine he was on good behavior and playing nice at the moment.

"What is it you need?" Riley repeated.

She set down the glass.

The detective had only walked far enough into the room to get a distant view of the window, but he looked there. "Will you be able to identify your attacker?"

"I'll never forget his face," she said. "I have a knack for remembering faces."

More beats of silence passed and the detective still hadn't said anything to warrant this visit. She had already told this same thing to the officers at the scene.

"I just needed to corroborate your place of employment, Dr. Price, and to make sure you're credible," he said.

"Credible how? What's my job got to do with anything?"

"It makes things easier for us all if you are believable in your statements."

Riley pointed to her throat. "Want to see the bruises that guy inflicted?"

She flushed when his gaze landed on her neck, and began to think this detective might have had another reason for coming here. However, since she had already allowed her imagination to run amok once tonight and had landed in trouble because of it, Riley waited for whatever he'd say next.

"I'm sorry to have brought this up so soon and to have disturbed you," he said. "Tonight's attack must have been terrible for you. So how about if I apologize for the intrusion and let you get on with whatever you were doing? You can answer more questions tomorrow."

Riley nodded. "Thanks for showing some concern."

She wasn't going to vocalize how Detective Miller's presence lent an air of safety to a truly awful night, or how knowing that guys like this were on the streets doing their job made her feel slightly better.

There was no way in hell she was going to submit to fanciful thoughts about this guy, or let herself believe he was strikingly similar in size and looks to the man that had come to her rescue on the street...because that would have been pathetic.

"Well, I'm glad to see that you're going to be okay," he said.

"Yes, thanks to two of your guys out there."

The detective's inquiring gaze returned. "Did you mention anything concrete about them to the officers who took your initial statement? Descriptions? Conversations?"

"It happened so fast, I'm afraid I wasn't in good enough shape to speak or to note many details about who those guys were. One of the officers later suggested some ideas about who my rescuers might have been, though."

"So you wouldn't be able to identify them?"

Riley eyed her glass on the desk, wishing she actually liked whiskey and that she'd taken another sip if there was going to be much more of an interrogation.

"I was just glad they showed up in time to save my ass," she said.

Detective Miller's gaze was like being caught in a tractor beam. Never one to shy away from a challenge, Riley met that gaze with an equally studious one.

"Nothing?" Detective Miller asked. "You can't describe them in any way?"

"Other than the fact that neither of them wore shirts, not much was clear...which is strange, when I think about it. So I'd prefer not to think about it and just be grateful."

When the detective smiled, a further ripple of familiarity returned to her in a flash of repressed memory of the night's events. Her rescuer had dark hair and light eyes that were a lot like this guy's. They both had the same kind of unshaven face that highlighted handsome, angular features. She had sensed wildness in the man on the street as well, and both of these men possessed the same kind of male vibration that affected her after only a glance in her direction.

She ran a fingertip down her cheek—the same cheek her rescuer's lips had illicitly touched. That touch left her feeling breathless.

Detective Miller's expression was again one of concern, though he didn't close the distance.

"Are you all right, Dr. Price?"

"Yes. I... I just need time to process this."

"Did you remember something just then?" he asked.

Rile shook her head. "Nothing that would help."

The detective nodded, turned and walked to the door. Riley tracked his movement without calling him back, though every cell in her body urged her to ask him to stay. At the door, he paused as if he might have been reluctant to leave her.

"I don't see myself as a victim," Riley said.

He looked at her over a broad shoulder. "I can see that you don't."

As he crossed the threshold, she added, "Actually, the man who came to my rescue looked a little bit like you."

He paused again, then said, "I get that a lot. I'm thinking it must be the jacket. Good night, Dr. Price. Maybe we'll meet again tomorrow."

As he closed the door, Riley took her first deep breath and headed after him. Changing her mind at the last minute, she leaned against the door and strained to hear the sound of the elevator, but felt as if she were listening for something else. Like the howl of a wolf. Or the velvety growl of a light-eyed, dark-haired, chisel-faced, half-dressed werewolf with the kind of voice that resonated, even now, in her soul.

Just like Detective Miller's had.

Derek leaned a shoulder against the wall of the elevator and looked up, as if he could see through the ceiling to a couple floors up.

"Good night, Riley Price," he muttered. "He looked like me, did he?"

He had taken a chance by coming here to speak with her, but at least he now knew the things she did and didn't remember, and could take comfort in the fact that she hadn't been able to identify him outright while standing several feet apart.

"I'm no less interested, just so you know," he added.

She was safe up there in her office with the guard manning the front desk. At the very least, he didn't have to worry about that. Her memory was another issue altogether. Psychologists were familiar with all sorts of tricks to spark repressed memories. Meeting her again would not be wise.

And yet he wanted to see her again. He wanted to see her again right now and get to the heart of the werewolf remark she'd made on the street. But that would probably serve no purpose whatsoever other than to place his pack in jeopardy.

He signed out and exited the building with a curt wave to the guard. From the sidewalk in front of the building, Derek glanced up at the moon and said, "Fine. Let's get on with it." He walked toward the car he had parked near here earlier in the evening, before the night's antics had begun.

He removed his jacket, tossed it on the seat and took one more look at the street corner from the shadows of the two buildings that hid Riley Price's building from sight. Then he ducked into the alley, where the subtle scent of werewolves filled the night air like its own brand of dangerous perfume.

From her window, Riley watched the detective turn the corner. He did look a little bit like the man who had rescued her. At least, she thought he did.

Grabbing her jacket and her purse, she locked the door and went down to the street, determined to find the truth of what she now had come to suspect—that Detective Miller and the man who had helped to save her life could, in fact, be one and the same. If not, maybe Miller had a brother on the force. A twin.

He had headed east with purpose, as though he knew exactly where he was going and what he'd find there. His stride had been graceful when viewed from above, and radiated confidence. Miller was a dangerous man in his own right.

Riley gripped her cell phone tightly in her hand as she exited the elevator, signed out and started out after the detective, hoping she'd catch his trail before both sanity and the need to think about her own safety returned. The fact that she wasn't alone helped somewhat. There were plenty of cars moving in both directions. Couples laughing and holding hands breezed by her, and she had a momentary pang of desire to be like them.

She couldn't really recall the last time she had shared a light, loving moment with anyone. The flicker of wildness in her nature made her want to find her soul mate instead of settling for anything less, and she had never found that certain someone.

At the intersection, she paused, knowing Miller was long gone and that she was a fool for thinking she could have found him.

But then...

She heard a sound that made her hands quake. Was it an engine turning over, or could it have been a growl?

You know better, Price.

Go back to the office or go home.

She ignored both of those options. As if tonight's events had never happened, Riley crossed the street. She headed for an area where shadows pooled and moonlight failed to reach the sidewalk, drawn there for reasons that felt insane. If Detective Miller had been looking for trouble, the shadows were where he was going to find it.

Chapter 8

Derek again scented a problem.

Two of his packmates had already come this way, and he could almost picture them in his mind. They were riled up and anxious because they had found something nearby. He knew what that something had to be.

The alley he had entered was a dead end. He searched the dark before climbing over a short brick wall, and jumped down on the opposite side with both of his hands raised and ready for whatever showed up. But he didn't step into the moonlight. He wanted to see what kind of creature would come out for a look at the man who had just possibly walked into a trap without realizing it.

His packmates had beaten him here and were hidden from sight. One of them was on the rooftop, all wolfed up and as motionless as a Gothic ornament. The other wolf was behind a partially boarded-up window.

If these vampires didn't feel the danger in their midst

and were inept as to how the supernatural world worked, they would soon show themselves, the way their cousins had earlier. If they were seasoned bloodsuckers, they would avoid three werewolves like the plague and ply their trade elsewhere.

Derek kind of hoped for the latter on this occasion. He would have preferred more time to think about Riley Price, but just couldn't allow personal issues to take precedence over his job. Nor could he afford to let a perfectly good full moon go to waste.

"Anyone here?" he finally called out, lowering his hands and feeling his claws spring as he turned in place, very near to the light.

His two packmates were silent, intent on what might happen next. Derek took in a breath that was tainted with a new and potent scent of Otherness before a figure appeared in the distance. Derek squinted to make it out. The damn thing seemed to be wrapped in its own fog, and that left its outline unclear. The creature also appeared to float several inches off the ground.

The whole image was murky at best, and decidedly different from anything in Derek's experience in dealing with vampires.

He inched closer to the stream of moonlight next to him, ready to meet this thing head-on, and said, "Who are you?"

The voice that came from the fog might have been either male or female. Derek couldn't be sure as he heard it say, "You trespass here, wolf."

This was a seasoned vampire that knew a wolf when it saw one. And that could potentially make the task of taking this creature down a hell of a lot messier.

"I could say the same thing about you," Derek returned.

"Werewolves belong in the forests," the newcomer said.

"And vampires belong underground. Which makes me wonder why you're walking around."

"It's a very long story."

"I'm all ears," Derek said.

"The thing is, I'm not sure I owe you anything, certainly not an explanation for my existence. I just am. Nothing more. Nothing less."

"And you're here now, in this alley, for what purpose?" Derek asked.

"I came to warn you."

"About?"

"Where to find your next fight."

"You mean the next fight after dealing with you?" Derek said.

As he watched, the fog began to dissipate slightly. Not enough to actually see the thing hidden inside it, but Derek did see a tall, thin figure of unknown gender.

"You can't fight me, wolf," the creature warned. "I think you already know that."

"I'm not sure I do. Why don't you enlighten me?"

The creature's reply was as cryptic as the rest of this conversation. "I believe you have better things to do at the moment than to deal with the likes of me."

"Such as?" Derek said.

The fog floated to the left, which gave Derek a decent view of what was beyond it. He saw the street, and cars going by. Then he saw someone stop to peer into the shadows in the break between the buildings.

He felt a chill on the back of his neck. His heart gave a thunderous roar and a few treacherous beats.

"It helps to find out that wolves have not only soft underbellies, but other vulnerable spots as well," the creature remarked.

Damn it...

The wolf on the roof began a quick descent. In seconds, one of Derek's packmates was standing beside him looking big, dangerous and lethal, with his sharp canines exposed. The fog remained on the sidelines, like a dark cloud that had swallowed whatever the thing was that used it for camouflage.

"I don't know what you're talking about," Derek said.

But he did know, of course. And for the first time, Derek also understood that he had exposed himself to the vampires tonight in another way. A new way. Because it was Riley Price who stood there on the street, looking on.

And there was probably a vampire to keep him from reaching her if this vamp had brought friends.

Riley hit the wall with a shoulder that was already sore, and winced. The protests she wanted to utter got stuck in her throat. Either the shadows were playing tricks with her eyesight and she actually did have a concussion from hitting her head earlier, or there was a werewolf in this alley.

A real, live werewolf.

No joke.

She stumbled back and toward the street, numb with shock. The fact that she had wanted to find a werewolf melted away behind the actual sighting of one. The phrase that kept repeating over and over now in her mind was that she wasn't insane after all, and might never have been.

Still, she refused to believe that seeing a werewolf in Seattle was anything other than the very definition of insanity. So she turned around and walked away, heading back toward her office with her skull humming and her pulse hammering away at warp speed.

She'd call Detective Miller and tell him about what she had seen. Would he think she was crazy? Could he possibly understand that no governing body would issue a license to a therapist whose own sanity they doubted? As for proof of what she had seen…by the time she got to the precinct or found another way to reach the detective, that werewolf would probably be long gone.

As Riley consciously willed her legs to carry her forward, she knew there was no way she could win this, prove this, or convince anyone about what had been in that alley. She also knew that she had to try.

Derek glided into the moonlight to join his packmate in a standoff with a vampire that was far too enlightened for anyone's good. He wondered what the wolf beside him thought of this discussion.

There was a chance the abomination hadn't meant its remark the way Derek had taken it after seeing Riley there. Yet it had sure felt that way. The comment had seemed pointed and personal.

He knew that Riley had to have seen his packmate in full moonlight, and that for her the werewolf comment she had made earlier had now taken on new weight.

What would she do next?

Where would she go to feel safe?

Who will you tell, Riley?

His shape-shift took seconds. Derek roared in the moonlight, daring the creature in the alley to challenge two Weres in spite of what it had said. But the creature, which had to be some special kind of vampire, didn't rally. It hovered near the street for some time before Derek decided to break the face-off.

He rushed forward, wanting to get to Riley, knowing that in order to reach her, he'd tear this bloodsucker apart if he had to.

Intending to ram the vampire's body, Derek barreled forward with his backup on his heels. The foggy bastard he lunged for wasn't solid, so he passed right through it and pulled up a few feet from the street, snapping his not-quite-human teeth.

His packmate had no better luck.

Angry, Derek whirled around to try again. But the vampire remained elusive, shifting in time to avoid any direct confrontation as it drifted over the Weres. It was as if the spooky sucker had the ability to fly.

Again and again, Derek and his mate challenged, spun and went for the abomination. Time after time, their teeth and claws came away empty. Finally, the bloodsucker floated to the street and spoke. "You see, wolf, that I was right to warn you, and to call to your attention the vulnerability attached to your new weaknesses."

The next remark the vampire made came in the form of a touch on his mind.

"She is not for you, wolf. Stay away from her or our next meeting will not go nearly as well as this one."

Derek clutched his chest—he was suddenly short of breath. He hadn't been wrong. The warning had been pointed and had pertained to Riley Price. Who else could this sucker have been talking about?

Madder than ever and refusing to give up, Derek and his packmate sprinted toward the creep like rabid animals, biting, clawing and punching at nothing even remotely physical enough to maim or injure. They kept this up until the vampire simply disappeared, as if it had never really been there at all.

Derek stared at the empty alley with his heart racing. When his packmate turned to him in an equal state of confusion, Derek sent a message. *"I hope to God there aren't more of those things around."*

It was at that moment that Dale arrived, alone and calm.

After a quick look at the two Weres, Dale asked, "Did I miss something?"

"I think it must have been a ghoul," Derek's current fighting partner, still wolfed up and wild-eyed, messaged back. *"That thing was seriously demented."*

Though Dale looked to Derek for an explanation, Derek was already miles beyond thinking about the fight. There were new questions to be answered—carefully, cautiously and with as much diplomacy as possible. The thing they had faced had shown off new tricks, and also knew about Riley. It didn't seem to want him hanging around her, and had issued that warning.

It was possible the creature had purposefully allowed Riley to see the werewolf in this alley, so that she'd be frightened enough to stay away from the streets. Why, though? What did that creature have to do with her, and more to the point, what did it want?

"Derek?"

Derek glanced at Dale.

"Maybe you can explain what happened after you've changed back, boss. Tonight was quiet everywhere else we patrolled. The pack is reconvening at the park for your summary and for further instructions."

Derek didn't feel like downshifting. He felt like running. Like howling. Like tearing apart that damn fog in any way he could so that he'd be able to sleep.

But who was he kidding? There'd be no way to sleep when he had to find Riley Price and convince her that she hadn't seen what she had seen.

There'd be no way to rest until he made her understand there was no such thing as a werewolf, and that she must have been mistaken due to the darkness of the alley if she thought there was.

Those urges had to be tamped down for the moment, however, because his pack was waiting for their alpha.

Was the weakness the vampire had mentioned about Riley?

Did he believe that?

There was no way to skip over this encounter with the vampire, or ignore what it meant. Either the vamps had evolved somehow and learned new crafts, or he had just come face-to-face, more or less, with their damn queen.

Damaris.

If that was true, he had, for the first time, experienced the power of a centuries-old vampire that had been around as long as there had been history. A powerful female blood-sucker that had gone after his ex-lover two years before and had caused McKenna Randall to accept the so-called *blood gift* that only a pair of fangs could offer in order to fight back. McKenna had accepted immortality by way of a Blood Knight's kiss. Her new lover's kiss.

McKenna had been given the gift of an everlasting life span from an immortal warrior who had walked the earth for as long as Damaris had, and who once had gone by the name of Galahad. The same motorcycle riding super-power that had stolen McKenna's heart, and then had taken her away.

A goddamn immortal who rode a Harley instead of a steed.

"Derek?" Dale called out.

Derek backed into the shadows and absorbed the flash of pain that came with downsizing again. He headed for the street, already planning what he had to do to warn his pack about the future, before he'd try to find Riley Price and get to the heart of the problems piling up.

In his mind, like a lingering echo, he heard that vampire's message. *She is not for you, wolf.*

It was no longer to be an average fight with a vampire. Whether or not anyone liked it, the stakes had just gone up.

Chapter 9

Riley made it to her car and got in wishing she had avoided coming out in the full moon altogether. With a shaky hand, she finally got the key inserted and started the engine, not sure which direction to go, but needing to get away from where she was.

There had been a werewolf in that alley, and though the beast had looked dangerous, it hadn't come after her. Two close calls in one night made this the worst night in her life as far as stumbling into danger went. It also made her the luckiest woman in Seattle to have emerged relatively unscathed.

She pulled away from the curb, nearly scraping the car parked in front of her. Though she drove too fast, she couldn't help it. Adrenaline pumped through her body in a fight-or-flight reaction to what she'd seen in that alley, and there hadn't been time to tame it.

She had to tell someone.

She couldn't call her dad after what they had been through. There was no way she could mention the word *werewolf* to her father.

The western headquarters of the Seattle PD was housed in an old building north of the city's hot spots. She found it easily, parked and turned off the engine. Above the roar of her pulse, Riley tried to remember the name of the officer who had spoken to her after the earlier incident, hoping that if she found him, he'd help her find Detective Miller.

And then what?

Was there any way to explain about what she had seen?

She didn't get out of the car. Instead, Riley sat there, watching cruisers and cops come and go, comforted by the uniforms and the badges that were reminders of her family and of her home. The truth was that she was afraid to actually find Miller. She was now afraid to mention any of this to anyone at all.

After fifteen minutes had passed, she reached for the key, still in the ignition, ready to back out of what she had been about to do. Startled by a knock on her window, she glanced sideways to find one of the police she had been looking for. Officer Marshall, the cop who had hinted at knowing the men that had come to her aid during her attack.

Riley opened the car door. On legs that were astonishingly solid after the night she'd had, she got out and faced the young officer.

"Do you need help, Miss Price?" he asked politely.

"I'm wondering if you might help me find Detective Miller."

"Is there anything *I* can help you with?" he asked.

"He came by my office to ask me some questions and I wasn't in the mood to answer. I thought I'd make up for that now if he's around."

"On a night like this one, Miller seldom comes in."

Riley met the officer's dark-eyed gaze.

"When a full moon comes, all sorts of crazy things happen in this city," he explained. "Most of the guys that work here have to put in some overtime to help curb all that. Miller and his crew are on the night shift tonight. They'll be driving around, waiting for a call."

Though Riley tried to smile, her lips wouldn't comply. While she should have felt relieved about not having to face Miller with her story, there was no relief at all, just an inexplicable, deep-down feeling of being at a complete loss as to how to even begin to explain what she'd seen.

"Can you please tell him I came by? He knows where to find me," she said.

Officer Marshall nodded. "Sure." Then he waited, probably in case she had something else to say.

"Is Miller a good detective?" Riley asked.

"One of the best," Marshall replied.

Riley glanced up at the officer and said the stupid thing that had been on the tip of her tongue for the last five minutes, then immediately regretted it.

"Does he always wear a shirt? On the job, I mean?"

The young officer smiled to placate her. "I would assume that he does. Is there a reason you asked? Maybe you're thinking about the men who helped you tonight? You said they didn't wear shirts, I believe?"

"Yes, well, the detective sort of looks like one of those guys, and I was just—"

"I doubt very much if our detectives who aren't undercover run around half-naked," the officer said. "I can't account for all of them, of course, you understand. But it's highly doubtful that your guy and Miller are one and the same. I will tell the detective you stopped by, though."

"Yes. Thank you."

She got back into the car feeling a little foolish about bringing up the shirt detail, yet not nearly foolish enough to let it go. So she spoke again to Office Marshall in parting. "He'd probably look good without a shirt. But you don't have to tell him I said that."

Officer Marshall closed her car door. Though he remained sober-faced and professional, Riley was sure he was trying not to laugh.

Derek didn't mean to ignore his inner chastisements, and didn't actually realize his mind was elsewhere until Dale punched him in the shoulder hard enough to wake him up.

"It's not a good sign," Dale said. "If that thing in the alley actually is what you think it is, why would a vampire Prime show up now, after all this time? Why would she suddenly come out to confront us?"

Derek had no idea how to answer that.

"It could be the reason for the strange scent in the east," Dale suggested. "The vamp queen brought it with her."

"Right now I imagine it is," Derek agreed, though he was having a hard time wrapping his mind around this new predicament. No one had seen or heard anything about that vampire queen for two years, so what had they done now to receive the honor of such a direct form of contact with the central villain of Seattle's vampire hive?

"Her appearance might be connected to the woman we helped tonight," he said to Dale, thinking out loud, rehashing everything that had happened and hoping something would eventually make sense.

What if was a game all cops played to try to reason things out. Events had to be studied from all angles, no matter how absurd they might seem. There was no way he was going to mention anything about a weakness for pretty psychologists, though, or the vampire's remark about her, when Dale already knew about his interest in Riley Price.

Dale said, "You think our little victim might have caught the vampire's eye, and that out of all the people in and around Seattle, a vamp queen could be interested in the one person we helped out of a jam? Why would that even occur to you?"

"The two things happened on the same night. And Riley showed up at the head of that alley where the monster confronted us, as if she had been summoned there."

Dale appeared to mull that over. "Such a scenario could mean this heartless vampire bitch might be interested in our Miss Price because we helped her. But we help people all the time, so what's so special about tonight?"

He added with a meaningful sideways glance at Derek, "Maybe the vampire is interested in Price because of who helped her. Her sudden interest could be in retaliation for us dusting some of her newbies tonight."

"Then why didn't she just go after us in the alley?" Derek said.

Dale shrugged. "I don't know."

Derek would never forget the problems they confronted the last time Damaris came out of hiding. If it hadn't been for that renegade Blood Knight heading off the vamp queen, none of his pack would be around today.

"Our Miss Price showing up again near that alley could be a coincidence," Dale suggested. "We have to consider that."

"One hell of a coincidence," Derek said.

Dale went on, "You've shown interest in Riley. Could that vampire actually be interested in you, Derek, rather than Riley Price?"

Derek had gone over those same questions fifty times since meeting with his pack an hour ago, and hadn't yet gone to find Riley because of his fear of involving her further.

He could feel Riley out there, and couldn't trust that sensation. They had no real connection. She wasn't a Were, so they couldn't have imprinted by gazing so intently into each other's eyes.

The only serious relationships for his kind were Were-to-Were. A special look, a lingering kiss, or a roll in the grass without their clothes, and two Weres were as good as engaged if they were meant to be mated.

Imprinting was serious business. Some Weres used the word *fate* to describe the immediacy of such attractions. And though imprinting rarely happened between a Were and a human, Derek supposed it didn't have to be impossible if the circumstances were right and the stars lined up. He just hadn't heard of any such cases. Still, he couldn't shake the thoughts that kept him tied to Riley.

Dale picked up on this unspoken thread, probably by reading Derek's face. "If your sudden interest in Riley is the reason for the vamp's interest, then you can't go near her until we know for sure."

Dale leaned against a pillar in the parking garage. "I can't help wondering why this happened tonight, out of all the other nights."

"I guess finding that out will be our new priority," Derek said.

"Will Price be safe in the meantime, if we're the ones who brought this shit down on her?"

"We'll have to make sure she is," Derek replied. "I thought I'd hand that job to you."

Dale didn't even blink at being nominated for the task, though it was a dangerous one. "Should I start now? Do we know where she might be without going in to see her file?"

"I can find her," Derek said without stopping to hear

how that might sound. Thing was, he knew he could find her wherever she might have gone. That acknowledgment alone should have made him wonder.

Dale waved a hand. "Lead on, wolf. The sooner we find out what's going on, the better. Isn't that right? We won't have the moon to help us forever."

"Exactly right," Derek agreed, already sorry that he had handed over Riley to Dale, who would watch her from afar without getting any of the answers to the questions Derek had.

They didn't really know anything at this point, and weren't any closer to figuring things out. By contrast, the vamp queen would know that werewolves were the strongest under a full moon, and that tomorrow might be another story if she decided to play this game.

It truly was best for him to keep his distance from the woman while he scoped out the shadows and pieced this puzzle together. He wasn't a decorated detective for nothing. When he put his mind to a task, he got things done. In a supernatural playing field, he usually came out on top.

What about Riley, though? Without an intimate knowledge of the shadows and what they hid, how would she get along? Beneath a talented vampire queen's studied scrutiny, how long would a human last, whether or not she was the real focus?

Riley's sweetness sat on the tip of his tongue, behind the lips that had touched her soft skin. Derek fisted the hands that had held her in place when quakes of fear rocked her.

Nevertheless, as he had previously acknowledged, Riley Price was no weakling. Tonight, she had taken what the world had dished out, and then walked away proudly with her head held high. In his book, that made Riley special. And he hadn't experienced *special* in a very long time.

The fact that he might have found such a woman again was what had to spur him on now.

"Get on it," he said to Dale. "I'll go back out there and snoop around."

He added silently, *"Make sure she's safe. Riley Price might turn out to be the key to finally ending this war with the vamps if we're lucky."*

As he turned to go, Derek said, "Wouldn't that be something? The hand of fate just falls in our laps with the help of a small blonde?"

But if that was true, and Riley was to be the key to finding Damaris, the beautiful psychologist's chances of survival were slim at best.

And that just wouldn't do.

Chapter 10

Finding some solace in movement, Riley drove around until her gas tank was empty before she parked in front of her office building again. Engine off, she sat back in her seat, reluctant to get out and in need of a few more seconds of thought.

Moonlight bounced off her dashboard, reflecting in the small crystal pendant hanging from her rearview mirror. Usually, she would have considered this a sign of good luck, but now thought seriously about using that pendant to hypnotize herself to make sure she had seen that damn werewolf.

After meaning to go home, she had ended up here instead, and Detective Miller had been at the center of that decision. He might return to her office if the other cop told him she had stopped by the precinct to see him.

Riley hoped he would return, and also hoped he wouldn't, for reasons that were clear in some ways, not so clear in others.

Why should I trust you, Miller?
Have you done anything to deserve it?

She had only spoken to him once. So why did she want to see him so urgently right now?

It took her another ten minutes to get out of the car. Riley carefully searched the street for areas engulfed in shadow. Satisfied there weren't many, she rushed into the building, nodded to the guard, said, "Please sign me in," and lodged herself in the elevator before taking the time for a deep breath.

She unlocked her office door, moved inside and then locked it after her. She muttered, "So far, so good," and almost believed that until a tingle at the base of her neck suggested there was another presence in the room with her. Something silent. The sudden pressure of something hidden in the dark.

"What do you want?" She waited with her back to the door, feeling around for the light switch and getting ready to bolt back to the elevator.

She heard a hissing sound that reminded her of steam escaping from a kettle, and tried to concentrate on getting her eyes adjusted to the dark. Where was the damn light switch?

The blinds were closed and she hadn't left them that way. There was no moonlight to help her see what kind of danger she faced, though the guard wouldn't have let just anyone in. So, who the hell was this?

"I'm going to turn on the light," Riley said without making a move toward the wall switch she now remembered was located on the opposite side of the doorway from where she stood. "You might as well tell me who you are."

"I can see you well enough without it," a voice returned.

The low timbre of that voice made the words seem sinister. The only way this person could have gotten here, past the guard downstairs and through a locked door, was by way of the window.

She looked there.

"Maybe you have the eyes of an owl. Unfortunately, I don't," Riley said.

The warning tingle turned into chilling waves of sensation that slid down her back. She labored for each breath. The palms of her hands felt moist. She'd barely gotten over the last two scares tonight…*and now this?*

"It would be easier to have whatever kind of conversation you're expecting face-to-face," she suggested. "Are you in need of my help?"

She wanted to shout "Did you break the window?" but thought better of it. The thing to do was to get this person to speak again, so that she could figure out where he, or she, was, and detect their state of mind.

"Maybe you prefer the dark?" Riley asked with her fingers on the door's lock, hoping whoever this was didn't have great hearing.

"Don't you?" the hidden guest returned.

"Don't I prefer the dark? No. Actually, I don't like the dark much at all these days."

"I find that strange," her visitor said.

Riley controlled the quake in her tone. "Why is that strange?"

She could open the door and flee. She might be okay if the person in the room with her wasn't fast enough to catch her at the elevator, if there was a nefarious reason for this visit.

"I suppose they never taught you to honor the night," her invisible visitor said softly, though the danger behind that softness came across loud and clear. "I'm here to fix that omission, and see that you learn."

"Thanks, but I'd rather not deal with this tonight," Riley said. "I have office hours most of the day on Monday if you'd like to come back. We can continue this chat then. I'm afraid I've had a rather long day."

There was a swish of fabric that told Riley the visitor had moved. From very near to her, the strange, uninvited guest spoke. "If you don't learn about your heritage, it might be too late to help you."

What the hell?

Riley inched the door open, praying that the hinges wouldn't squeak.

"What are you talking about?" she demanded loudly enough to cover any sound her exit might make.

She didn't get to hear the response to that question, if there had been one coming. The door burst open. A dark figure rushed past her into the room growling like a big cat. Like a lion or a…

Riley suddenly felt light-headed. Not willing to wait, or to find out what was going on, she ran into the hall- way. Avoiding the closed door of the elevator, she sprinted toward the green exit sign and flung open the heavy fire door.

The echo of her shoes on the concrete stairs seemed outrageously loud. When she reached the ground floor, Riley shoved open the door and sprinted across the mar- ble tiles, barely noticing that the guard wasn't at his post.

"Damn you," she said angrily as she reached the side- walk. "Damn you all," she shouted just before she rammed into something hard and unrelenting.

Two arms wrapped around her. Breathless from a com- bination of fright and exertion, and afraid this was the final straw, Riley looked up to meet the concerned stare of a man's familiar eyes.

* * *

"You!" the woman in Derek's arms whispered, hardly able to get that one word out.

Her face was bloodless. Quakes rocked her so harshly, he feared she might crumble to the ground.

"Riley," he said to focus her attention. "We have to get you out of here. Can you walk?"

She nodded, seemingly treading the line between panic and disbelief that a night like this must have caused her.

"Okay. Good," Derek said, looking up at her building.

Dale had gone to her office after finding the guard was missing, and had messaged Derek. Dale would do what he had to do to take care of the problem.

Derek stepped back to ease his hold on Riley. He had shown up despite what he had said to Dale about the possible danger of seeing her again.

"Time to go, if you're able," he said.

The defiant look he'd seen earlier tonight reappeared in her eyes. Though she shook fiercely, inner strength was going to get Riley Price past this moment. If nothing else, Derek liked her even more for that.

They backed away from the building's front door, careful to keep out of the moonlight. What Riley might do if confronted with a werewolf close up was something he didn't want to find out. He would take her to the precinct and keep her there. She'd be safer off the streets. He'd see to it that she'd be watched over until the night was over, so that nothing with fangs could come calling.

After he'd taken one more step, a crashing sound from above spun him around. Seconds later, a shower of broken glass rained down.

Derek's reflexes kicked in with a white-hot surge. Flexing his arm, he reeled in Riley, spun her around and pressed her to the wall to protect her body with his, as something much larger than the shattered glass of the window also hit the ground.

Derek didn't have to see what it was. His body rippled with tension that had only one cause.

Tearing himself away from Riley, he swung himself toward the vampire, who had landed on both feet without breaking a bone. The thing was dressed in black. Its face was a white death mask. Dark, red-rimmed eyes found Derek's, and the creature's spectacularly fanged mouth turned up in a sneer.

"Just the beginning, wolf," the bloodsucker hissed as it turned on its heel.

"Not if I can help it," Derek said.

Ready to send this abomination to a new afterlife, he reached for the wooden stake tucked into his boot. The vampire was quick, but Derek was angry, and that made him faster. He caught the vampire by its coat-tail and dragged the creature sideways until it struck the wall.

Without giving a thought as to why the vampire didn't put up much of a struggle to free itself or sink its fangs into his arm, Derek raised the stake and was about to finish off the bloodsucker when he remembered why he was there, and who was watching.

He turned his head to look at Riley. Their eyes met and held. His knew his eyes were wild, but hers were worse. She had mentioned werewolves and now it was too late to keep her from finding out what other kinds of creatures existed.

When he turned back to the vampire, it was with a sudden acknowledgment that this sucker had known he wouldn't strike in this situation, with Riley looking on. But that was a gross error, since every vampire taken off the streets was a point in human favor.

Derek brought down the stake.

The vampire's pasty face registered surprise. It hissed again menacingly, and then exploded as if it had swallowed a bomb. The only sound that remained was Riley's gasp of horror.

Chapter 11

It felt to Riley as though she had left her body. The real world had simply melted away and nightmares were the new norm. What she had witnessed was so bizarre, there was no logical way to accept it.

Yet here she was, standing under a rain of dark gray, awful-smelling ash. And there he was, Detective Miller, holding a wooden stake in his hand that he had used to explode a...

To kill a...

"Vampire," he said, turning to face her. "You can choose to believe it, or not. Maybe you'll wake up tomorrow and call this a dream, but that wouldn't be wise. Ignoring what happened here might put you in more danger."

Riley didn't know how she was able to speak. She didn't understand why she was still standing. "It's too much."

The detective nodded. "I get that. You're now one of the few people who know about these things, and that kind of knowledge isn't pretty. But it is what it is. You haven't made this up."

She found that there wasn't anything else to say at the moment, and wouldn't be until she processed all of this information.

"The immediate danger might be over, though that doesn't mean this guy didn't have an accomplice," Miller warned. "Will you come with me to the precinct, where you and I can sort this out?"

"Do the cops know about these…things?"

"Not all of them, no. It's not a secret those of us who do know are willing to share."

"Wouldn't everyone be safer if they were on the look-out for creatures like that?"

"There would be panic, and that's worse. The world as a whole isn't ready to acknowledge the shadows. We just have to try to manage them. And we really should go now."

"I'd rather go home," she said breathlessly. But she realized she wouldn't be able to drive in this state and didn't want Miller to take her there. She was afraid she'd want him to stay.

Her heart was beating so fast and so loudly, Riley had to work to hear her thoughts. Believing Miller, and her own eyes, meant that the world was a different place than the one she thought she knew, and not in a good way. How was she supposed to come to terms with that?

"Vampire." Above her heartbeats, Riley's ears rang with that word.

"Yes," Miller confirmed. "One of many."

Riley mustered her courage, hoping it would carry her through the next few minutes. She had seen how fast Miller moved. Running away from him on foot wouldn't get her very far. Besides, you couldn't outrun budding feelings for someone, even if you didn't know that person very well.

There was no explaining attraction, and how feeling safe with him stopped her insides from churning in the aftermath of the terror she had just encountered.

Riley wasn't ready to let any of this go without further explanation.

"They're real?" She pressed herself to the brick wall, glad to find something truly solid in a dreamlike world.

The detective waved at the remains of the falling ash. "This is what's left of the one that came after you."

What he said caused her synapses to fire. "Why would a vampire come after me?"

"I don't know. I wish I did," he replied. "Until I find that out, you'll be safer if you're not on your own after sundown."

This was so absurd, Riley almost smiled. "Because vampires sleep during the day?" Her tone was cynical.

The detective's eyes darkened. "The precinct will be the safest place for you, for now."

"Maybe so." Taking her eyes from this detective was tough. Other than the wall behind her, he was the most solid thing in sight. He had helped her and was willing to do more. She would be safe with him, except for the undeniable attraction she felt. Was this a case of hero worship?

"What about the man that attacked me earlier tonight?" she asked. "Was he one of them?"

"Not one of them, no. Merely your average drunken pervert on a bender."

She got no relief from that. And after what she had just witnessed, how could she fail to believe that vampires were real?

"I'd like to go home," she said.

A flicker of disappointment flashed in the detective's eyes. His handsome face creased slightly. "All right. If you insist on that, I can post an officer at your door."

"Is that necessary? I have a good dead bolt."

He pointed to her office. "Don't you wonder how that sucker got in?"

Miller was right, of course. The office door had been locked.

"Climbing suits them," he explained. "If you saw how they do that, you'd never leave your windows open again."

Riley's thoughts spiraled back to the reason she had been in such a hurry to get back to the safety of her office. All of a sudden she wasn't so sure how to bring that up. She remembered the howls that had started all this, and what she had seen in the alley around the corner.

She looked Miller straight in the face, and recalled how she had seen the same flicker of wildness that darkened Miller's eyes in the eyes of the gorgeous shirtless man who had dealt with her earlier attacker. *She* again shivered when she thought about how there had been two attempts on her life tonight. And the two men that had come to her aid were indeed similar in subtle ways.

Her shaking stopped when Riley remembered that facing trouble was in her DNA. She had to stay strong now—advice her father would have given her if he had been here.

"And werewolves?" she said to the detective, who observed her with concern etched on his handsome features. "What about them?"

He'd been caught between an explanation and a hard place without a viable way to extricate himself, Derek realized. He had started Riley down this path and wondered how far he could take her.

Should he tell her the truth, which would place his pack and others in a tough spot? Or maybe keep her in the dark about this one important thing?

She had briefly seen the vampire, and she had also seen

his packmate in the alley. By taking the reality of tha
werewolf sighting away from her, would Riley ignore hi:
warnings and talk herself into believing she had made the
whole thing up, vampire and all? He knew for a fact tha
human minds were capable of twisting things when they
were overloaded.

Her eyes were on him. Riley was waiting for him to
answer her question about werewolves. The decision he
had to make was either to pull the rug out from under her
with excuses, or to share a few more secrets with the hope
that she would keep them to herself.

It might be tough to stop her from passing on secrets.
He'd have to be prepared to tackle that problem. As the
alpha here, he had to protect his pack above all else.

She was waiting expectantly. And since psychologists
were probably experts at detecting mind games, Derek decided to try the truth, unable to see any other viable way
to go at this point.

"Werewolves do exist," he said.

Riley's reaction turned out to be nothing like he had
expected. She exhaled a long stream of the breath she'c
been holding as her eyes again met his. Blinking slowly
she wet her lips with the tip of her tongue.

"I knew it," she said in a soft voice that lacked any hin
of skepticism.

What Derek wanted to do to her, with her, that very moment and on a public street, could have landed him in jail
He had desired her from the first moment he laid eyed or
her, and was aware of how long it had been since he had
allowed himself to feel anything at all.

Two steps forward brought him close enough to Riley
to follow where those impulses led. She didn't back up o
retreat, probably because she had no idea he was one of the

creatures she was asking about…and also since she was already pressed to the brick wall behind her.

"Well, now you know," he said.

This was exactly why humans and Weres didn't mix. There were too many secrets to protect.

"I wonder what you'll do with that information, Riley Price."

"What do you do with it?" she responded.

"I patrol the street, keep those secrets to myself and try to maintain peace."

"With a wooden stake in your boot."

Derek shrugged.

"And for the werewolves?" She looked up at the moon. "How do you go after them?"

"We don't have much trouble from the Weres," Derek confessed.

She had looked away but her gaze now returned to him. "Why not?"

"Weres are reasonable most of the time and blend well with humans when there's no full moon."

"Blend well with humans?" she echoed, picking up on his slip in word choice.

"With people," he corrected.

She bit her lip before continuing. "Have you met some of them? Werewolves, I mean?"

"Yes." There was no need for him to expand on the answer at the moment. "Now it's time to get you off the street."

Instead of turning, Riley moved closer to him. The heat of her focused curiosity made the wolf inside him anxious to be set free. His claws pressed against his fingertips as if ready to spring. Shoulders that had borne the burden of all these shape-shifts tonight twitched in anticipation of what he might do next.

Kiss her...the wolf urged.

Take her home.

He didn't have the chance to do either of those things. Riley Price reached up to place her hands on both sides of his face and gently pulled him closer. Her breath was warm and fragrant when she spoke with her mouth inches from his.

"Thank you," she said. "Thank you for letting me know I haven't gone mad."

When she touched her mouth to his, Derek's wolf, tucked deep inside, silently howled.

Chapter 12

A shudder of shock ran through Riley as her lips met Miller's. The suspended moment was no less intense than being chased by a vampire.

Warmth flooded her body. One little touch of skin to skin, and her chills were history.

So was her mind, it seemed.

Neither of them moved right after that. Possibly, Miller was as surprised as she was by this brazen act that had turned out to be so much more than a simple thank-you.

The fact was that her body betrayed her. Rumbles of longing and need heated her from the inside out. More closeness was what she wanted. More of Miller. Because along with his confirmation of the existence of were-wolves, and without knowing anything about her or her past, he had set free another part of her.

His hands slid around her waist. With her body tight up against his, Riley again felt immersed in the dream that had allowed all of this to happen. There was even a fleeting thought that her dad would approve of her dating a cop.

But she and the detective hadn't been dating. Not only had they just met, they had also bypassed everything else by going along with the new urgency that sprang into place between them.

When Miller's instincts began to take over the direction of this closeness, Riley let him have that role, lost in the wonder of a heat that was like no other. Her reaction to the hardness of Miller's body produced a raw physicality she hadn't previously experienced with any man, or even known existed.

What had been a light, exploratory kiss quickly became a drowning act composed of mutual greed. And it wasn't enough for her. Not by far. Though they had spoken about werewolves, she felt like the animal here.

I've gone insane...

She breathed a soft groan into Miller's mouth. If he was really good at detective work, he had to know what might come next, and what she was willing to do.

Strangely enough, he didn't act on their obvious mutual desires. Miller paused, then eased back. Cool air rushed in to replace his heat as his light eyes searched her face.

What was he looking for? Something deeper than skin and the telling thunder of her pulse?

Riley recognized that look, just as she had been familiar with the flash in his eyes. She recognized the shape of the face in front of her, as well as the wide shoulders and the way Miller's shaggy hair fell across his forehead. The most significant thing about that was the way her body responded to his. Just like before. Like the previous meeting tonight that Miller had failed to mention.

Detective Miller and her earlier rescuer truly were one and the same. This was the shirtless man she couldn't

get out of her mind—the man who had responded to her
earlier remark about werewolves as if he had known all
about them.

She was an idiot for not pressing the point when she'd
thought of it, and for failing to ask Miller outright about
what he might know from the start. It had taken a certain
level of closeness to see this. See him.

Same eyes.

Same immediate and inexplicable physical attraction.

Same man.

The expression Derek saw cross Riley's face was one he
had hoped to postpone. She had put two and two together,
and he had to avoid the conversation that might follow.

"It's okay," he said. "I'll drive you home."

He couldn't do that, of course, without stepping into the
moonlight. The best he could manage tonight, under that
full moon, would be to take Riley through the back alleys
on foot while trying to avoid any vampires that showed
up on the way to the precinct. Either that, or he could call
someone who could drive her wherever she wanted to go.

Tonight, the moon ruled even Weres with special skill
sets like his. This wouldn't have been the case any other
night. Still, the back alleys weren't really an option at the
moment. One little beam of moonlight on his face, and
Riley would see the result.

He pulled out his cell phone. "Marshall? Miller. I have
someone who needs a ride. Check the coordinates to find
us, and hurry."

Riley hadn't yet said a word, though her breathing had
slowed and she had opened her eyes. *What did you make
of that damn vampire, and the way I took care of the problem?* he wanted to ask her. Were enough worlds colliding

in her mind to muddle up proper reasoning, even with all her psychology training?

"It was you. You helped me out earlier when the guy attacked me," she accused.

"Why are you so sure about that?"

He saw how she struggled to come up with an answer for something that was as inexplicable to her as the existence of vampires and werewolves. Riley was seeking explanations for reactions that couldn't really be tied to a physical description. She didn't know Weres could fast-track emotions and get to the heart of male-female closeness with the simplest eye contact…if that connection was meant to be.

He knew this was meant to be. He felt the connection acutely, and was going to have a tough time letting Riley Price out of sight when Marshall showed up.

All this pent-up emotion meant that he could no longer avoid the word he hadn't been willing to consider: imprinting. Even though it wasn't supposed to take place between their species. Either that's what had happened here, and he and Riley had forged a type of special bond, or he was an idiot for thinking it possible.

Imprinting meant that they were connected on a level that had to do with the soul. Fate and the soul. Possibly there'd be no way out of that kind of connection for either of them if she harbored the same feelings, while for him, now, here, the chain was already being forged.

Dale appeared beside him. Derek acknowledged his packmate with a nod, glad of the distraction. Dale would fill him in about that vampire in Riley's office later. Although the thought of leaving Riley in order to give her time to think, and to get on with his job, was an unwelcome one, some common sense, at least, kicked in. Riley had to get off the damn street, no matter who took her.

As for the imprinting phenomenon…

Well, if that's what had happened here, he'd want to tear up the world to get to her when they were apart. He would never be satisfied until he and Riley had joined in every way possible. That's the way imprinting worked. It was a particularly feral type of hunger.

Did he dare tell Riley all of this, or wait and see how this played out? Maybe that hunger was different for a human, and she'd be able to ignore it and get on with her life. But even his love for his ex hadn't been the same. Not like this. He had, after all, let McKenna Randall go.

Marshall's cruiser pulled up. He rolled down the window and leaned across the seat with a simple question.

"Where to?"

Derek couldn't walk Riley to the car without being exposed to moonlight. Neither could Dale. So he released her hand and gestured for her to get into the cruiser.

"Tomorrow," he said. "We can talk tomorrow, when you're ready."

Riley stepped off the curb and turned back. She spoke to Dale. "If you helped me out up there—" She pointed to her office. "You have my heartfelt thanks."

She got into the police unit and closed the door.

Derek watched the cruiser drive off.

Dale was unnaturally silent for a Were used to stating his opinion more often than not.

"I know," Derek said, reading the signs, if not Dale's thoughts. "Damn thing, timing."

"I see you found Detective Miller," Officer Marshall said, then fell silent.

Silence was okay with Riley. She was afraid to tell him that she knew Miller was the shirtless man who had helped her earlier. Someone might have been listening in.

They pulled up in front of her house. Officer Marshall walked her to her door and waited while she went in before speaking again.

"I'll be right out here for the rest of the night, Miss Price."

She faced him. "Did Miller ask you to babysit?"

"Call it an unspoken request. A healthy precaution."

"Will you be comfortable out here?"

"I'm used to the gig," Marshall replied. "First, though, I'd like to walk through your place to make sure everything is in order. Is that okay?"

"Not only okay, welcomed."

Riley stepped aside so the officer could precede her into the small house she had been lucky to find after arriving in Seattle. There wasn't much to see, and few hiding places in the five rooms.

The officer searched the closets, checked the windows and looked under the bed before returning to the front door. "Shout if you feel scared, or if you hear anything," he advised with a touch of his fingers to the holstered weapon on his belt.

Riley thanked him and got the door closed before her legs gave out and she sank, loose-limbed, to the floor. She sat there for a while as her heart continued to spike dramatically and her mind whirled with thoughts that would seem unreasonable to anyone else.

But fact was fact. She had seen things tonight that didn't fit into neat files she could categorize and label, and was shocked to have discovered that the world had more secrets than anyone knew.

There were important questions to consider now that couldn't be ignored. The main one, the surface problem, was the question of why she had become such a monster magnet and what she might have done to deserve that. Wrong time, wrong place? Twice?

And that, of course, tied in to her ability to deal with the fact that vampires and werewolves actually existed.

More important, however, was how she was going to deal with the hurt that had to do with her past; with what had happened to her mother so long ago that tied her together with the word *werewolf.*

There was no way in hell she could call her father and discuss any of this. She couldn't put him through echoes of the things he had tried so hard to put behind him.

After hiking her skirt up so that she could get off the floor, Riley stood up. After she took a quick look out of the peephole to make sure Officer Marshall was indeed there and visible to anyone who might try to bother her again, Riley dragged herself to the bathroom.

Dropping her clothes on the floor, she took a good look at herself in the mirror before heading into a hot shower that would hopefully wash away the silliness of kissing Miller. It was either that, or she might start screaming.

Though the night seemed terribly long, it had been mostly uneventful after Riley went off with Marshall. His friend and coworker was one of the few humans who knew about what went on behind the scenes, and was good at keeping those things to himself. Marshall would take good care of Riley.

Back in his apartment by dawn, Derek paced from room to room as he went over the night's events and came up empty on reasons why Riley would have been involved in the antics. What was so special about her that he and Dale hadn't been able to reason out?

No other vampires had appeared to make the rest of his shift more miserable. The bastard he had staked by Riley's

He knew the answer to that question already and without having to reach for it, because Riley had kissed him first.

Like it or not, they were going to become lovers, and that was thanks to some strange hand of fate that had once upon a time twisted werewolf DNA far enough to create beings who could fit in with Homo sapiens... And one of those Homo sapiens had howled at a full moon.

Derek smiled in spite of the obstacles ahead, and removed his hand from the doorknob without knowing how it had gotten there. It was way too soon to visit Riley again. He had to wait to see what she would do tomorrow.

"Good night," he whispered to her. "This might begin to make sense someday, when you know it all. If you're to know it all."

As he headed to his bedroom, Derek had to wonder what a young psychologist would make of the events that had already occurred, and if she had the tools to deal with such a radical shift in reality.

Hell, maybe she could hypnotize him out of a relationship that really had nowhere to go. Possibly he could even afford to pay for a session like that.

The problem was that he didn't want an end to what had only just begun. He was just too damn interested in another tryst with those lush pink lips for his own good.

Chapter 13

The day dawned cloudy and gray. Riley believed it was a miracle she'd been able to sleep for part of the night, and that she hadn't dreamed about fangs, wooden stakes or full moons.

Thoughts of the handsome detective returned soon after she woke, and plagued her as she made some coffee.

In the daylight, the events of last night seemed dimmer, more distant, almost as if they had happened to someone else. If more people knew that vampires and werewolves actually existed, would there be a mass exodus from Seattle? Would the National Guard be called in to exterminate?

Yes. Miller had been right about people panicking.

Miller's watchdog was missing from her porch this morning, and that was okay. Vampires slept in the daylight, right? At least according to works of fiction and Miller's unspoken implication. No vampires would be coming after her until dark, if at all. And the full moon had passed, which took care of worrying about werewolves.

All that was left to worry about today were good, old-fashioned people, and she was making a career out of dealing with them.

Since she seldom saw clients on weekends, she dressed casually for her interview at the precinct in a good pair of jeans, soft ankle boots and a blue turtleneck sweater worn in honor of the ring of bruises encircling her neck, where the bastard by the pub had choked her.

The interview with the cops today wasn't a bad thing, but she didn't need to make this into a pity-party by showing off the damages she had incurred in that incident. She was here. She had survived. End of story.

Except that it wasn't the end of anything really, and was in fact the beginning of something else that felt a lot like having entered another dimension.

A quick brush of her hair and a swipe of mascara finished the look she had been going for. Nothing about her appearance suggested that she might have wanted to impress Detective Miller. All she had to do now was to put one foot in front of the other and get into the taxi she had already called, having left her car downtown.

The air outside was bracing and fresh. Careful to lock her door, Riley hiked down the pathway toward the curb to wait for the cab that was due at any minute. She hadn't meant to bring the nightmares back so quickly, but thinking back to how that vampire had exploded into foul-smelling ash made her head hurt.

One damn howl had been her downfall. Chasing dreams. Her overactive imagination.

And okay, she had to admit that maybe loneliness was in there somewhere, too, which was why she'd had nowhere to go after work and time to roll along with her imagination.

Sometimes moving so far from her home and family seemed like it might have been a bad idea. On the other hand, when every cop on the force knew her at home, due to her father being one of them, there wasn't much room for adventure. And then there had been the looks she'd gotten, early on, because of what had happened to her mother.

"Suck it up, Price."

Everyone would be better off if she played this interview straight with no mention of fangs, broken windows and furry types in dark alleys. *You know...straight.*

In other words, she'd have to lie.

Omit was a better word choice, Riley decided as the cab arrived and she got in. As she saw it, two interviews were necessary today. After the cops grilled her about her attacker, she'd need a one-on-one Q-and-A session with Miller about everything else.

They could pretend that kiss didn't happen. She sure as hell wouldn't bring it up. He might have been her white knight, but she wasn't the kind of girl to kiss and tell. Nor would she hold him to the rich promises in that kiss, even though she'd like to.

"It was a damn fine kiss, Miller," she muttered.

In point of fact, it was the best kiss she'd had in quite a while. In months. Maybe even years.

This whole thing, it seemed to her, was centered not only on herself, but also on the detective that had shown up at every turn of her little supernatural wheel of fortune. Big, outlandishly handsome Miller, who looked almost as good in a shirt as he had without one. Whose chiseled face suggested a hardness that was the exact opposite of the compassion he'd displayed and the concern he had shown for her.

And who just happened to carry a wooden stake with him around Seattle…and knew how to use it.

Even better…

Knew whom to use it on.

"She's here," Dale warned as Derek strolled into the room. "Interview room two. How do you suppose this is going down?"

"I'm here to find out," Derek said.

"I left her place early this morning, right after Marshall's departure. Nothing out of the ordinary happened, so she's okay. I can go in there for her statement if you'd prefer."

"I'll handle it. Thanks all the same."

Derek repeated to himself that he shouldn't go into that room with Riley. He told himself that same thing over and over all the way down the corridor until he stopped at the door. If she was going to mention supernatural activity, he needed to be the one to hear it.

Swear to God, though, he felt her behind that door without having to open it. Her perfume lingered in the hallway—earthy, fragrant, feminine and like a trail leading him to her.

After rolling his shoulders, Derek opened the damn door, ready to find out what Riley Price was going to say about last night.

He stopped on the threshold as her eyes met his. There was no coy lash-lowering on her part when she saw him. She showed no outward signs of discomfort, even though he sensed the shudder she quickly suppressed.

"Dr. Price," he said in greeting, carefully monitoring his tone. She was even more beautiful in the light, if that was possible. "Thank you for coming in this morning, after a night like the one you endured."

"Not a problem, Detective," she said. "I'd like to make
sure the guy that attacked me gets what he deserves."

He hadn't forgotten the deepness of her voice and how
it affected him. But he couldn't let that be a distraction.
He needed to listen to her without veering from his du-
ties or giving away the concerns he had over the swiftness
of the connection they had made and why there had been
a vampire in her office. Neither of those things could be
mentioned here.

Though Riley was the first human to be in a situation
like this in a very long time, having survived a meeting
with a vampire, she wasn't the least bit hysterical. He ap-
proved of her self-restraint, but had to wonder about his.

"Just some quick paperwork and you'll be free to go."
Derek sat down and handed over some forms for her to
sign. "It would be a good idea for you to read through it
first and make sure everything in your statement is correct."

He looked at her intently. "Or if there's anything you
would like to add."

She stared back. Her lips moved with unspoken questions. "How there could be such things as vampires?" was
what she'd want to know. She might also address the way
he had so easily dealt with the bloodsucker that showed up
last night, and how he knew about werewolves.

Did she expect him to mention that kiss and apologize
for his part in it?

Derek slid the papers closer to her, over the top of the
table. "Your attacker is in custody, so you won't have to
worry about him going after anyone else."

She glanced at the papers, then back up at him. The flu-
orescent lights highlighted her porcelain skin, which was
unlined and ivory-smooth. Behind her bland expression,

however, Derek perceived a hint of her desire to bring up her second attacker.

To her credit, she didn't mention it.

It occurred to him then that the camera in this interview room hadn't been turned on, and no taping was necessary for this session. No one would be observing them from outside because it was nothing more than dealing with paperwork.

The second thing that crossed Derek's mind was that the room wouldn't be able to contain the heightened degree of interest they had in each other for long. His reaction to her was visceral, and physical enough to bring him out of the chair.

Riley stood up seconds after he did. Backing toward the wall behind her, she said, "I don't fully understand what's going on."

"Maybe I should get someone else to come in for that paperwork," Derek suggested.

"Maybe you should," she agreed.

She didn't mean that. Her eyes were wide and her lips were parted. His Were senses picked up on how fast her heart was beating—not out of fear, but something else. Something neither of them wanted to discuss out loud.

Riley probably didn't have any idea what was going on between them. How could she? The word *imprint* wasn't in everyone's everyday vocabulary. If this kind of drama and tension persisted every time they met, he was going to have to explain things to her sooner rather than later, and that would take some finesse.

He wanted her. The wolf inside him wanted her. He hungered for her in a way that was almost obscene.

Derek rounded the desk in three strides, but didn't touch her. "You can file a complaint," he said.

"For what?"

The slight tremble in her voice should have warned him to keep his distance. He wasn't known for allowing his wolfish hormones to get the better of him, and liked to believe he was in control of his baser needs. Yet he said, "For this," as he closed the distance. "And for the record, this would be worth the trouble that complaint would cause."

Chapter 14

In that moment, as Miller invaded her space, it didn't matter to Riley what she had intended to say, or how many times she had vowed to keep things on a professional basis with this guy. As soon as he was close enough for her to look up and see his face, she knew she would go along with whatever he had in mind.

He didn't hesitate or pretend to ask for her permission to pin her to the wall. Inside her, sparks ignited. His mouth hovered over hers, almost touched down and then hovered again as he slid his hands up the wall and leaned closer to her. All she could think was *To hell with vampires—he's the dangerous one.*

She closed her eyes. Her heart pounded. When his mouth met with hers, all bets for self-control were off.

Okay. So I'm an idiot, she thought.

There was nothing light or tentative about the kiss.

Fierceness dominated it. Strange and unlikely passions reigned.

Miller's skin was warm and his mouth was hot. She couldn't have described his taste, and knew she'd never get enough of it to satisfy whatever they had going on.

He took her mouth in the same way he would have taken her body if he'd had the chance. At that particular moment, she would have let him have it all and helped him to take it. The power and strength he possessed were turn-ons, as was the aggressive, intuitive way he seemed to know she wouldn't argue or protest this level of closeness.

She kissed him back with equal fervor and allowed him the leeway to explore her mouth—taking, yes, but also giving back in kind. When her hands slipped to his back, he caught them and held both over her head, against the wall he'd trapped her with. He held her captive with his mouth and his hard, exquisite body.

Riley felt every inch of him from his chest to his thighs. She melted into his warmth as if she was starved for affection. The kiss deepened, demanded more, required her to tap into an emotion she had never experienced in order to find something she'd never known existed.

The rumbling sensations that started up deep inside her were like an oncoming storm system, and were painfully similar to the sensations of an impending orgasm. That internal storm moved through her, rolling, rising, beating against her insides with a demand to be acknowledged.

She groaned and let go of the last remaining vestiges of resistance to the sensory overload. If he had touched her anywhere else, any other part of her body, she would have exploded like that damn vampire they'd encountered last night.

She waited for that touch, equally wanting and wishing to repel it. Wanting to stay right where she was, and also desiring to get away before this went any further. She was already losing sight of her objectives and knew she was a goner, when in the periphery, an unfamiliar voice called out.

"Derek."

Then, "Detective Miller."

The mouth-to-mouth assault stopped. Her sexy detective drew back, tugging on her lower lip with his lips as his mouth separated from hers completely. There was no way Riley could open her eyes. The thunder inside her hadn't stopped when the kiss did, and was still rolling toward one specific spot that hadn't yet been discovered by the man before her.

Reality intervened when her detective released her hands and stepped back to turn toward the speaker, taking his heat with him.

"Emergency call," the other man announced.

Only then did Riley open her eyes to face what she had done here, in a room of Seattle's police precinct, with a man who was one of them.

Derek nodded to Dale, who stood in the doorway, and took a deep, settling breath. "On it," he said hoarsely. "Give us a minute."

When the door closed, he again faced Riley. "Can we continue this conversation later?"

He watched her big eyes blink several times, and noted how the pink tint in her cheeks had spread. Although he was the only wolf in the room, his senses now told him that Riley was no ordinary human being, either. She had the look of something much wilder. Something as hungry as he was. There were flashes of gold in her baby-blue eyes. A defiant expression returned to tighten her beautifully symmetrical features.

"Over dinner?" he said.

She shook her head, but he didn't let that deter him.

"There are some things I need to explain. I'm sure you have questions, and so do I," Derek continued. "If that conversation needs to be in a public place, it's your call. You choose the location and I'll either pick you up or meet you there."

He raised his hands as if to press home the point that he wouldn't touch her again, at least over dinner.

"I don't think that would be a good idea," she said soberly. "You're much too…"

"Pushy?" Derek finished for her when her voice trailed off.

She looked him right in the eye. "Yes."

"Just dinner," he said. "And talk."

"I don't think so, but thanks for the invitation."

Riley Price sidestepped him, took the papers from the table fairly calmly and headed for the door. She ignored Dale, who was standing in the hallway, as she left.

Derek blew out a low whistle and shook his head.

Dale said, "It might have been better if you'd have let me get those papers signed."

"According to what line of reasoning?" Derek returned.

"In honor of the decorum and sanctity of being inside our place of business…or some such shit like that."

Derek looked at Dale. "I blew it, didn't I?"

"Some people might think so, but hey, you're the boss."

"There's this thing between us that I can't explain," Derek said as he headed down the hallway.

"Yes, well, finding you speechless would be a first," Dale remarked.

"So, what about this emergency call?" Derek asked.

"A strange break-in last night at a therapist's office downtown needs looking into. Sound familiar?"

"I'm on my way," Derek said. "Before anyone else gets there."

"And, boss?" Dale called after him.

Derek paused to look back.

"I'm free for dinner, if she isn't."

The pleasures of partnering with a smart aleck just never waned. Derek gathered up his jacket from the back of his desk chair, barked an order to the guys nearby and exited through an exterior door, trailed by enough of Riley Price's lingering scent to make his muscles twitch.

Riley didn't want to go home or to her office, where she'd have to face the damage to her windows. There were already three calls from the office management company on her phone, which she hadn't answered. How would she explain the inexplicable, even if she had no other excuse for all that shattered glass? Who in their right mind wanted to hear the words *a vampire went through the window*?

The thought of what had actually happened last night made her stomach queasy and also upped her fear level. Thoughts of what she had just done in the police precinct with Miller almost made her feel worse.

What part of *fiction* didn't those monsters get?

Detective Miller had some of the answers. The problem was that he had been all heat, and no explanations. He had managed to sideline her agenda, and that might have been on purpose. The only way she could possibly have asked the questions she'd held back was to have accepted his offer of dinner. *And then what?*

She couldn't assume anything more would come of another meeting when it was obvious the lust they felt for each other would continue to get in the way. All that heat, plus the fierceness of the way Miller kissed, haunted her.

She didn't like the vulnerability of being disturbed like

that, and hated the loss of self-control she had exhibited. Due to their getting carried away, she still didn't know squat about the monsters roaming the streets of Seattle.

Riley stopped on the street to look behind her, knowing she would have to see the detective again, and that the handsome bastard might be expecting her change of heart any minute.

She stared up at her office from the corner of the block. There was a police cruiser at the curb. A cop stood next to the front door of the building…and there *he* was, appearing as suddenly as if he had simply materialized out of thin air. Miller.

Of course he'd be the one to lead this investigation, since he had something to do with what had happened last night. At least, he had been there.

Riley eyed him warily from her position on the corner. The good detective would have to either lie about what he had seen or cover it up. In any other case, that would render this investigation tainted. But this wasn't like any other case. Not even close.

As though he had some kind of special sense, Miller glanced her way. He didn't address her or make his way over to where she stood. Derek Miller had a job to do here. And since it was her office they were investigating, there would be another interview.

Riley watched the detective and another cop enter the building. She waited a few more minutes before leaving the scene, needing time to come to grips with what was going on and wondering if she'd be able to go back into that office without imagining a vampire there to confront her.

She was afraid, and had to admit it. Nothing in her background was going to help her, because nothing actually made sense no matter what angle it was viewed from.

Someone called her name when she reached her car.

"Riley?"

Deep baritone. Velvety syllables that made the base of her spine ruffle.

Riley reluctantly turned around.

Chapter 15

"I'm sorry if I made you uncomfortable back there," Derek said, keeping a few feet of distance between them.

She nodded. Changing the subject, and in spite of the people passing by on the sidewalk, she said, "How many of them are there?" without mentioning vampires by name.

He looked at her for a few seconds before speaking. "If you're asking about the office intruder, the answer is that there are too many of them for anyone's good."

She went on, hitting hard and to the point. "Who, besides you, knows about them?"

Gone now was the pretty pink tint in her cheeks. One of her hands rested on the roof of her car. Her other hand tugged at the collar of the sweater that matched her blue eyes.

"Very few people know," Derek said.

"Why not? Why doesn't everyone have that information when it's so important? Why haven't you told them?"

"I've already mentioned to you about the panic that would ensue. You can imagine it, can't you?"

"There was a vampire in my office," she said in a hushed voice when there was a break in pedestrian traffic, and as though she needed to say those words out loud in order to grasp the ramifications.

Derek nodded. "Yes. There was."

"What about the other ones? The monsters that aren't vampires? You said most werewolves don't cause problems, so you do know about them."

Before he could reply, she went on. "I heard them howl and thought it was a prank. That sound was the thing that kept me on the street."

The remark she'd made last night began to make sense to Derek now, and it also left him feeling guilty. If Riley had followed the sound of a Were's howl for some reason, and that howl had been his, then he had put Riley in danger.

Still, he was curious about why she had been lured onto the streets by a wolf's howl when no one else had paid any attention. And why she had tried to howl at him.

She hadn't actually seen anything when he and Dale arrived to help her with that attacker by the pub. She hadn't been in any kind of shape to see them in their alternate shapes, and yet Riley first had chased a wolfish sound and then had mentioned werewolves to him after her attack. In retrospect, there had to be something more to her story than a whimsical love for adventure.

"I do know a few things," he said.

Derek had no idea how he was going to get out of this conversation gracefully. Riley wouldn't have been owed any explanations if that damn vampire hadn't followed her. She might never have seen him again.

Had that bloodsucker in her office been his fault, as

well, as he and Dale suspected? Derek supposed it was possible the vamps had been observing him and that they might have picked up on his interest in Riley.

If any of that was true, he did owe her something for the trouble he might have caused.

"I have to get back to the current investigation," he said. "But I'm not going to keep those answers from you. Meet me tonight and I'll explain. It will take a little time, and I don't have that right now."

"All right," she said, surprising him yet again. "Tonight at Orson's. Eight o'clock. But first, one more question."

"Ask it," Derek said.

"Why would a vampire single me out, if, in fact, that one did?"

"Maybe it didn't. How are we to know that unless we make an attempt to find out?"

She opened her car door and turned to face him again before getting in. "You won't stand me up tonight, Detective?"

"I wouldn't dream of it," he said.

That much at least, Derek thought to himself as Riley drove away in her silver sedan, was true.

She had chosen one of the most popular eateries in Seattle for this dinner because the place would be packed on a Saturday night. It would also, Riley knew, be noisy enough to cover the strange conversation she and Miller were going to have.

At home, her anxiousness over everything that had happened manifested not only in the way she checked every nook and corner in her house for intruders, but also in the way she dressed for this next important meeting.

Her black dress, which was smart, and not too short or too sexy, would work as camouflage in a hip restaurant ull of other black dresses. Her strappy high heels would be easy to slip off if the need came to run…

She drove fast to reach the restaurant and scored a good parking space. When she walked up to Orson's, Miller was there, waiting for her in front. He hadn't changed his clothes, probably because he had taken time off from the job to see her.

Miller's tight T-shirt hugged his torso. His loose, worn black leather jacket almost covered his jeans-clad hips. She had prepared herself for the sight of him, but seeing him standing beneath the restaurant's overhead lights gave Riley a jolt of pleasure. He truly was gorgeous, and he radiated a confidence only slightly magnified by the power of his badge.

As she walked toward him, Riley couldn't help noticing the interest he got from other women. Miller's sexual vibe affected females on a primal level, and she felt it as she approached him.

He was observing every step she took as though she was a suspect in an investigation. Maybe he was sizing her up to see whether he could trust her with the information she'd asked for.

He didn't smile. Of course he wouldn't, since this was not a date, and for perhaps the first time in a while, he was the one in the hot seat. She might have grinned over that idea if the situation hadn't been so serious.

"Detective Miller," she said in greeting.

"Dr. Price," he returned.

All business, he avoided commenting about how she looked, though Riley was sure there was appreciation in his eyes.

"Are you finished up at my office?" she asked.

"For now."

"Will there be more interviews tomorrow?"

"Yes, if you'll oblige."

Riley already sensed an undercurrent of electricity passing between them and had to ignore it just to get through this. If she had met Derek Miller at any other time, and in any other circumstances, she would have enjoyed whatever was making her skin tingle each time she looked at him. Now, however, she needed a lot more than male-female warm-and-fuzzy feelings.

"I believe your father is also in law enforcement? A captain?" he said as they headed toward the entrance.

"You've done your homework, I see, Detective."

"All in the name of piecing together a puzzle."

"That puzzle being?"

"Your two brushes with the dark side, Dr. Price."

It was a cold night, and his reply made Riley feel exposed. She tugged at her jacket and gestured to the door with her clutch purse. "Shall we go inside?"

"It's crowded," he noted.

"Exactly."

He nodded. Locks of shiny brown hair fell lazily over his forehead when his eyes returned to her. "After you."

The decibel level of the noise inside the restaurant was deafening, though the night was still young. People were two-deep at the bar, but Riley passed it by. This meeting might have required alcohol, and yet she was again going to play it straight and see how far she got.

Miller had fans inside the trendy restaurant, too. He and Riley were shown to a coveted corner table, near the back wall. Riley shook her head when Miller moved to help with her jacket, and sat down. Ignoring the menu she was handed, she carefully rested her hands and her purse on the table. There was a small tape recorder inside that purse.

"You're sure about this?" Miller asked, giving her an option to back out of this conversation.

"It's safe here," Riley said. "At least, I think so. Maybe you can tell me if I'm wrong about that."

"They wouldn't come here, or to any place where people gather in numbers."

The way he said the word *they* gave Riley a healthy round of chills even though she'd left her coat on.

"Vampires?" she asked.

"Yes."

"How many of them are we talking about, exactly, Detective?"

"Enough."

"Which is?" she pressed.

"People are good food, and there are plenty of people around."

Her hands slipped from the table. "That's obscene."

"It's what you wanted, isn't it? The truth?"

Riley blinked slowly to take in what he'd said. "Besides you, who else knows about this problem?"

"Maybe a hundred of us, give or take."

"Do you all carry wooden stakes?"

"It's highly recommended when we're poking our noses into dark alleys and backstreets. Since you've seen one example of the species, I'm sure you can imagine the trouble vampires can cause."

Riley shifted in her seat, thinking *only a hundred people know?*

"It jumped from my window, three floors up," she said.

"Through the window," Miller corrected.

To keep from trembling over that memory, Riley bit her lip and took a moment before speaking again. "Doing so didn't seem to hurt it."

"Not much would when they're already dead."

The trembling spread to her hands, which she kept

office building hadn't brought cohorts. There had been no throng of spectators. Worst of all, though, in the aftermath of tonight's trials, was the thought that he'd have to exact a promise from Riley not to reveal to anyone what she had witnessed. He'd have to make sure she kept that promise, or his remark about most of Seattle's Weres not causing trouble would be a lie.

Derek leaned a shoulder against the wall by his front window, feeling antsy, though his mind was fatigued. In a few hours, and if he chose to participate, he would see Riley at the precinct when she came in to go over her statement. He wasn't sure that would be such a wise move after the connection that had snapped into place between them.

Are you thinking of me, Riley?

Will you have fitful dreams?

More important, would what she had witnessed free her tongue in front of others in the department?

If he was there, he could warn her about that. At the very least, he could change the direction of the conversation if she looked to be headed that way. How could he win? She'd be better off if he didn't show up, and his pack would be better off if he did.

You are a wild card, Riley Price.

It was never wise to involve a human in supernatural affairs. He and a whole host of others worked hard to keep things out of the public eye, and had done so for years. Why let anyone spoil that now? was the question his pack would be asking.

With his eyes closed, Riley's face appeared before him like an image he could reach out and touch. Her scent still filled his lungs. Her observant stare continued to haunt him. He was stuck in a loop centered on her.

Will your humanness allow you to choose a partner more wisely, Riley?

folded in her lap. *It's better to know*, Riley told herself
Danger rides in the wake of ignorance.

"Have you come up with a theory as to why that thing
was in my office?" she asked.

"One you probably won't like, and yet it's only a theory," he replied.

"I'd like to hear it."

"What if I ask you to listen to it with an open mind
and stay where you are, in that chair, for a while longer,
no matter what I say?"

"Open minds are my business, Detective. And I'm familiar with the concept of a theory."

His nod was pensive. Did he think she would run away
now, when she didn't like anything about this conversation so far, and had been ready to run from the moment
she sat down?

"That vampire might have been sniffing you out because I had been there, in your office. It could very well
have been trying to find out the reason for my visit, though
the fact that this particular bloodsucker could have been
researching and planning would be highly unusual."

She needed a minute to make sense of that, and took
even longer to respond. "You know their habits that well?"

"I have to if I'm to keep this city safe."

"You've encountered them before," she noted.

He nodded. "On too many occasions."

Miller's gaze was boring into her, she knew without
having to look. He was again gauging her reaction to what
he'd said.

"So, that one could have been in my office because
you go after them, and it might have wanted to retaliate?
It might have been after you, not me?"

The fact that Miller had to think over his answer to her
question made her quake.

"That could very well be the case," he conceded. "If so, then you were in danger because of me, and helping you out of that situation was the least I could do."

"Is that the only theory you have?" Riley asked.

"At the moment, yes. But we're working on others."

She had been studying psychology long enough to know when someone was holding something back. Nevertheless, Miller was under no obligation to tell her everything, and Riley knew it.

She said, "Is there a theory about how those creatures can exist? How they came about? Why they're here?"

"Only the things fiction writers point to, and that's not necessarily reliable," he replied.

"So, you take them down when you come across them and hope to keep their numbers from increasing? You do this in secret, with others?"

"Yes."

"And the public won't ever know about vampires?"

"Not possible," he said. "Not any time in the foreseeable future, anyway."

She eyed him without caring if he noticed how much she was shaking. "Maybe a little panic would be a good thing."

Miller shook his head. "You'll have to trust me on that."

When their eyes met, heat flooded her cheeks. Uncomfortable with that reaction, Riley broke eye contact.

"It's my turn to ask something," he said. "Why don't you tell me about what you thought you were chasing on the street last night after you heard a noise like a howl?"

Riley suddenly found herself mute. Seconds ticked by, and maybe even minutes, before she took a breath, settled her shoulders and confessed, "I have a thing for werewolves."

That was the truth, just not all of it.

Miller's gaze was disconcertingly focused. But after

hearing herself say those words, Riley stood up, picked up her purse and left him at the table to stare at her retreating backside.

She hadn't meant to run. But she was more afraid of hearing what Miller might have said about that little confession than what he'd said about vampires.

He'd had the strangest look in his eyes. And she had just given him a hint of the secret she had protected for most of her life.

Chapter 16

Derek went after his fleeing date—the woman who was now privy to one of Seattle's greatest secrets. Better than that, he now knew the *thing* she had for werewolves was what had brought them together.

What were the odds of that happening, even if she had just meant the creatures in the movies?

He didn't actually believe in fate. He had never stopped to consider why he was a Were, and different from everyone else in Seattle.

Riley Price just happened to have an appreciation for the species he belonged to without having known that werewolves actually existed. Now that she did know, what would she do?

He caught her outside the restaurant with a hand on her arm and said, "We can't possibly be finished with this conversation. You don't get to leave me with an exit line like that and hope to get away without an explanation."

When she turned around, he saw how flushed her cheeks were. Instead of avoiding him, she took a step closer to meet his studied gaze.

"I now know there are more things going on in this city than you're willing to talk about, and I also understand how strange my remark might seem to someone like you, who knows about most of them."

Derek couldn't tell if Riley was afraid or testing him in some way, hoping he would tell her more than he already had. But he wasn't quite ready to go there.

Her scent was delicious, and her body was close enough for him to want a replay of the kisses they had shared. Willpower was the key for getting him through the next few seconds without pulling her in for more.

"Spill," he said. "Tell me why you don't want to talk to me now, and why you ran."

"I don't know," she confessed. "We're speaking about nonsensical issues that are no longer nonsensical. The world has changed. My world has changed. How am I supposed to get used to that in the five minutes since I've known about it?"

"You deal with the truth," Derek said. "Better than most, you should understand the reasons for facing whatever comes up."

Her eyes were bright. She was shivering in the night air. "Do you want to go back inside?" he asked.

"No. I was wrong to choose this place. I'm sorry."

"Someplace else, then?" he suggested.

She shook her head. "Will vampires come after me again?"

Derek wanted to say no, but couldn't. He just didn't know what to expect. Even now, they were together again, and vampires could easily have been observing them from nearby rooftops.

"Just in case the one theory I have turns out to be right, it's probably a good idea if we don't meet so visibly after dark until I understand what's really going on," he warned.

Derek could have sworn Riley looked disappointed at that suggestion. It was possible, however, that he was mistaken, and what he actually saw in her expression was relief.

She glanced around before bringing her attention back to him. "It's creepy. This whole vampire thing is creepy."

"It is."

"How long have you known about them?" she asked.

"About three years, though their numbers have increased dramatically in the past two."

Her eyes widened. "What should I do if one of them comes after me again? I don't have any wooden stakes. Not even a good steak knife."

Derek smiled. He couldn't help it. She was trying to put a light spin on a dark situation, and not too successfully. It was possible that levity made her feel better, though her face was extremely pale.

"I'm going to ask you to trust me," he said. "Can you do that?"

"Because of your badge?"

"Because I happen to know more about this problem than most people, and out of necessity have made an art of studying vampire habits."

"You won't always be around to watch over me. I need to know how to protect myself."

He remained silent, waiting for her to answer his question about trusting him.

"Yes," she finally conceded. "I suppose I can trust you."

"Then come with me."

"Where to?"

He waited again for her to come around. She finally did with a curt nod and a whispered "Okay."

What Riley Price didn't say, but probably wanted to, was *"Will going with you, trusting you, hurt me, or be any crazier than the last two days?"*

That just happened to be the question he couldn't have answered truthfully.

Riley felt the strength in Miller's hand when he laced his fingers through hers. She wanted to absorb some of that strength as he led her down the sidewalk and away from the restaurant. She didn't question him again about where he was taking her, and remained watchful of her surroundings.

He stopped beside the entrance to an alley two blocks down and turned to face her. "Showtime," he said. "Are you ready?"

Hell, no. Ready for what? her mind warned, though Riley didn't say that out loud.

Miller bent down to remove the wooden stake from his boot, as she had seen him do the night before. When he handed it to her, Riley felt like throwing up.

"Take it," he advised, closing her fingers around the unusual weapon.

The stake was smooth in her hand, with a pointed tip. *Well-used* was the word that came to her as she clutched the stake. Did he expect her to use this? She prayed there wouldn't be an opportunity to do so as Miller headed into the dim alley assuming she would follow him.

Riley had a hard time moving her feet. The street, with its lights and traffic, had become scary enough without leaving it for the city's darker places. She had already seen a vampire and a werewolf, and that was more than enough.

She could head in the opposite direction and say to hell

with Derek Miller, and yet the little spark of inner defiance wasn't going to allow her to do that.

"Please tell me you're kidding," she called out when he paused to wait for her to catch up.

"We should be quiet now," he warned.

Since she didn't want to be left behind and on her own, Riley took a few steps with the wooden stake raised. Her heart rate spiked into the red zone, the way it had last night, when she thought she'd heard a werewolf's howl and chased the sound. Adrenaline surged through her with hefty electrical jolts that fired up her nerves and obliterated her chills. She had wanted adventure and truth, and it didn't get any bigger than this.

Her restless mind kicked up all kinds of scenarios as she moved forward. Was Miller going to show her another vampire? Was this going to be a lesson on how to protect herself and what to look out for...with her dressed in heels and a little black dress inappropriate for the occasion?

Swallowing back her fear over what they'd find in the alley, Riley remembered that so far in their short acquaintance, Miller had come through when the going got tough.

She could do this.

Like a shadow, Riley kept as close to Miller as she could without tripping over him. She reminded herself to breathe, and kept a death grip on the wooden stake.

Miller stopped again just past the edge of the building beside them and gestured for her to wait. He took several more steps that made him blend into the shadows that were lit only by a single overhead lamp hanging from the back of the building, high up.

A sound in the periphery numbed her with fear.

"Come out." Miller spoke to the dark space beyond the reach of the light.

Riley's ears picked up static, like the kind radios make between stations.

"It's just me," Miller said to whoever or whatever was out there. "Me, and a friend."

Every separate system in Riley's overstrung body sent up a red flag for her to get out of there as quickly as possible. She had experienced this same warning twice before in the span of twenty-four hours.

"Some of you wanted to see her, and here she is," Miller called out. "The last vamp who wanted the same thing didn't fare so well."

Riley's throat constricted. Her breathing grew shallow enough to leave her light-headed.

"Last chance," Miller said to the darkness. "Take it or leave it."

Leave it. Please leave it... Riley silently pleaded.

But that was wishful thinking, since they had invaded a vampire's space, and the man beside her was calling out the monster.

Miller kicked up some alley detritus with his boot, an action meant as a further challenge for any creature that was here to show itself. Riley couldn't have moved if she had to.

With her eyes riveted to the darkness ahead of them, she waited without knowing exactly what she would see, whether some kind of supernatural creature accepted Miller's taunt. The vampire in her office had been little more than a blur. Miller hadn't given it much time before he had taken care of the problem.

She didn't want to see this, but had to.

There was a movement in the darkness. With a slick sideways glide of dark overlapping black on black, something emerged. Feelings of impending doom engulfed her as a light face appeared, a ghostly pale face that stood out from their surroundings and seemed to hover too far off the ground.

"Vampire," Riley said.

Miller nodded. "A fresh inductee that didn't bother to hide its scent."

Riley didn't want to know what that scent might be. The odors in the alley were enough to cause a gag reflex.

When the white face floated closer, Miller offered encouragement. "That's right. Come on. You can smell her, can't you?"

The creature was close enough now for Riley to see that its body was swathed in a black robe that had rendered the vampire invisible in the dark. This was a vampire. No mistake. Nothing else could have looked or moved like this. Nothing alive, anyway.

"Riley," Miller said to her without taking his eyes off the vampire. "Meet your nightmare. Not the worst one, but a decent example of what happens when a person has risen from the grave into an unintended afterlife."

The vampire's hiss was almost as frightening as its appearance. Riley fought the urge to back up and run. She held Miller's stake so tightly in her hand her knuckles were as white as the creature's face. If she left, Miller would have nothing to protect himself with.

She clenched her teeth and waited for what would happen next, telling herself that Miller was a pro and able to handle this vampire. He had done it before, right in front of her, with relative ease.

"This alley is in my jurisdiction," Miller said to the creature. "There are a lot of people nearby, and I'll bet you're hungry."

The vampire didn't advance or make another sound. Dark eyes studied her and Miller both, as if they were prey.

"Do you have to kill it?" Riley whispered to Miller. "I

mean, I get that it's already dead. Is there no way to reason with them?"

"They are animated corpses driven by a thirst for blood. They prefer human blood and are indiscriminate about where they get it. This guy would drain you dry in about twenty seconds. Don't think he isn't considering how to do that right now," Miller said.

"So you have to…"

"Yep. I've seen far too much of the carnage these bloodsuckers leave behind. It's either us or them."

The vampire opened its mouth to show off the tips of two ungodly long and pointed teeth. Riley raised the stake and held it aloft, as though it was a magical talisman that would keep the creature away…

Just before the vampire attacked.

Chapter 17

Derek blocked the vampire before it could reach Riley, grabbed the stake from her frozen fingers and spun it around for a better grip. He caught the creature by its robe and hauled it backward so that he could take aim at its chest.

The thing hissed again loudly, but Derek had heard this before on so many occasions it had no the effect on him. Some new vampires were wily and some weren't. Like most of the vamps he'd met in the past few weeks, this one believed itself to be invincible and the bigger threat.

That would be its first and last mistake.

The creature kicked out and fought back as though it had ten limbs instead of four. The newly made bloodsucker was fast, but not thinking too clearly. The bloodlust was upon it, and Riley was a delicacy it wanted to reach with those nasty fangs.

Behind him, Riley hadn't moved. She was all eyes,

and tense, but he could tell a good portion of her fear was for him. In that moment, as he again hauled the vampire back from reaching her, Derek realized that Riley would help him if she found a way to do so. She wasn't actually frozen in place, but was waiting for the opportunity to present itself.

He heard that thought run through her mind as if he had the ability to read it.

Surprised by the intimacy of that connection, Derek let the vampire slip from his grasp. It lunged for Riley, fangs snapping, before Derek caught hold of the creep again. But it had gotten close to her—close enough for Riley to smell its fetid breath.

She recoiled in time to avoid a bite to her left shoulder. With reflexes Derek silently praised, Riley slapped the bloodsucker in the face and jumped aside. The vampire turned to catch her, angry, hissing like a startled cat.

"Enough," Derek said.

As Riley moved to stand behind him again, he kicked the vampire, knocking it to the ground. He placed his boot on the vamp's chest, raised the stake in the air and then it was over. *One more down. Case closed.*

Standing upright, he turned and looked at Riley, who was still behind him, and breathing hard. Her face had lost half of its color. Gray vamp dust littered her head and shoulders, but she hadn't run away this time. She had stayed.

They stood there looking at each other for some time without speaking. The air was loaded with tension that hadn't fully been used up. Derek's muscles rippled beneath his shirt and jacket. Riley's hands shook. Neither of them broke eye contact this time because they both understood that the only way to get rid of the adrenaline rush was to ıse it up. Wear it out. Short of finding another vampire to fight, there was only one way to do that.

Like the hunger the vampire had possessed, Derek's desire for Riley and for what might occur in the next few seconds burned him up inside. Somehow he sensed the same thing happening to her.

"You're a surprise, Riley Price," he said. "And also much more than you seem."

"I could have told you that," she returned. "I am a cop's daughter, after all."

But that wasn't it. That wasn't what Derek had meant. She also kept something hidden from the world. He saw this in her face, and in her eyes. Riley Price had secrets, and he had just witnessed one of them in the way she had behaved here, by his side.

"You weren't very afraid," he noted.

"I nearly lost my lunch," she said.

Her eyes dared him to delve deeper. "No. That's not it. That's not everything," he suggested.

"I have no idea what you're talking about, and you're the one with the answers here."

Maybe that was true, but Riley was being equally as unreasonable. He was painfully aware of her body, her eyes, and the way she was looking at him. Sexual tension surrounded them like a fog. Invisible lightning crackled in the air. His next move was in response to all of that.

Derek took her by the shoulders and drew her in until their bodies were molded together. As with the night before, she didn't protest when his mouth found hers. Her lips were already parted and ready for the kiss that was to come. But a kiss wasn't going to do it for either of them. Not tonight.

He took her mouth like the wolf he was. It was a fierce

action, a teasing lead-up to the next inevitable step in their crazy, short-term relationship.

It crossed Derek's mind that he was becoming involved with a victim in two open police cases, and also that it didn't matter, since he would help her out no matter what took place. Riley was now privy to what went on in this city, and his part in that.

Her mouth was feverish, tender and greedy. She kissed him back the way a she-wolf would have in similar circumstances. For Weres, there was a grand finale to fighting and vanquishing a foe, and that finale was sexual.

What did it mean for her?

Derek drew back far enough to take her hand. "Not the place," he said. "Too many eyes. Too much filth."

She let him lead her to the street. They walked fast and said nothing. His need for her didn't ease once his muscles were in motion. If anything, heading toward a safe place where they could go at each other like animals served to intensify those cravings.

He would find out what her secrets were.

He couldn't wait to peel back the mask.

His apartment wasn't far and there was no need to take Riley's silver sedan. They just had to get there before anything else came up that could get in the way of what he had in mind.

Derek glanced at Riley as they turned the corner of his street, looking for her go-ahead. The green light.

She smiled.

She'd seen her second vampire and was still standing. Walking, actually. Riley didn't know how that could be, other than the fact that her trust in the man beside her had become a tangible thing she wanted to touch with both hands, and there was only one way to do that.

Just now she wanted to be the one to bite the man beside her—run her teeth over his neck and his bare shoulders to see what kind of control the big, bad detective had then.

Most cops were wild at heart and Derek Miller was no exception. Riley supposed she had her father to thank for passing that wildness to her, though it had taken years of hard work for her to tame it.

Miller lived on the second floor of a newer apartment building, not far from one of the main boulevards. They passed up the elevator in favor of a steep flight of stairs, barely slowing down until they reached his door. One turn of the key and they were inside. Without taking the time to look around, Riley found herself on her back, on top of his unmade bed.

Miller leaned over her and kissed her again. She tasted his passion, heat and desire. There were, however, too many clothes getting in the way of satisfying their mutual needs.

Miller had to have been thinking the same thing. He stood up, tossed his jacket to the floor and then pulled off his shirt. He stood still long enough for her to take stock of everything she suddenly wanted so badly.

An image flashed through her mind of her first encounter with her rescuer as she stared at Miller's gloriously bronzed muscle. Long hair, a taut body and eyes like diamonds in the night were things she would never forget.

He pulled her to a sitting position and removed her coat. Then he tugged her to her feet and wrapped his arms around her so that he could reach and find her zipper.

The sound it made in its downward slide was erotic. In the otherwise quiet room, that little piece of metal moving along its track was a heady signal that two adults were agreeing to have sex.

Cool air brushed across Riley's naked back, and she

sighed softly. The handsome detective wasn't kissing her now. Her head was pressed to his bare chest, where his heat was fierce. The guy was on fire, and she needed heat

She had worn black lacy lingerie to match the dress and didn't stop to wonder if Miller would like what he found. He was one-hundred-percent involved in undressing her, and he was savoring every minute, just as she was.

His fingers slipped seductively over her spine and began an agonizingly slow journey upward, taking time to explore the feel of each vertebra until he reached the nape of her neck. By then, Riley was ready to jump him and cling. But his breath in her hair and the way he was taking his time with the foreplay were turn-ons.

With her ear against his chest, Riley heard Miller's heart beating with a slow, rhythmical cadence that was the exact opposite of hers. She kept her eyes closed as his warm hand slid upward and into her hair. He took hold of a few strands and drew her head back so that she had to look up at him. When his eyes flashed, Riley felt as if she was falling, and as though she was about to drown in the blue blaze of those eyes.

He pressed the soft black fabric of her dress over her shoulders. They were too close together for the dress to fall, and close enough for her to feel how aroused Miller was. The pleasure he was already giving her was extreme. She felt it all, each move, each flare of warmth. She heard him whisper but couldn't catch the words.

The seduction was like a song, in that it built up slowly in tempo. Miller was priming her for the moment when they could no longer stand being apart, but she was already shouting inwardly for him to hurry up.

He lifted her to let the dress fall to the floor, where it puddled next to his jacket. Riley kicked off her shoes. Her legs were bare.

Miller didn't even back up to look at and appreciate the body she had worked hard on in the gym, or the lacy lingerie she wasn't going to wear for long. Hunger overtook them both at that moment, uncontrolled and primal in its intensity.

She was against his bedroom wall and he was kissing her senseless. A minute later she was back on the bed with Miller perched above her. There was no way to put off what they both wanted any longer. Their breathing was shallow. The hardness behind his jeans, against her thighs, proved Miller was as expectant as she was.

She dug into his back with her nails as he reached down to free her from the fragile black-lace barrier that was keeping him from taking what he wanted. And then he freed himself.

He entered her gently at first. Riley writhed beneath him, encouraged him to get on with this. It wasn't supposed to be making love. This was nothing more than an attack of mutual lust and a few moments of unparalleled passion between people who were barely more than strangers.

Her lover gave her what she wanted as he moved into her with an agonizing slowness, then withdrew again so that they could both take a breath. His eyes never left hers.

Then he came back, moved slightly faster with a plunge into her depths that took her breath away. Gripping his arms, Riley kept him close as he again withdrew. But after that, they couldn't take their time any longer.

She made appreciative sounds as he began to move with a gradual buildup of depth and speed. She couldn't stop herself. Every new thrust, each withdrawal, infused her with a blistering heat and the desire for more.

It didn't take her body long to flood with the sensations he was providing. A thunderstorm began deep inside her and grew steadily, quickly gaining in strength. The thunder rolled toward her lover, rushing to meet at the point of their merging bodies.

He again whispered something to her that she didn't hear—words that got lost in the storm system she was experiencing. But something about the way he said those words, and the velvety tone of his voice, brought her to the vortex of that internal storm, and made her peak.

The climax hit hard, and with real fury. Riley bit back a cry of pleasure as her body seized, caught in the throes of a new and exotic kind of sensory overload.

She didn't open her eyes now. Couldn't. Her lover pinned her to the bed as the waves of her orgasm crashed over her and kept coming.

He found her mouth, and kissed her, absorbing her cries as he let out his own sound—part sigh and part groan of pleasure. His body finally slowed its wicked rhythm with a satisfied gasp of release.

Only the sound he made wasn't a gasp.

It was a growl.

Chapter 18

Riley held her breath until her lungs were ready to burst before she exhaled slowly, hoping she'd be able to breathe normally sometime in the near future.

Echoes of the bliss she had experienced still tickled her insides. Her legs were tangled with the legs of the man who had given her so much pleasure.

Miller was looking down at her with his bright blue eyes, but instead of reflecting the satisfaction of the past few minutes, his expression was one of trepidation. Maybe he thought he had gone too far. That they had gone too far.

The sound of satisfaction he had made hung in the air. Had he growled because of her earlier confession about liking werewolves? Did he expect her to smile and appreciate that he had listened to what she'd said when it had been silly for her to admit to such a thing?

She didn't really know this man at all.

But she had to say something. It was what people always did after sleeping with a stranger.

"You're good at that," she said.

Miller raised an eyebrow. As incredible as the sex had been, it had, in the afterglow, become awkward.

"Thanks," he said without easing up on his keen stare, or moving aside.

"I'll have to go," Riley said, avoiding his eyes, afraid that if they found that same connection again, she'd be up for round two. The truth was that she was already up for it.

"So soon?" he asked, though he couldn't have missed her breathless, slightly anxious state.

"What is it, Riley?" he added in a tender tone that brought her more ripples of heat. "Please say you don't feel regret."

"No. It's..."

"It's what?"

"You're much more than you seem," she said.

"Was that a compliment?"

It actually was a compliment in a roundabout way, Riley decided. And this wasn't the time to ask the questions that returned now to plague her, though she felt she had to say something else. That growl had brought back a dozen thoughts and memories from last night.

"I saw a werewolf in an alley," she said, moving from pleasure to the nightmare of the night before as quickly as those thoughts arrived.

Miller's expression registered his surprise. He clearly hadn't expected her to return to the supernatural subjects still on the table. But he didn't avoid addressing her remark.

"I told you Weres exist, Riley. I believe you saw what you saw."

"Not a guy in a costume. A real live werewolf," she said.

"Please don't bother trying to evade the subject. Don't lie to me about vampires being the only immediate threat. That wolf was fierce and like nothing I've ever seen. I heard one of them howl when I was first attacked."

The room was quiet for a few seconds before he nodded. "That's highly likely."

Riley actually had nowhere to go from here and couldn't think of anything else to say. The other items on her list floated away as the warmth of Derek Miller's next exhaled breath touched her cheek.

He backed to his knees and stood up. He offered her his hand, which Riley took, feeling far too exposed now in the few scraps of lace still covering her. She put on her coat, skipping the dress. Miller watched with interest as she leaned over to slip on her shoes.

Wearing just enough to make a quick getaway, she looked at Miller, figuring that she could think of him as Derek now, after this, though cops almost never went by their given names.

"Talk to me," he said. "You can, you know."

Riley hesitated, not sure how to begin. "I can't go home, can I, in case a vampire might be waiting for me?"

"You'll be protected, I promise," he replied. "Nothing with evil intentions will get to you there or anywhere else."

They were avoiding the elephant in the room. Dancing around what had just happened on his bed. Withholding things made the transition from the rawness of their passion to normality uncomfortable.

He wasn't going to pressure her or argue, though. "I'll take you home if you want to go," he said, then, after a few beats, added, "But why don't you stay here? I'm due back at work, so you'll have the place to yourself. More protection will arrive as soon as I make a call. You can make yourself at home."

Riley looked around. The bedroom was small and tidy, except for the unmade bed, and was sparsely furnished. There was a large rug, a dresser and one shuttered window.

She recalled passing through a living room to reach the bedroom, and catching a glimpse of a kitchen. But she wouldn't have felt at ease in Derek Miller's house when his scent was everywhere, especially after what they had just done. Being among his things felt too private. She wasn't ready for that, so she had to go home.

As if he had read her mind, Miller nodded. "Fine. Wait a minute while I make that call. Then I'll take you home. Grab a drink from the refrigerator if you'd like. There's a bathroom down the hall."

As he left the room, he glanced at her over his shoulder. "I'm truly sorry if something I've done has put you in danger. The only way I can make up for that is to see that you stay safe. Will you let me do that? Will you stay off the streets until I find some answers?"

"Yes," Riley said, because what other option did she have? Having this detective watch over her meant that she would see him again, though she promised herself she wouldn't return to his bedroom until they knew each other a lot better. Until she felt sure about any feelings she might have for him beyond the kind of lust that had gotten her here in the first place.

She did have feelings for him. Damn it, she did.

He had stopped in the doorway and was waiting for her to look at him.

"I can do that," Riley said as she turned to find the bathroom, in need of a few minutes of alone time in a space Derek Miller didn't occupy. "I can give you time to sort this out."

Due to the strangest circumstances possible, she was going to be a prisoner of sorts for a while. Derek was offering protection every time the sun went down. She wondered how many times he might take a shift.

In the bathroom, she dabbed cold water on her face and sat on the edge of the tub. Several minutes and a thousand heartbeats later, she emerged to find Derek in the living room, standing beside the front door. He held up her dress.

"There's time for you to put this on."

"Thanks, but I'd better get going."

She took the dress from him. Their hands brushed. Riley felt another flush of heat in her throat, caused by the man who could mesmerize her without trying.

Being near to Derek Miller was a threat to her sense of reason, and looking at him made things worse…because he was the epitome of every woman's wet dream, in the flesh.

When he opened the door for her, Riley realized that besides her thing for werewolves, she was going to have to add Detective Derek Miller to the list of her interests.

They drove in silence. There wasn't much more to say that hadn't already been covered, except to acknowledge how their bodies had fit so well together and how their passion had merged perfectly in his apartment, on his bed.

He hadn't lied to Riley about trying to keep her safe. The wolves in his pack would help with that without asking questions when they heard about the vampires' sudden interest in her. Now all he had to do was worry about why Riley had been targeted.

Derek didn't like what one of the bloodsuckers had said, and the words kept repeating in his mind, adding to the puzzles needing to be solved.

She is not for you, wolf.

He was fairly sure she was for him, and that what had taken place in his apartment confirmed it. His next step would be to have Riley realize, and admit to, the same thing.

He pulled the car into her driveway and cut the engine. "Please wait," he said, and got out to greet Marshall and the member of his pack who had answered his call for assistance.

Although no explanation was required, Derek said, "Vampires have tagged her." That was all they needed to nod and get on with the job of watching over Riley while he went to investigate the issue.

Derek wished he could watch her himself. Stay with her. He didn't want to let Riley go, or allow her to think that all he'd wanted from her was sex, though he still wanted that. Beyond the urges tugging at him, however, there were bigger issues to be dealt with. Riley Price was only one piece on a moving chessboard…even if she was such a lovely one.

Derek walked her to her door, went in with her and checked the rooms. Back at the door, he finally spoke up.

"It was better than good, and only the beginning."

She hadn't looked at him on the short drive, but did so now. Her blue eyes gleamed with the same kind of longing for a rematch that he had, and her struggle to hide it from him didn't work.

Her voice was breathy. "I might hold you to that."

Turning from Riley, leaving her there, was a necessity, and also one of the most difficult things Derek had ever done. With his inner wolf whining and his hands fisted, he smiled, nodded to her and went outside, where the foul stink of vampires drifted to him on a cold, incoming breeze.

Chapter 19

"Damn it," Derek growled.

His ginger-haired packmate moved to back him up. "Not the usual neighborhood for bloodsuckers," Jared noted, and that was true. Riley lived on a quiet street lined with trees and small cottage-style houses. Families lived here. Children would play in manicured yards during the day.

Derek had never seen a vampire this far west of downtown, but he realized what the draw had to be. "Marshall, are you ready?" he asked.

The off-duty officer was wearing jeans. He pulled out his specialized gun.

"Rounds?" Derek asked, keeping his focus on the street.

"Silver, just as you requested," Marshall replied, two-fisting the weapon in front of him. "I wonder what the other guys would think of this."

The unpleasant odor was growing stronger though there was no vampire in sight. Derek backed his way up the driveway to search the roof. Zeroing in on the rooftop of the house next to Riley's, he muttered, "There you are."

He realized right away that the thing on the roof wasn't a new vampire. Brand-new vamps wouldn't have been able to peg two of the three beings standing there as werewolves without a full moon to prove it.

This bloodsucker traversed the rooftop with the agility of a cat. Instead of backing away, it moved silently toward the front of the roof and paused there to peer down at Derek's keyed-up threesome.

"Guess we're not scary enough for this guy," Jared said.

"On the other hand," Marshall remarked, "I'm totally creeped out just looking at him. It. Or whatever the hell that thing is."

"Sorry you have to see this in person," Derek said to Marshall without taking his eyes off the vampire. "Hearing about such things and actually facing them are experiences that are worlds apart."

Though vampires, like werewolves, had exceptional hearing, the one on the roof didn't react to the conversation going on beneath where it crouched. If it hadn't been cloudy, there would have been enough brightness the night after a full moon for Derek to have seen its face. As it was, even with his Were abilities, Derek couldn't view the monster as clearly as he would have liked. Its smell, however, was that of rotting debris.

"We've got all night," Derek called out after minutes of inactivity had passed. "But I don't think you do."

The taunt was a half-hearted threat, since it was probably closer to midnight than to daybreak, so there were plenty of dark hours left before the sun came up.

The vampire stood up, providing a better target for the silver bullets in Marshall's weapon. Marshall took aim. But the bloodsucker became a moving target when it leaped from the roof to land in the yard. With speed that was truly exceptional, and almost a blur, it hopped onto the fence next to Riley's cottage, and from there jumped to her roof.

"Oh, no you don't," Derek warned, heading for Riley's front door. Over his shoulder he shouted to his packmate, "Go around to the back. Find that sucker."

Riley had locked the door. Derek pounded on it with a fist and called her name loudly enough for anyone nearby to have heard.

The door opened. Riley stood there, dressed exactly as she had been when he'd left her minutes before. Derek took hold of her arm and hustled her outside, wondering if that was the safest move, but he had to do something to keep her in his sight. She didn't say a word or ask what was going on. The wideness in her eyes suggested she already knew.

He led her to Marshall's car and put her inside before he nodded to Marshall and then sprinted back to the house, muttering every obscenity he had ever picked up.

He raced into the house, remembering how vampires had gone after his ex two years before. Back then the reason had been to lure her new lover into the open. The guy she had fallen for. It turned out that the vamp queen also had the hots for that new guy, and had kidnapped McKenna to get rid of the competition.

But this was happening in the present, to him and to Riley. So he had to again consider the possibility that Damaris had set a plan in motion for reasons only she knew about. Could it be to lure Derek into taking a misstep that would leave Seattle without a diligent alpha and open to a full-on vampire invasion? Were his pack and others like it the only barrier to a possible future bloodbath?

How did Riley fit in with that plan?

No. That line of reasoning couldn't be right because

the warning he had been given was that Riley wasn't for
him, and that he was to leave her alone. Him. Personally.

He blew through Riley's house like a tornado, and the
search turned up nothing. Exiting through the back door,
Derek met Jared in the yard.

"No sign of it," Jared said.

A chill at the base of Derek's neck provided the impetus for his next sprint, which was in the direction of Marshall's car.

Riley pressed her face to the glass, anxious about what
was going on. She recognized Officer Marshall out of uniform. He stood by the hood of the car with his gun raised.

She sat back when she heard shots that sent her anxiety
level skyrocketing. This incident could be a break-in or a
random trespass, but Riley doubted it could be anything so
simple after the events that had preceded it. Due to Officer
Marshall's presence and the warnings Derek had given,
this had to be another vampire sighting…which meant the
monsters had found out where she lived.

Why, though? What made her a target?

Officer Marshall fired two rounds. The noise was
shocking, but she couldn't see what he was shooting at
outside the car window. It wasn't hard for her to remember the vampire she'd met tonight in the alley Derek had
taken her to, and the way it had blended with the shadows.

Riley sat up straighter to see what would happen next,
and found Derek looking back at her through the window.
She withheld a sigh of relief. This was the man who had
promised to protect her from monsters, and he was adher-
ing to that promise.

Another shot rang out. She heard Officer Marshall
shout. A face appeared on the opposite side of the car,
pressed to the window on her right. It was a terrible face—

deathly pale and wicked, with dark, red-rimmed eyes and a gaze that pinned her to the seat.

She sat between Derek at one window and a vampire in the other. Derek's eyes were on the vampire. The vampire only had eyes for her.

"Fuck you," Riley said to the monster.

A fourth shot ricocheted off the door, creating sparks on the metal. Derek vanished. So did the vampire.

Riley reached for the door handle and stumbled out of the car, thinking that in the old days, a weapon like Officer Marshall's would only have had six bullets in the chambers and that only two would have remained. But there were other options now, and she hoped to God this gun was more up-to-date.

She saw Derek running across the lawn of the house next door with another man on his heels. Officer Marshall barked a curt "Get back in the car" without turning to face her.

Riley put a hand to her chest, as if that could possibly have slowed her hammering heart. She didn't want to get back in the car. Somehow she felt safer in the open.

"Did you see it?" she asked Officer Marshall, who kept his gun raised. "You know what that was?"

"I know that thing shouldn't exist, and that we'd all be better off if it didn't," he replied.

"Was there only one of them?" Riley figured that had to be right, since Derek had given chase.

"One is enough." Officer Marshall held his weapon steadily, without any hint of shaking or visible surprise.

He added, "They're coming back," careful to keep anything moving toward them in his sights.

"Not—" she began, her query cut off by Derek's familiar voice.

"Did you get it?" Marshall called out.

"The bastard got away." Derek crossed the lawn accompanied by the man who had followed him in the chase.

"What now?" Marshall asked, lowering his gun.

"Now Miss Price will have to relocate, at least for a while," Derek replied as he approached. To her, he added, "Are you up for that?"

Riley leaned against the side of the car. The lingering echo of the sound of gunfire underscored her lover's words. "Is there actually a place that would be out of their reach?" she asked.

"Yes, though you might not like it much, either."

He glanced at the tall, muscled young man who had backed him up, as if seeking that man's confirmation of the place he had in mind, and received a nod in return.

"Where is that?" Riley asked as Derek again took her arm.

He leaned toward her and lowered his voice so there would be no opportunity for it to carry. With his blue eyes on hers and a gentle grip on her arm, he said, "You know that species you have a thing for?"

Riley wasn't sure why her pulse spiked so dramatically when her heart shouldn't have been able to beat any faster than it already was. She met Derek's steady, direct gaze. "Please tell me you're kidding."

But he wasn't kidding. "No one can reach you or even dare to try if you're surrounded by my pack," he said.

Riley gave his words time to settle in, but they didn't. They couldn't have, because two words dominated all the rest, and those were *my pack*.

Pack. As in a group of people with similar goals...

Or a group of wild animals that lived and hunted together. Like wolves.

But Derek had said *my pack*.

For the first time in her life, Riley thought she might

faint. The problem was that she didn't like playing the part of a victim and had always passed on the concept of females being the weaker sex.

So she looked into Derek's eyes. "You were that shirt-less guy. Only you're not actually a *guy* after all, right? You're a—"

"Werewolf," he said.

Chapter 20

There it was. Cat out of the bag. A confession of sorts to a human who otherwise wouldn't have guessed his secret. They had been heading in a good direction before this. What would Riley do now?

She had gone pale. Her beautiful face was slack with disbelief. Again, though, if he had put her in danger, he was responsible for her safety. Beyond that commitment to her, there was now another kind. Riley had gotten under his skin. She was all he could think about. Her image accompanied every thought he had.

He waited for her to let his news sink in, wondering if she would start shouting, and if her legs would give out. He had just confirmed her suspicions about the existence of werewolves, and she couldn't possibly have expected him to be one of them.

They had shared the most intimate connection there was. Whatever came next was in some part out of their hands if she felt the tug on her soul in the same way he did. For him, sex had sealed him to Riley as if his soul had been chained to hers.

Not many humans would have wanted to be a werewolf's mate. Not many of them could have handled what that entailed.

But Riley was different.

There was so much more that he needed to say to her, and he couldn't take the time. The damn vampire had gotten away. Once a vamp had targeted its prey, it seldom gave up on that target. Like a bloodhound on a scent, this one would return for a second pass at Riley. Derek was sure of that.

This sucker had been unusually strong, and fast on its feet. It had stolen a good look at Riley. Derek pictured the bloodsucker licking its lips in anticipation of getting even closer to her. The Lash, a term to describe the extremes of the unholy vampire beast's raging hunger, had shone in its eyes.

Since Riley didn't speak, he had to. "Those fangs got too damn close."

There was no real way to read into her silence as she continued to stare at him. He heard her heart beating frantically inside her chest. The vampire wouldn't have missed that, either.

"Gather a few things," he said. "Enough to get you through the night. You can return tomorrow if you want to, and you can continue to work. But before sundown, from now on and until we get to the bottom of this, I'll take you to stay with my friends."

"Pack," she said without meeting his gaze. "That's the term you used."

Derek nodded, glad to hear her speak. "Yes. Pack."

"Because you really are a werewolf."

"Yes."

"And I'll be safer with a bunch of wolves than anywhere else."

"Infinitely safer."

She turned to Marshall with an accusation. "Are you one, too? A werewolf?"

"No, ma'am," Marshall replied. "I'm just a regular old human being who has some supernatural friends."

She looked to Jared. "Yep," he said before she could ask him the same question.

Everyone gathered here had to be wondering the same thing about why she didn't question this further, and how she could seem so calm in light of being hit with such news. Without calling them all crazy, and without any outward display of what she had to be feeling, Riley turned toward the house, as he had directed.

Derek turned with her, loathe to leave her alone in case she had a delayed reaction to what was going on. In the doorway, she paused. He anticipated that move, waited for it.

"Nothing is as it seems on the surface, Riley. I think you already knew that."

"If I didn't know it before, I do now," she said.

Derek perceived the slightest tremble in her voice. Weres were highly attuned to fluctuations in emotions, and his emotions were now connected to hers.

He stayed by the door and listened to Riley rummage through drawers in another room. She returned minutes later with an overnight bag in one hand, looking tired, her energy spent. Derek took the bag and followed her to the car. He tossed the bag inside and kept Riley from getting into the back seat.

He brought her around to face him with a gentle tug on her arm. "I'm glad you know about me," he said.

She didn't look up.

An overwhelming desire to kiss her tensed his insides. Although Riley needed to wake up from the shock she'd had, the fact that there were others present kept him from acting on that desire.

He wasn't going to lose her over this, Derek vowed. Riley would come through. She was intelligent and street-smart. She had been trained to listen and to analyze what she heard from others without rushing to a judgment. Her profession was one of tolerance and secrecy, while his was partly the opposite. In law enforcement, he faced violence and intolerance on a daily basis.

It was, however, a strange turn of circumstances that with so many she-wolves lusting after him, he had chosen to go so far out of bounds by finding a human partner. This human. *You, Riley.* And it seemed even odder to him that vampires also wanted Riley Price for reasons of their own.

"One sign," he messaged to Riley on the Were channel she couldn't hear. *"Give me a sign that you're still on board."*

A tingle at the base of his spine warned Derek that she was going to respond to his message as if she had indeed heard it.

She stood straighter, rose onto her tiptoes and placed her hands on the sides of his face. Her gaze traveled upward slowly. After looking at him closely, she touched her lips to his briefly enough for Derek to believe he could have imagined it.

Although long lashes partially covered her eyes when she backed up, Derek had seen those eyes flash with a warning of her own. It told him that Riley Price was more than a mere human woman. She was more than anger, defiance, sex, strength and courage. And she was going to prove that to everyone, including him.

Starting now.

She got into the car without an argument, without being told exactly where she was going. Which meant Riley still trusted him in spite of everything she had learned. He couldn't accompany her. He had to let her go and remain at her house in case the vampire made a quick return visit.

Jared would see to it that Riley arrived in one piece at the special location outside the city, where some of his pack had set up a community. It was a place where no one had to hide their identity. Only there could Weres feel almost totally free all the time.

"You'll be surrounded by some of the fiercest Weres around," he said to her. "As my guest, you'll be welcome."

That was true, though the members of his pack would be as wary about having a human in their midst as she would be about being around them. Still, minus a full moon, she'd fit right in.

He tapped the roof of the car, giving the signal for Marshall to drive on. In the front seat, Jared gave him a thumbs-up gesture that confirmed his acceptance of the responsibility that now rested on his shoulders.

Riley was leaving, and Derek hated the thought of a separation.

"Turn around," he whispered to her as the car pulled away from the curb. "Look at me, and I'll know where your thoughts lie."

He waited for that to happen. Willed it to happen.

It almost didn't.

The car was at the end of the block when she glanced back at him through the rear window. And for that one small favor, Derek's heart felt a tremendous surge of appreciation and hope.

They drove for a long time, eventually heading out past the city limits. The purr of the engine lulled Riley into a temporary peaceful state, which was a respite from both internal and external chaos. Away from the city, it was easier to believe none of this had happened.

She rested her head against the back of the seat and closed her eyes. Despite her knee-length wool coat, she felt chilled. But that wasn't surprising. She had been face-to-face with two werewolves and shared a bed with one of them. Dreams had indeed melted into a strange new reality. Parts of her past had come forward to bite her, proving that she did live in a world where werewolves exited.

Werewolves and other things.

Who would have guessed that about Detective Derek Miller? While he had rugged good looks and was formidable, he also walked and talked like the people around him and held an important job that made a difference on Seattle's streets. Wasn't that what being an alpha meant? That he was a protector and a leader?

How did someone go about becoming one of them? How had werewolves come to be?

After she'd gone to bed with Derek, would that wolfishness spread to her?

She tended to doubt that last part. Derek wouldn't have put her in that position. Sex couldn't be the way to spread werewolfism from one being to another. Or so she hoped.

Derek. You bastard. How could you keep that from me?

She was sick of all the dead-end questions, and thought about pumping the Were in the front seat for details. But this guy didn't owe her anything, other than seeing to her safety in Derek's absence. Derek had implied that she wouldn't need protection from the werewolves they would be joining, so did that mean most of the Weres Derek knew were intrinsically good, and that horror stories had gotten that wrong?

At this point she was still in the dark, and anyone else

might have been happy to stay there. Too bad she wasn't like everyone else.

The car slowed once they'd left most of the city lights behind. Riley ran a hand over the seat next to her, wishing Derek was there and that she could form a clear picture of what she'd be facing.

There was no way to tell what time it was. Her wristwatch was missing; she had removed it in Derek's bathroom. Leftover adrenaline hadn't completely dissipated. Thinking back to the vampire's appearance at her home, heat flashed like a bad sunburn across the back of her neck, clashing with her chills.

As the car turned off the main road a few miles past a low-lit strip mall, Riley emerged from her stupor enough to pay closer attention to her surroundings. Moments later, they turned onto a street marked as private. Soon after that, they encountered a gate.

"Are we here?" she asked.

"I believe we are," Officer Marshall confirmed.

Without turning around, Derek's packmate grunted a low reply. "They know we're coming, so it's okay."

His response caused Riley to wonder what would have happened if Derek's friends hadn't known that a human was coming to meet them.

"It's late," she pointed out.

"We like the night."

So, okay. This was it, and scary as hell. She was about to enter an area populated by werewolves. Right? Real, live werewolves.

Riley pressed a fingertip to her lips to keep from speaking, and swiveled on the seat to avoid the ache centered low in her body that was proof of what she and Derek had done in his apartment.

What she had done with a werewolf.

When the gate opened and they drove through, she saw additional lights in the distance. Riley rolled down the window to let the cold air reach her face, anxiously awaiting what lay ahead. This was Derek's pack. Maybe some of them were his family. She didn't even want to think about what it must have been like for a werewolf being raised in a human world.

Derek had been right to assume that vampires wouldn't trespass here. Hell, she was beyond being scared already as the lights kept getting closer, and she was supposed to be a welcome guest.

She hated to think what might happen if any Were enemies passed that gate, if Derek and the red-haired wolf in the front seat of the car were any indication of the breed.

Gathering her courage, Riley slowly counted to ten.

Chapter 21

Derek sat on Riley's front step with Marshall's gun in his hand. He could have held the silver bullets this gun contained in his bare hands with no problem at all, contrary to what some people believed.

Most of the whole werewolves-are-vulnerable-to-metals rumor was just that, rumor. Myth. Hollywood fantasy. The only way silver could harm him or any other Were was if he were shot by one of those silver babies in a vulnerable spot, with no doctor around to remove the bullet in a hurry. It was called evolution—and vampires hadn't fully kept up.

He was good with a gun, and more than just a decent shot. If the bloodsucker returned before dawn, it was going to be one sorry dead guy.

Odds were better than good that it would come back.

"Make it quick," Derek muttered, frustrated that he couldn't take Riley to the pack himself, and angry he'd had to delegate that task.

"You know you want to return," he said out loud, thinking of the vampire that had caused this round of trouble. "Her fragrance is a heady draw for me, too."

Sitting on her step brought him all kinds of Riley-related scents, and he liked them all. But he couldn't afford to overlook the other odors he sensed in the night.

He stared at the street, the neighboring houses and their lawns, with a need for action, and clapped a hand to the back of his neck to acknowledge a sudden nudge of awareness. He stood up slowly with the gun at his side and started toward the street with his muscles tensing.

"So damn predictable," he said to the newcomer whose presence caused his body temperature to rise.

The lights Riley had seen turned out to be streetlights in a neighborhood of houses that could have existed anywhere, except for one thing. There were no people in them, according to Derek. Just werewolves.

Officer Marshall drove slowly. Guided by the other guy in the front seat with him, Marshall finally turned into a driveway and let the car idle.

Riley took in the ranch-style house with its long covered porch. There was a green front lawn, a brick walkway and more brick on the stairs. All of that seemed so normal she felt like laughing, as if the joke was on her and there were no werewolves here or anywhere else.

The front door opened and a man came out. Like Derek— and the guy he'd mentioned was named Jared, the only other example of Derek's packmates she'd met—this guy was tall, broad in the chest and shoulders, and handsome. An aura of energy surrounded him that Riley could have sworn passed right through the car window.

Marshall spoke to the Were beside him. "Christ. Are

you all that big?" It was possible that Marshall had never been here before, either.

"Not all," Jared replied as he got out of the car. "Just most."

As Riley strained for a decent breath, she became aware of a low-pitched humming sound. Her body reacted to it by producing another swiftly moving wave of heat that radiated outward from her chest.

Startled by her reaction, she took a better look at the man who had emerged from the house to stand by the car. An odd flicker of recognition came to her when he asked, "Is everything okay?"

Suddenly, she was thrown back in memory to the city, to the street where she had first been attacked last night. She again felt the roughness of the pub's exterior wall, where she'd been held fast by a pair of strong hands.

"You'll be all right in a minute. We've called this in and someone will come to get you," her rescuer had said.

Beyond that smooth, mesmerizing voice she hadn't been able to forget, she now remembered hearing someone else give a warning about having to get out of there before anyone saw them. There had been two rescuers. She had known that. But she hadn't recalled that the second guy had spoken until now, after hearing the same voice say to Marshall, "Thanks for bringing her. I'll take over from here."

She slid toward the door to get a better look at the speaker, but didn't recognize him. Only his voice was familiar, and yet she had the impression that this guy was tightly connected to Derek in some way, and thus to her.

Wait a minute, her mind nagged. She had seen him before, hadn't she? She now recognized the dark hair and lean body. Wasn't he Derek's partner? The guy who had arrived after Derek had staked the vampire near her office? It was hard to tell, since she'd been in shock at the time and Derek was the only thing she had paid attention to.

In case anyone hadn't noticed, she was still in shock now.

When the car door opened, Riley didn't balk or hesitate. She got out and stood tall with her coat closed tightly around her. "Is Derek alone back there, left on his own to fight my battles?"

The big Were smiled. "One thing you will soon learn is that Derek does whatever he wants to do. Case in point—bringing you here."

Riley dialed back her assertiveness a little. "He might get hurt."

Her new host's smile remained fixed. "Just so you know, he rarely is. Besides, we're blessed with exceptional healing powers that enable us to spring back almost miraculously. And we taste bad to vampires."

Riley looked from the Were to Marshall, then back to the Were she was speaking to. "Will Derek come here later?"

His reply was earnest, and also slightly cynical. "I'd be willing to bet that nothing short of meeting up with Seattle's vamp queen herself could keep him away from here for long."

Some of Riley's tension settled. Derek would come here. He would be all right, and so would she.

"Would you like to come in?" her new host asked. "There's a room ready for you."

Riley shook her head. "If you don't mind, I'd like a minute to myself. If that's allowed."

"You're not a prisoner, Dr. Price, though I wouldn't go off on your own, and I'd advise you to stay in this yard."

"I just need a minute," she said.

Jared got her bag from the car and tossed it to the Were she'd been speaking with. After that, Jared wandered off with a promise to return in an hour.

That left her in the yard with only Officer Marshall for company. When he turned back to the car, Riley stopped him with a hand on his arm. "You're not one of them, so maybe you should have someone look at that wound on your neck."

Wearing a solemn expression, the young off-duty officer shook his head. "Maybe we shouldn't bother anyone here with that just now."

"You're bleeding."

He ran his fingers over the wound and wiped off some of the blood pooling there, giving Riley a firsthand view of two tiny puncture marks beneath his left ear.

The skin around those punctures was raw, red and swollen. The holes themselves looked like they had to be painful. Riley knew what they had to be. The subliminally fast vampire at her place had gotten to Marshall. And she was to blame.

Marshall's face had paled somewhat, but he shrugged. "It might be too late for anyone to help. I can't be sure. But I'm not dead yet. That monster didn't have time to finish me off, so I guess I was lucky."

"I'm...sorry," Riley stuttered, feeling sick again, and helpless.

She watched Marshall climb back into the car, and stayed where she was long after it had disappeared from sight. That's when she made a vow, a promise to herself and to that officer to join in the hunt for the monsters that had put the Seattle PD on high alert, and had ruined what could otherwise have been a perfectly good night.

* * *

The vampire approached Derek with a gait that reminded him of someone on roller skates. Derek wasn't impressed.

"Back for more?" he asked.

The abomination stared back, so white-faced it looked like a moon had descended to street level.

"She's not here," Derek said. "You can tell that to whoever sent you. I doubt if you'll find her again, so you might as well target someone else. I'd recommend that you take Riley off your fetish list, or you'll have a pack of Weres to deal with each time you resurface."

The damn thing finally spoke, though its fangs made the words difficult to understand. "You know nothing, wolf."

"No? Then why don't you enlighten me?"

"She is wanted."

"By whom?" Derek asked.

"Someone far more powerful than you."

"I can think of only one someone that would fit that description. Could that vampire be your Prime?"

"You know nothing," the vamp repeated.

"Let's not go backward, okay? I'm trying to understand why Riley is so special."

"Why is she special to you?" the pasty-faced bloodsucker countered.

"Part of what makes her special to me is the fact that all of you want her so badly. I'm trying to figure out the reason for that."

"I can smell her on you, wolf, which means that she is special to you for other reasons as well."

"Maybe you're right," Derek admitted. "But is your interest centered on any feelings I might have for her?

Because that would make this whole stalking nonsense about me."

"You merely make things more difficult."

It was evident that this was a well-spoken vampire he faced. In his experience, only the ancients of the species possessed the ability to make real conversation of any kind…and Christ, how many of them could there be?

"You can go now," Derek said. "Trot back to whomever you report to and tell them you failed to reach your prey."

"Humans are vulnerable," the vampire said. "Choose your friends wisely, wolf, or some of them won't survive for much longer."

Derek didn't like the sound of that threat. He raised the gun, aimed and fired…but there was only empty space where the vampire had stood.

He lowered the gun and swore loudly, wishing he had a car.

Chapter 22

"Riley?" her Were host called out.

She had been out here too long, Riley supposed, and had lost track of time waiting to see the telltale headlights. Derek's. About to give up, she finally saw a car heading toward the house.

"He's coming," she said to the Were that had walked up to stand beside her.

"And driving too fast," he remarked.

Was Derek equally as anxious to get to her, or was there another reason for his speed? Either way, Riley knew she wouldn't feel so alone among strangers when he arrived, though he was actually little more than one of those strangers.

This was Derek's pack. He was in charge. She wondered if, in addition to his apartment in the city, Derek also had a home here. She also pondered how much her life had changed in just two days. Tonight she had become the consort of a werewolf and might live to regret it. At the moment, however, she was really glad to see him.

Tires squealed on the road as a black SUV stopped in front of her. Riley thought about running to Derek for the warmth and familiarity he'd provide, but waited for him to get out of the car.

His eyes found hers immediately. The air crackled with the same kind of electricity that had driven them to the brink a couple of hours ago. Some people would have labeled the buzz passing through her body as a form of sexual chemistry, the internal acknowledgment of a mutual attraction. But looking at Derek now, without being close enough to feel or smell him, was torture. And that was yet another surprise.

"Vamps gone?" the other Were asked Derek.

"Gone, but not forgotten," Derek replied as he walked toward her.

"The sucker got away again?" the Were asked with an incredulous tone.

"Faster than it should have, and not without issuing a threat." Derek glanced around. "Where's Marshall?"

"He left a while ago."

Derek's gaze came back to Riley. "Are you all right? That thing by your house didn't touch you?"

"I'm fine," she said, and silently added, *Now that you're here.*

"Was Marshall okay?" he asked. "Did he seem to be all right on the way out here?"

She couldn't recall if the officer had asked her not to tell the Weres about the marks on his neck. Maybe he just hadn't wanted to worry these guys with the fact that he had been wounded by the monster they had faced. Marshall was human. He wasn't fueled by wolfish superpowers and didn't belong to this pack.

"He seemed all right," Riley said, when that wasn't necessarily true. Though Marshall had tried not to show it, he had looked alarmed.

Deep in her gut was the awareness that those puncture marks on Marshall's neck could mean he would become like the monster that had bitten him. Still, she had no real notion of what it took for a human being to turn into a vampire, so she didn't want to worry Derek about his friend unnecessarily.

"Good." Derek's relief was obvious. "Glad to hear he's okay. Marshall is a necessary member of this team."

He came closer to her, reached out to her. "How are you holding up?"

"I'll manage as long as I don't think about tonight too closely."

"You handled the situation bravely, and better than most people would have," he said, darting a glance to the Were that stood next to her. "You don't have to meet all of the Weres here. Only a couple at a time."

"And only the best of us," the other Were said with a smile.

"Riley, meet Dale Duncan, a personal friend of mine and my first choice for backup in the city."

"Cop?" she asked her handsome, dark-haired host.

"Yes, ma'am," Dale Duncan said. "But don't hold that against me."

Riley looked around. "Vampires don't come here?"

"Would you, if you were them?" Dale said. "There are over a hundred of us here, give or take."

"Two packs call this valley home," Derek explained. "It's private land. Being here is by invitation only."

She eyed both Weres. "Werewolves don't fight among themselves?"

"Not since we became civilized, which was several decades ago," Derek replied.

The relief flooding Riley's system felt like a wave of warm water. Vampires weren't coming here, and that was good news. They couldn't get in or out of a place teaming with werewolves like the two next to her. If all one hundred of Derek's friends, or even a good percentage of them, were as formidable as the examples she knew, no monster in the world could afford to take that kind of a risk.

For the first time in a while, Riley found it easier to breathe. She was actually accepting everything, and that these two guys were what they said they were.

A larger flash of heat returned as Derek took her hand. He led her up the steps and across his friend's front porch. Dale preceded them into the house. When Derek stopped her from entering, Riley braced herself for what might come next. More kissing and further closeness were what she desired, but those cravings didn't involve a human male and couldn't possibly lead to any kind of acceptable future.

Derek brought his face close to hers. In a tone that wasn't so much like velvet as gravel, he said, "Now tell me the truth about Marshall."

Derek observed the change in Riley's expression that told him she was debating how to answer his question. He had pondered his own take on Marshall soon after the police cruiser had driven off from Riley's house. Marshall had been uncharacteristically reserved and a little white around the edges.

"Riley, it's important that I have all information about what happened tonight," he explained. "It's possible you sense this, even if you might feel an obligation to withhold certain pertinent facts."

His eyes delved deeper into hers. "If, in fact, there are more details."

Riley faced him bravely, for all that had gone on in the short time he'd known her. Once again, he silently applauded her ability to cope and bounce back from events that would have driven other people out of their minds. She had met vampires and werewolves, and she was here because of some internal switch that allowed her to dial up the ability to confront issues like this without panicking.

He figured she was compartmentalizing. Locking up her fear in an iron box. If that was the case, it might not be long before signs of distress showed up.

"There were marks on Marshall's neck," she said.

He had been afraid of something like that and took a minute to consider what it meant.

"Scratches?" he asked.

"Punctures. Two of them."

Her reply served to confirm Derek's worst fears. Seattle needed cops like Marshall; cops who had seen a few things that were out of the norm, and kept on ticking. Marshall was extremely valuable to the Weres both on and off the force. He was even more valuable to the people he served.

"Did he talk about them, Riley? Those marks?"

"He said he'd be okay because the vampire hadn't finished him off."

Derek hoped to God that was true.

"What could potentially happen to him, Derek? Since this was my fault, I need to understand the ramifications."

She had called him by his first name. He looked into her clear, wide-set eyes.

"Those wounds alone won't necessarily affect him more than being painful for a while. Vampires can drink from a vein and leave their victim standing if that victim doesn't die of shock over the ordeal. This vampire didn't have time to binge."

He didn't like scaring Riley. After taking a deep breath, Derek cautiously continued. "It's the venom that's dangerous. Vamps are like rattlesnakes in a way. Their saliva contains toxins that can both paralyze and hypnotize their prey. If they use that venom and leave their prey alive, the unlucky victim might fall sway to vamp demands without having a say in the matter."

Riley uttered a groan and closed her eyes. Derek tightened his grip on her hand.

"Let me stress that you're not responsible for any of us, Riley. We hunt vampires. This is what we do. What we've done for centuries. The only thing special about the past few days is your involvement."

The way she looked at him made Derek's pulse jump. Riley was a damn good actor. However, in that moment the bond they shared exposed her true feelings. He saw confusion and dread in her expression, where there had formerly been only anger and defiance. Her emotions were so strong he was almost able to feel them.

"It will be okay," he said. "Trust me, Riley. We take care of our own. We'll get help for Marshall and we will take care of you."

He again perceived the faint tremble in her lower lip. That quiver was the only way she was going to let her fear visibly manifest.

He needed to convince her that he was telling the truth and put Riley's mind at ease. She was intelligent enough to comprehend that the danger was only postponed. Tonight's confrontation had been managed, but tomorrow was another night. And there'd be another one after that.

She had become a target, and Riley felt the bull's-eye painted on her back.

"The best thing you can do at the moment is to put your trust in us and get some long-overdue rest," Derek said.

"Promise me Marshall will be all right." Her voice was little more than a whisper.

"I made a call on the way here as a precaution. Someone will be waiting for him, and will check him out."

Her eyes searched his.

"Let's go inside," he said.

"You'll stay here? Stay with me?"

"I'll be here when you wake up," he promised.

"You expect me to sleep?"

"I'd recommend it."

"I won't be able to close my eyes."

He smiled. "I think you'll find that you can, if you try."

In spite of being needed in the city, he was going to put aside his responsibility in order to be closer to this woman—something he would never have done in the past.

Damn it, he couldn't help himself. The Weres in the city would have to take this shift in his stead. Riley was more precious than anyone realized, and not just to him. Other eyes were on her, and as long as she remained alive and well, there was a chance he could find out what was going on, and why a vamp queen like Damaris was so interested in her.

There had to be a reason Riley was a target. He'd dig out that reason if it took facing fifty more bloodsucking bastards to do so.

Riley tried to hide the drawn expression that sent bolts of white-hot anger up his spine. Pulling her in, Derek whispered in her ear, "Let's make the most of the hours until sunrise. You and me. What do you say? We can sort the rest tomorrow."

Acquiescing, she turned to the doorway, but not before he saw the terror that had darkened her eyes.

Chapter 23

All night, Derek held her cradled in his arms. No kisses, no sex, just a comforting offer of warmth and some semblance of safety. Now and then, he whispered assurances to her. In a crooning voice, he told her things about werewolves that slid in and out of her mind and finally lulled her to sleep.

Riley slept soundly. There were no dreams because she was already living them. When she awoke fully, the sun was up and she found herself alone on a single bed in a light-filled room with a decidedly masculine touch. Blue-painted walls. Narrow blinds on two large windows. Wooden floors. Modern furniture. Her overnight bag sat on a seat by the window. There was no sign of Derek.

She sat up.

Though she was still dressed in her coat, Riley remembered kicking off her shoes before Derek had scooped her into his arms. The bedspread beneath her was rumpled. She was covered in a blanket.

Her body still ached, and it was easy for her to guess why. Their session the other night on Derek's mattress had been wildly fulfilling. Since she hadn't slept with anyone else for over a year, physical stamina had been lost in the interim. Derek was a good lover. The best.

Getting out of bed took effort. Beyond the bedroom door was the great unknown. Derek might be there. Dale, the Were she had met last night, might be there as well, along with any number of Derek's packmates. The thought of facing them made her anxious.

What she needed to bolster her courage was a shower and a toothbrush. Riley padded to the bathroom connected to the bedroom by a door. It would be her private sanctuary for a few minutes. She'd emerge more presentable in both body and spirit.

The water in the shower was hot. She stood beneath the spray, waiting to regain her composure and the ability to think ahead, and struggled to remember the things Derek had said as she lay curled up in his arms.

Werewolves have existed since the beginning of time, he had told her. *No one knows how wolf and human DNA got mixed, or if werewolves appeared as their own species from the start.*

There are good Weres and bad ones, as with any other species, including the human race. Weres learned to police our own kind early on so that our secrets could be kept, and to prevent the spread of what some called a werewolf virus.

She remembered something else. Derek had mentioned that a bite or a deep scratch from a werewolf's tooth or claw could transmit enough wolf blood to a human to make the human into a werewolf. He'd said that this kind of activity also had to be closely monitored, since wolf gangs had increased in size in some cities by creating their own underground armies.

Riley braced herself against the shower wall, despising the thought of criminal werewolf gangs roaming city streets along with vampires and who knew what else.

She was forced now to openly think about what might have happened to her mother in a past that was never forgotten.

The shower was steamy and felt good enough for her to want to stay in it all day. But that would have meant she was hiding, and if her father had been around, he would have scolded her for that. Her dad knew a lot about life, but as she had recently found out, he had also missed a few important details.

Still, he would have said that the Prices were tough, and no one in the family had ever let weakness get in the way of setting things straight. Her father was usually a good example of that credo.

When the door opened, Riley turned her head.

"We've rustled up some clothes for you."

Derek's voice made her heart race, the way it did each time she heard it. But she didn't ask him to join her.

When he said, "Can I come in?" Riley held her breath. But it turned out he only entered the bathroom far enough to leave the clothes and a pile of fresh towels on the sink.

"I have to go, Riley. Dale will take you home. I'll come for you again before sundown."

She didn't reply. Any response she might have had to Derek's announcement would have gotten stuck in her throat.

Hearing the door close again, Riley peered out from behind the shower curtain. Part of her was thankful Derek had gone. Other parts weren't so keen on the idea.

Dale handed her a cup of coffee when she arrived in the kitchen with wet hair, dressed in borrowed jeans and somebody else's gray sweatshirt. The only shoes she had to top off the outfit were her high heels, so this morning she didn't exactly exemplify the term *chic*.

"Breakfast?" Dale asked. In the manner of a paid television ad, he said, "You know it's the way to start your day."

"Thanks. Just coffee for me."

Today, Riley could afford to smile. She sipped the aromatic coffee gratefully, ignoring the soft rumble of hunger in her stomach. With this Were watching her every move, she was too nervous to eat.

As Dale moved around the kitchen, Riley revisited the question of whether or not all of Derek's friends might be equally as large and handsome. And why weren't there female here? She wanted to know everything about this breed. Had to. What would female Weres look like, anyway?

With the issues nagging in the back of her mind, it wasn't long before she lost the smile and set down the cup.

"I'll pull the car around," Dale said. "Take your time and come out when you're ready. There's a whole pot of coffee on the counter."

After nodding to her, he left the room. Riley leaned against the counter, more than ready to go home. It was Sunday. She needed to think things over and begin to regroup. She toyed with the idea of calling her father, and dismissed it. It would give away her current state of mind. If he got worried, he would hop a plane to Seattle and discover something that wouldn't jibe with his reality. He might stay. Her father's presence might keep Derek away.

Riley retrieved her overnight bag and brought the coffee cup with her onto the porch. A tan, standard-issue unmarked police sedan was parked at the curb this morning and Dale stood beside it in a lazy, relaxed stance. As Riley went to meet him, she decided that werewolves had to be at the top of the food chain, and therefore didn't have to fear much of anything.

Dale opened the car door for her, and closed it after she got in. He climbed into the driver's seat and started the engine before speaking to her again.

"Can you be ready for pickup before sunset, Dr. Price?"

"My name is Riley. And yes, I'll be ready. What will you and Derek do today?"

"Snoop around. Sniff things out. Make some calls. Finish up paperwork. It's easier to find vampire hidey-holes in the daylight, when they're sleeping."

"And when you do find some?" Riley asked.

"We take care of them one by one, unless there are too many in one place. Then we have to burn them out."

Riley kept her focus on her coffee cup so that the Were sitting next to her wouldn't see the disgust she felt over picturing the things he had said. If that's what it took to keep Seattle safe, and Weres could do things like that, she would have to rethink how she might be able to help. The wooden stake Derek had placed in her hand last night had felt foreign, and yet what other kinds of defense did she have against a fanged enemy that was supernaturally strong and dangerous…and coming after her?

Derek had searched four city alleys by the time Dale showed up. He looked to his friend for word about Riley.

"Home, and fine," Dale said. "I have to admit she's tougher than I would have imagined. Are you sure there's none of our species in her background somewhere?"

"I'm not sure of anything, other than how exceptionally well she is taking all of this."

"Any new theories we haven't explored as to why the

vamps are interested in her?" Dale asked as he scanned the back of the alley.

"None at the moment. I can't piece this together yet. On the surface, Riley is simply a newly credentialed psychologist."

"Maybe our vamp queen is in need of a shrink," Dale suggested.

Derek knew his partner was joking but wasn't ready to ignore the idea altogether. His mind raced, trying out other ideas, and finally landing on one.

What if the vamps that had approached Riley hadn't come to kill her, and instead had been sent to fetch her?

After two visitations from Damaris's bloodsucking minions, Riley hadn't been hurt, when it had only taken three seconds for one of them to take a bite out of Marshall under everyone's noses.

Dale said, "I know that look on your face, so you might as well cough up what you're thinking."

"Riley is alive," Derek said.

Dale was quick to follow where he was going with this. "And that's unusual for a target."

Derek nodded. "Even with Weres guarding her."

"So they will wait until she isn't guarded, which will never happen again after sundown. And they can't move around during the day, so…?"

"So," Derek said thoughtfully, "either they're completely clueless, and will try again to reach Riley when the sun goes down, or else they will have to adapt to a new time schedule and find her in full daylight."

"That's impossible," Dale remarked.

"Yes," Derek agreed. "Impossible."

But he wasn't going to rule anything out. He was already heading back to his car parked on the main street so he could get to Riley...just in case any of those theories weren't as absurd as they sounded, and losing sight of Riley in the daytime wasn't a good idea.

Chapter 24

Riley stood frozen on her front step for so long, she felt like she'd become one of the pillars holding up the roof. The sun was up this morning, so no vampires would be hiding in her house. No one else would be waiting inside, either, and yet she couldn't make herself use the key.

Cars drove past. Down the block, kids were playing in the street. Everything seemed like a typical Sunday morning, except for the fact that things weren't normal. She had slept with a werewolf in his human disguise. She'd seen bite marks on Marshall's neck. For real. She was absurdly okay with knowing about all of those things because she had to be. What other option was there for processing the truth?

After a little reminder to herself about bravery being a virtue, Riley went inside the house that would never feel the same. Vampires had tainted both her home and her office, and they knew exactly where to find her, so she was screwed.

She changed out of the borrowed outfit and folding everything, then packed more clothes for when Derek came to take her back to the wolves. She placed her bag in the entryway, unable to remember where she had left her car. And, anyway, it didn't really matter, since she didn't feel up to a drive and wasn't able to focus properly. The damn vehicle could have been sitting right in the driveway and she wouldn't have noticed.

Her cell phone, resting on the kitchen table, was dead. She plugged it in to recharge before heading outside again. Walking downtown would burn off excess energy that had nowhere to go. On foot, it wouldn't take her much more than half an hour to get there.

With a backward glance at the house, Riley set out, happier than usual to feel the sun on her face when her insides were so damn icy.

Dale hopped in to ride shotgun as Derek cranked the engine of the black SUV. "We need more information," he said. "Riley can't be our prisoner forever."

"She's not a prisoner," Derek reminded him

"She's going to think so if she's under surveillance twenty-four-seven."

"Yes," Derek agreed. "She will."

"And we don't actually believe that vamps can walk around in the daylight, do we?"

"I don't see how they could."

"Then you can probably rest easy, Derek, and it might be a good idea to give her some space."

It sounded simple when someone else said the words Derek had been thinking ever since he'd left Riley earlier that morning. However, he couldn't give her space after the imprinting phase had been sealed on his bed the other night. In the initial stages, Weres were faced with unrelenting desire, like being on a honeymoon, times ten.

He glanced at Dale, and found his friend grinning.

"Making the connection wasn't wise, boss," Dale said. "But I guess it is what it is. Right?"

Derek blew out a breath, expecting Dale to say "I told you so." When that didn't come, Derek echoed, "For whatever reason, it is what it is."

"Does Riley know what's happened, as far as you two are concerned?" Dale asked.

"No way she could, if she's not one of us."

"Are you going to tell her?"

"Yes. Today," Derek said. "Though I'm afraid that kind of information might push her over the edge. How many days has it been since we helped her out?"

"Try three, including today," Dale replied, though the question had been rhetorical. Dale dropped the grin and added, "Good luck with that. I'll get out of your way if you'll pull over."

"Check her office for me, will you?" Derek said.

"On my way."

Dale got out at the next stoplight. Derek drove on, considering how a Were could explain the bonding process to someone who didn't understand the first thing about Weres. He hoped the right words would come.

And if you want out, Riley Price?
What then?

Hell, if she wanted out of what had only just begun, he was going to need a shaman to remove the chains binding him to her.

As he was leaving the main downtown district, Derek saw Riley on a street corner, and he took the next right turn to circle back. She had paused when she recognized the SUV and was still there when he pulled around the corner.

Parking was easy Sunday mornings, and Derek found a spot not far from her. As he got out of the car, he was able to feel the buzz of Riley's interest from eight feet away. The earthy vibration increased as the distance closed to three feet. Two feet. Then one. After that, it was all over, and her body was up against his as if they were magnetic, and the only two people around.

"It's not time yet for you to get me," she said breathlessly.

"I couldn't wait for sundown. How's that for a confession?"

"I was feeling lost," she said. "I want to go to my office, and I'm afraid of what I might find."

"I'll take you there. It'll be okay. The window was fixed late last night and the guard is back at his station."

"How do you know that?"

"It's my job to check on things."

She nodded. "Okay. I have files to go over for tomorrow's appointments."

"Do you feel up to going back to work?"

"It will keep me sane when everything else is—"

"Crazy?" Derek said, finishing for her. "Unbelievable?"

She nodded again.

Neither of them moved toward her office building.

"You're going to tell me why I feel this way, right? About why it feels like I've known you in another lifetime?" Riley asked.

"I can do that," Derek said.

"Does it have to do with you being a Were?"

"Yes, though maybe not entirely."

Words like *fate* and *serendipity* ran through Derek's

mind, though he again rejected those possibilities as the basis for his feelings for Riley. This was something else. What?

"Do you possess some kind of magic that attracts females?" she asked as a woman passing by eyed him in the same way others had in front of the restaurant the night before.

"Were males have potent pheromones that some females might pick up on. Were females have it, too, as well as some human women."

"Do I have it?"

"Lots of it," he said.

"Are you making me feel this way about you?" she asked.

"What way would that be?"

"Like I want to…" She lowered her gaze without completing her sentence, and then started over. "I have to know everything about what I've gotten myself into. That's only fair."

"Your office, then," Derek said.

They still didn't move or try to separate. With Riley's body against his, Derek was feeling a level of arousal that was new to him. Riley felt so small and delicate when compared to his larger, more muscular bulk. He liked that, even though there was nothing small or delicate about her. Intelligent women were sexy, and Riley was smarter than most, which helped to make her so very appealing and damnably hard to resist.

"I don't want to be a vampire's plaything," she said.

"You won't be."

Riley looked at him even more soberly. "I don't want to be afraid each time darkness falls."

"We just have to find out what's going on," Derek repeated. "We can do that with a little more time, and then things will be all right."

Though he didn't want to lose the closeness of their bodies touching, Derek slid his hands down her arms and backed up slightly. When he took her hands in his, her fingers relaxed.

The way her lips parted and moved let him understand that Riley wanted to speak, and couldn't. That mouth alone could have driven him mad with desire if they had been in a safer, less conspicuous spot.

Riley wasn't so very pale today. Her skin was an iridescent ivory, and free of makeup. Each time she moved her head, he smelled the rosy scent of the shampoo Dale had left for her in the shower.

The collar of her purple sweater showed off enough bare neck to make his inner wolf restless, and didn't completely hide the marks he had put there while in a fit of passion. In the olden days, those marks would have branded Riley as his mate, proven she was his, and announced to the world that Riley Price wasn't to be touched by anyone else, ever again.

If she had been a Were, they wouldn't be standing here now. They wouldn't be talking, they'd be doing. But Riley wasn't like him, and he couldn't ask her to become like him, even when that path might be open to them in the future. If seeing that werewolves and vampires existed was frightening for her, he couldn't imagine asking Riley to join his species.

She was eyeing him back as if she was trying to follow his thoughts. He refocused on the present problem.

Yes, he had to tell her the things she needed to know. She would then decide what to do. He would let her make that choice and abide by whatever decision she made.

But he would stay by her side until the mystery of all this vampire activity was solved, no matter what the outcome was.

Derek led her from the corner with a protective arm around her shoulders, not caring if Seattle's vampire queen had spies. He was off-duty, and was going to make the most of his time with Riley.

"Feel free to ask whatever you'd like," he said as they walked. "You're right, and fair is fair."

Keeping his hands and his mouth off Riley until they reached her office, and after they got there, was going to be a momentous task. Right now he was going to have to prepare reasonable answers to whatever questions she had, and hope she'd be as receptive to the truth as she had been so far.

Chapter 25

There was a new guard at the front desk when they signed in. When they got in the elevator, Riley found that being cooped up with Derek in the tight space was tough. It was hard to breathe properly when he was around. Although Riley couldn't smell the wolf pheromones Derek had mentioned, her body gravitated to him on both conscious and unconscious levels. Unwilling to give in at the moment, she leaned against the wall opposite from where he stood.

She felt relieved when the door opened onto the third-floor hallway and he let her go past him without pulling her back. She walked quickly to her office and used the key to get in.

Derek had been right. Riley saw no evidence of an intruder having been there. There was no broken glass. Nothing was out of place. The window looked the same, as did the frame. Derek must have had a window company on speed dial.

She circled the desk to create distance between them, reminding herself that she'd need to keep a clear head to ask all of the questions she had. Thankfully, Derek honored that distance as if he understood.

"We can start at the beginning, I guess," she suggested. "You told me a few things last night that sank in. So can we start on the street where I was attacked, and go from there?"

Derek didn't sit down on the chair or the couch. He, too, was restless His energy careened off the walls.

"Why me?" she began. "Why were you interested in me after we'd met out there?"

"I don't really know," he replied. "Does there have to be a reason for one person being attracted to another?"

"There does when things happen this fast."

"I wanted to know you after just one glance. Then you mentioned werewolves before knowing anything about their real existence, and later admitted to liking them."

Not liking, exactly... Riley thought. *More like being interested.*

"And you found that promising?" she asked. "After a first glance?"

"I found it curious. I looked into your eyes, saw the fear and the defiance in them, and liked what I saw."

She couldn't argue with that, since it was a reasonable assessment.

"Next question?" he said.

"Can I go with you tonight if you go hunting?"

That surprised him. He obviously had anticipated her asking him something more personal about werewolves.

"It would be too dangerous, Riley."

"I don't care. Maybe I'd get the opportunity to ask one of them what I have to do with any of this. Cut to the chase. Get things in the open."

"I don't want anything to happen to you. They aren't what you think. Trust me, in numbers, they're far worse than anything you've experienced so far."

Riley rounded the desk without thinking about it, eager to press the issue. Before she could speak again, Derek did. "Most of them are minions. Mindless monsters ruled by thirst. Half of them can't remember how to speak, or why they're here.

"Other vampires are ancient and way too smart. They gather in nests and are truly dangerous. And all vampires breed like rabbits, only not in any natural way."

"By sinking their fangs into innocent necks," Riley said.

Derek nodded. "Unlike with a bite or scratch from a rogue werewolf, vampires pass death on to their victims most of the time. They feed until the hearts of their victims stop beating, draining their victims dry, then accidentally or on purpose give a small amount of their own black blood back into the open wounds."

It made Riley sick to think of it, but she also felt a ray of hope. "Then Marshall will be okay. He didn't die, and he didn't run off to do their bidding."

"It's likely he will be all right," he agreed.

"If being around them is so dangerous, how do you plan on finding the answers we need?" Riley asked. "I can't remain in the dark as to why they're chasing me, and what they want."

She moved closer to Derek. "I don't relish the thought of hiding forever. Do you?"

He was studying her again, probably looking for cracks in her armor. Riley didn't give him any reason to find them.

"There's a long history here that doesn't involve you in any way," he said. "A vampire Prime, which is the equivalent of a Were alpha, has only so much control over its family when vamp numbers get out of hand. But Seattle doesn't just have a Prime in residence, it has a female that has set herself up as queen bee."

"A woman?" Riley was surprised how much that news bothered her.

"She's no woman, Riley, and hasn't been for centuries."

"You've seen her?"

"I have. I helped someone chase her underground once, where she refuses to stay."

Specially attuned to emotion because of her profession, Riley perceived how Derek was blocking his. She said, "There's no way to get rid of this vampire queen?" and sensed how disturbed Derek was over how he was going to answer.

"I don't see how that could be managed," he admitted. "The most we've been able to do is to try to keep her pool of bloodsuckers from increasing in number exponentially. Most of the time that seems like an uphill battle."

So, she had the truth now, and it was disconcerting.

"Is the Prime angry with you for staking her vampires?" Riley asked. "Could that be why she might want to harm me? For getting close to you? For revenge? An eye-for-an-eye type of payback?"

Derek walked to the window and turned his back to her, which made Riley sure he was hiding something.

"The truth," she said. "Remember?"

He turned to her slowly and spoke as though he was divulging a secret. "I believe there might be a chance that Damaris doesn't want to harm you at all."

"It doesn't look that way to me. What else could she—Damaris, is it?—get out of scaring the life out of me over and over?"

Damn it, even the vampire queen's name was frightening. Riley replayed it a few times in her mind.

Derek raised his hands in surrender. "It's a theory I'm exploring. I don't know what else to think at the moment."

Riley's voice was steadier than she thought it would be. "All the more reason for us to find out what the truth is. Tonight, where you go, I go. The only way to stop me, Detective, will be to chain me to a post."

That won her a smile, sad as it might have been.

"I can find a post," he said. "And a chain."

"Over my dead body."

"That is exactly what I'm attempting to avoid, Riley."

She couldn't have stayed away from him for much longer no matter what he said. It wasn't even noon, but her body was already shaking with the thought of tonight, and what she was willing to do to put an end to the craziness.

Did Derek get that?

Derek stayed very still. Their frank discussion, the airing out of all the fear in the room, served to accelerate the onset of something that closely resembled trust. But he had to be careful.

Riley came toward him as if he had called her name, and he stepped forward to meet her. If he wanted to be fair, he'd have to suppress the urge to take her in his arms, when he wanted that so badly. A kiss would hold him over. One kiss that might distract them both long enough to keep Riley from going out to meet the vampires.

"Don't," she said as if she understood what he had in mind. "That would be too easy."

A sound at the door broke the next little moment of silence. Derek knew who was knocking. He had set the plan in place with Dale, hoping to avoid a moment like this one, and Dale had almost been too late.

Without waiting for an invitation, Dale entered the office, stopped when he saw them and was silent for once until Derek eventually glanced in his direction.

"I've got news," Dale said. "And I'm not sure if either of you is going to like it."

Riley backed up and turned to face Dale. Derek did the same.

"News for me, or for Riley?" Derek asked.

"Both, actually."

"Shoot."

"Dr. Price might want to sit down first," Dale suggested.

"It's Riley, remember?" she corrected. "And I'd prefer to stand."

Dale nodded to her and then looked at Derek. "I've been checking records. Did you know Riley's dad is a cop?"

"Yes," Derek said. "That makes sense, doesn't it? I now see where she gets her courage and fortitude. Growing up with a cop in the house isn't always easy."

"There's more," Dale said soberly.

"Go on."

"This news is about Riley's mother," Dale warned.

Derek glanced at Riley again. Her serious expression was still in place, though she might have paled slightly. He wondered what kind of news Dale possessed that might have made her lose color.

Before Dale could continue, Riley spoke up. "My mother was sent away when I was young. She was institutionalized for a while, and then she died."

She looked at Dale. "Is that what you're referring to? You've done a background check because of the incidents I've been involved with?"

Derek looked to his friend, then back at Riley. "We have a database for law enforcement. Chances were that your father's name would come up when we ran it. But I don't need to know anything about your personal issues unless you're willing to confide the details—"

Dale interrupted. "I think there are a couple of things that should be brought up in light of how you two are behaving and what else is going on."

Derek waited for Riley to address that statement. Reconsidering her refusal to sit down, she folded herself into the chair and reluctantly nodded for Dale to go on.

"It seems that Riley's mother was sent away because she thought she was a…"

"Werewolf," Riley said. "My mother believed she was one of you."

Chapter 26

Silence followed her statement. Inside that moment of quiet, Riley's ears rang with an echo of the confidence she had shared.

You might think Derek's question about her *thing* for werewolves had just been answered, at least in part, though Riley didn't see any sudden enlightenment reflected in Derek's expression. However, it didn't take a trained psychologist to figure out that she again had succeeded in surprising the alpha.

"What?" he said, as if he hadn't heard properly.

He was staring at her. Everyone was wondering what she'd say next, including Riley.

"People tend to hide things like that," she explained. "Those of us who were left after she was taken away never talked openly about it. Young people wouldn't go around chatting about being the daughter of a madwoman, would they?"

She waved a hand at Dale. "Now look. Both of you are living proof that my mother might not have made it up."

Riley let her hand fall. "Imagine my surprise when I found that out. Then again, my mother never proved she was like you, so I suppose no one would have really ever known the truth."

She stopped Derek from taking a step by shaking her head. "You can't possibly understand how glad I am to have discovered this weekend, and after all that time, that my mother might not have been so crazy after all. I've spent most of my life hoping I wouldn't turn out like her."

She watched Derek stiffen as the full extent of what she'd said began to dawn on him. But his expression gave away nothing as to what he might have been thinking.

He took some time before speaking again in a soft, uncertain tone, as if he still didn't believe what she was telling him. "You do realize that if she wasn't lying, and your mother was a Were, she had to have passed along that Were blood to you?"

From the sidelines, Dale muttered, "And that, my friends, explains a lot."

Riley had grown tired of the racing-heart routine long before this and ignored the pounding in her chest and the throb in her neck, not willing to give in to the chaos going on inside her.

"Until now, I was more concerned about the madness part being hereditary," she said.

"Riley…"

"I'm nothing like you," she said to Derek. "So there's all the more reason to doubt what you've just proposed."

Derek was sure to see the fear on her face. Riley recalled how he had been trying to find a hint of something he couldn't quite see ever since their first meeting. Had he been searching for a reason for their instant connection, as she had?

Did that connection have anything to do with her mother's beliefs and the possible concoction in her own bloodstream that he might have detected without actually recognizing it? The concoction she hadn't known existed? The one no one had believed existed?

No...

That line of reasoning was absurd and didn't warrant any more time spent on it, because that would mean her mother had been telling the truth, and might have been locked away unjustly by those who either didn't know about the existence of werewolves, or did know, and had to keep that secret locked away.

"Absurd," she muttered, thinking back, desperate to see what they all might have missed. "My mother was nothing like you, either."

Yet if it had been true, a heinous crime had been committed and Riley might have saved herself years of studying in order to deal with her mother's condition.

Riley didn't like the room's new atmosphere that made breathing a chore. She didn't particularly like the quiet, either, or the direction in which her thoughts had turned.

"You can stop looking at me like that. My mother could have made it up. There are plenty of cases like that on file. The syndrome is called Lycanism. She didn't have to be a Were."

With both Weres staring at her, Riley felt compelled to go on.

"I don't howl at the moon," she said.

Okay, that was a lie, Riley had to admit. She always howled when a full moon rolled around, and she had done so the night all this trouble began.

"I've never sprouted claws, and if I had ever turned furry, I would have committed myself."

She looked to Derek for support, willing him to smile, laugh, or tell her he didn't believe it, either. But he didn't do any of those things.

Her office suddenly felt crowded, and as though a lightning storm was gathering between four walls. It was possible that was always the result when two powerful Weres occupied a small space, and when all that subdued power was concentrated and contained.

"It was likely just a story," Riley said. "My father thought so. They all thought so."

"It was a just story until now," Derek said.

He turned to Dale. "We need to reevaluate events to include the possibility of Riley's latent inheritance."

"I'm not—" Riley began.

Derek cut her off. "Actually, Dale is right. It would explain a lot."

Riley's memory kicked up something then. It was what the vampire had said to her. *If you don't learn about your heritage, it might be too late to help you.*

Heritage.

Learn about her heritage.

Had the vampires recognized she could be part werewolf before anyone else had figured it out? The idea was unsettling and absurd, and still failed to explain why they'd want to bother her.

She got to her feet. "Don't be ridiculous. How could I have missed something like that? With all the work I've done, don't you think I've gone deep into my own psyche? Believe me, Derek, I found no wolf there."

The problem was that a seed of doubt had been planted in her mind, and that seed was going to take over unless someone put a stop to it.

She thought of her father. For him, her mother's commitment had been the source of years of loneliness and pain. He had loved his wife greatly. He didn't remarry after she died, and Riley doubted her father was over all of that even now.

"I'm not…" Riley again protested weakly. "I can't do this. I refuse to go through it all again. You have no idea what…"

She couldn't finish a damn sentence. Nightmares from her past had welled up again. The vampire's remarks continued to ring in her ears.

Derek was beside her. "Close your eyes, Riley."

"There's no sense in trying to hypnotize me, Derek. I have all the tricks down pat."

"Close them, Riley. For a few seconds. No more than that. Please."

She shut them to avoid the flash of new interest in Derek's eyes. With him, she had experienced what hunger was like and also how it drove two beings together. She had also, however, been privy to his moments of tenderness, and the way he had held her in the dark.

If her mother had been like him… If it turned out that her mother had been a werewolf…

God. What was she supposed to make of that?

"Breathe," Derek directed.

She squeezed her eyes tight.

"Open your senses, Riley," he said. "Listen. Smell. Feel. Believe."

She tried to follow his instructions, though she wasn't really sure what he was asking.

"Listen," he whispered to her.

In the distance, Riley heard cars on the street even though the windows were double-paned. She heard the clock on her desk ticking and the faint rustle of Derek's jeans as he came closer. She heard the irregular beat of her pulse, due in part to the fantastical ideas floating around the room.

And she heard Derek's heart beating.

"Smell," he urged. "Take a breath and process it. Break what's in the air into manageable layers."

Derek's voice had a mesmerizing quality that she had noticed before. Her mind willingly went along with his suggestion, but the only thing she could pinpoint was Derek's familiar scent—the overpowering maleness he exuded.

Wait. There was something else in the air. She definitely caught the fragrance of well-worn fabric and a trace of a muskier scent. Was that how werewolves smelled?

Derek's expression had changed when she opened her eyes to give him a challenging stare. Riley saw that he wanted to believe she had wolf blood hidden somewhere—locked away, without a key. But if her body contained hints of wolf, no matter how small or inert, her life as a human being had been fraudulent, and her mother had been unfairly cheated of a normal life. Riley didn't think she could bear the thought of either of those things.

"Was there anything out of the ordinary, having to do with your senses?" Derek asked, his blue eyes riveted to her face.

Riley didn't know how to answer. The situation she found herself in was moving too fast. She couldn't just become what Derek wanted her to be by breathing deeply and listening to her racing heart. And yet she hesitantly said, "That means they killed her for no good reason."

As a shudder passed through her, she met Derek's gaze and added, "Is there a better way to be sure?"

"Yes," Derek said, stifling his excitement. "There is a way to find out the truth."

"Like we don't know already by now?" Dale interjected.

Derek ignored the remark. This new revelation explained a lot, including the immediacy of his interest in Riley. In hindsight, his wolf must have picked up on the wolf in her from the start, though hers had been deeply buried by a psychologist who knew how to bury bad things.

"How do we do that?" Riley asked tentatively, and as though she didn't really want to hear the answer.

"Wolf calls to wolf," he explained. "By your being around Weres, any wolf traits you possess will eventually show up as if drawn to the surface."

"Like cream rising to the top," Dale added.

"No," Riley argued. "Animal attraction is just a figure of speech. What I feel for you, Derek, has nothing to do with the fact that you're a werewolf."

"Doesn't it?" he countered. "Can you be sure?"

He had known Riley felt the same way he did about this budding relationship, but was glad to hear her confirmation of those feelings. Proving she was a Were would be even better, and would solve issues they would have had to confront in the future. It also would help to eventually keep the vampires away from her.

"I didn't find out about your secret until you told me," she reasoned. "There was no big wolf reveal. I didn't get any sense of you being anything other than human."

"Maybe," he conceded. "And maybe some part of you related to what I am."

From behind him, Dale chimed in with a reminder of the bigger picture. "That might explain your attraction to each other. What it doesn't do is tell us why vampires are so interested."

Riley was at the window now, with her back to the room. The way she held herself, the straightness of her spine, told Derek its own kind of story. He had touched that spine with his fingertips and had explored each delicate bone and curve. But she was so rigid now. Her fear had grown to momentous proportions.

Memories of her mother had to have haunted her, and rightly so. The little girl who had braved her mother's traumatic incarceration was back now in full force because he had pushed her memory there.

Did Riley think she would suffer a similar fate as her mother if it turned out that she was a werewolf? Was she grieving all over again for her mother's plight and imagining what her mother must have gone through?

Caging a werewolf was tantamount to torture. His skin crawled with the thought of Riley's mother's ordeal.

When Dale plucked the next question from Derek's mind, Derek realized he must have beamed the thought over Were channels.

"Even if the vamp queen had figured out about Riley's latent talents before we did, Weres aren't exactly good dinner fare," Dale said. "We aren't scarce around here, either. So why would the vamp Prime seek out someone who is half wolf, at best, and who, up until now, didn't even realize it?"

Riley turned slowly. After tossing her hair over her shoulder, she eyed Dale almost fiercely. "Why don't we ask her?"

The question might have made sense in some other universe. In this one, it was absurdly unrealistic.

"No. Absolutely not," Derek said. "Damaris is unreachable. Treacherous."

"So I'm to run and hide forever, or until the vampire queen catches up with me? I'm to make even worse the danger you and your pack already face in this city after dark by hiding? How is that fair to me or to your friends? How does that get us closer to an answer for this riddle?"

"We'll deal," he said.

"The question here is how to deal with *her*. With this queen of the vampires."

He could have told Riley about the last time he'd met Damaris, but that would have been cruel. *I could tell you how I felt about losing a woman I once loved because we were different species. How Damaris had abducted that woman and then had nearly taken her life away, drop by drop, in a dank, dark and unimaginable place. But what good would that do? How would it help us, Riley?*

"I'll go with you tonight," she said. "Tell me more of what I can expect to face."

The sound of Derek's cell phone buzzing added an unspoken punctuation mark to Riley's demand. He read the message on the screen and then glanced to Dale.

"Go on. Take the call. I'll get her some food and stick around," Dale said.

"I'm not hungry, and I don't need a keeper," Riley argued.

"Maybe you're not hungry," Derek said, "but you'll need all the energy you can muster for tonight, no matter what you decide to do. They're not all so easy to take down, you know. It isn't all about wooden stakes, young, inexperienced vampires and closed alleys."

Riley's eyes widened. Her body grew stiffer.

"You shouldn't be alone right now," he advised. "Please don't think you can fix this or face what's out there on your own. I don't want to lose you, too, before…"

Derek let the rest of what he wanted to say lie there a minute. "We'll meet up later. Okay?"

Riley placed a steadying hand on the windowsill. The energy she radiated was wild and scrambled. She had a stronger scent when fear gripped her. There was no way to convince her of the level of danger these vampires presented, or make her begin to comprehend how powerful their queen was. No one could possibly have conceived of those things unless they had encountered them in person.

Yet he had no claim on Riley Price and couldn't prevent her from facing the future, whatever that future might bring. Her life was her life. She was missing some important details about what she was and how strong the enemy they faced was, but in her place, he would have wanted to confront his problems, too.

He willed Riley to meet his gaze. "This is a lot for you to take in at once. Promise me you'll let me have the lead and that you'll trust me to handle things in the best way I can."

"Okay," she replied after a short pause.

But hell…

That *okay* didn't satisfy him much.

Chapter 27

Darkness fell over Seattle faster than Riley had anticipated. From her place by the office window, where she had
stayed for some time, she watched Derek head back into
the building, marveling at how normal he looked when her
nerves were lit up like bonfires.

Dale had brought her food from a nearby restaurant,
but she hadn't been able to eat.

She regretted insisting that she go with Derek after
nightfall. For him, hunting for vampires was a normal
pursuit. For her, just waking, breathing and thinking had
taken on the aura of a bad dream. But running away didn't
really suit her, so she had to step up.

Derek didn't knock when he arrived at the office door.
She wasn't to be left alone, so Derek, Dale and Jared were
tag-teaming on the watch schedule. That should have made
her feel safe. Instead, Riley again felt cooped up, restless
and in need of fresh air.

She had to figure things out and believe that Derek knew what he was talking about with regard to her welfare, when it was difficult for her to turn her life over to anyone. She loved her father, but had come to Seattle to live her own life and be on her own.

Derek came into the room like warm wind. The first sight of Derek was always the same—thunder inside her chest, a pulse-pounding rise in blood pressure—as though in half a day she could have forgotten how gorgeous and commanding he was in person.

Was this their inner wolves talking?

Steps past the doorway, he paused to wait for her to acknowledge him before he spoke. "You'll need to lose the loose clothes and anything else a vampire might latch on to if you still insist on accompanying us."

"I have a running shirt in my bag," Riley said.

"Hair?"

"I'll pin it up."

"The pack is out in force. Without a full moon overhead, we're strong, but not anywhere near as scary as when wolfed up. Tonight, there's safety in numbers."

"Won't anyone notice extra muscle on the streets?" Riley asked.

"Four will be in uniform on foot patrol, and two more in cruisers. Five of my friends will be out there in plainclothes. Jared and Dale will shadow us closely."

Riley hid her shaky hands by stuffing them into the pockets of her jeans. "Will she show up?"

"Damaris rarely shows herself. When she does, the situation rapidly goes from bad to worse. We'd prefer not to have that happen."

"Then who will we be looking for?"

"Any of the old ones she sends to get a bead on things, and on you," Derek replied.

"Will they tell us what she wants?"

"Not voluntarily."

"I'm scared," Riley confessed.

"We don't have to go out there. You don't have to go."

"You're wrong about that if it's me they're after," she argued. "I'd like to remain free, and not have to move from place to place, constantly looking over my shoulder."

Derek leaned against the wall. "I'll wait for you to change the shirt," he said.

"And then?"

"Then we'll take a little stroll to the bad part of town and see what comes our way."

Her office had a small bathroom. Riley took her overnight bag there. Without bothering to close the door, she tore off her sweatshirt and slipped on the snug long-sleeved dark navy blue shirt she often ran in on cold days. She wound her hair into a knot and secured it with a rubber band.

The woman who stared back at her in the mirror didn't resemble her much. The face was too thin, too pale. Dark circles under her eyes looked like crescent moons. The top edge of the circle of bruises on her neck showed above the shirt's mock turtleneck.

If she was a Were, as Derek and Dale had suggested, wouldn't she know it? Wouldn't she also possess the powers of miraculous healing that went along with the werewolf mythology?

She could see Derek in the mirror as well. He hadn't moved from his post by the door. It was a testament to the one strength she had developed over time—her willpower—that she didn't call the whole thing off. If anything, her mother deserved this the most.

Derek's concern for her was mutual. Half of her—was it the half he said could be like him?—wanted to settle for another hour or two in bed, in lieu of hunting vampires. She would have chosen to close her eyes and wish this all away, if that had been an option.

What does that make me, Derek?

Does it prove that I'm as crazy as my mother for believing you?

"I can read you at times, you know," Derek said when she emerged. "Your thoughts are like wind in my ears. I get the emotion behind them, if not the wording."

"I do a similar thing with my clients. Read their emotions."

Silence made the next few seconds seem longer as Riley wondered if that was a sign of possessing a Were trait.

"Ready?" he asked.

"No."

His reply was patient and understanding. "I can wait."

"No," Riley said again. "It's time to face the music. Isn't that how the old saying goes?"

She walked past him and out the door, able to feel him right behind her. She was glad he was so close, but worried he would turn out to be right, and that she wasn't one-hundred-percent human after all.

But really…in spite of everything she knew about herself, she did want to run.

Derek signed out at the desk. When they exited the building, Riley matched his long strides. He stopped on the sidewalk to give Riley time to catch her breath. The shirt she wore was tight enough for him to see each rise and fall of her chest.

He hoped for a quiet night, just this once, and for the bloodsuckers to stay off his radar. He was off duty, as far as the department was concerned, and still there was plenty to do.

As they stood on the sidewalk assessing the situation and deciding which direction to go, a light rain started to fall. Derek's only thought right that minute was that Riley would be cold.

And then another thought struck.

Due to the fact that all he could think about was the female standing next to him, he wondered if Riley had somehow been sent to him as a distraction. A way to sideline him and temporarily dull his senses where vampires were concerned.

Nope. They had already covered that scenario, so his mind continued to whirl. Planting a distraction to waylay vampire hunters would have meant that vampires could plan strategically. Not many of them had that ability. But there was one that did. *Guess who?*

Taking this one step further was part of his job. He couldn't quite let go of the idea.

"Hell," Derek muttered, because if there was a plan like that, Damaris would have set him up. The black-hearted diva would have had a hand in placing Riley directly in his path for exactly that purpose. Distraction.

Derek's fingers ached the way they did when his claws were about to spring. His shoulders bunched from the tension gripping them. The wolf inside wanted to run back to that alley where he had last seen Damaris and bite, scratch and claw his way to the truth. Even if it took more strength than he had to deal with her. Even if it required the attention of a creature as old as she was, and equally as strong.

"What's wrong?" Riley asked, worried and as tense as he was.

"Mental jumble." It was the excuse he used to keep those ideas from reaching Riley. "Let's head toward the restaurant."

She fell in with him when he started out. Now that such

an idea had solidified in his mind, though, it was starting to eat him up. Chief among his questions was what Damaris might want to get out of distracting him when her monsters were already multiplying faster than he could keep up, and he was barely making a dent in their population?

A Prime couldn't possibly keep track of her nest when there were so many vampires in it, so what difference would one more wolf in Seattle make? A half wolf, at that?

Riley stopped walking, which made him stop.

"Something's not right," she announced.

"The whole thing stinks," Derek agreed.

"You took me to find them last night and weren't worried about it then," she pointed out. "You put the stake in my hand."

"Would you have used it?" he asked, attuned enough to their surroundings to sense that Riley was onto something, and that trouble was heading their way.

"Would you be able to take down a vampire if one appeared right here?" he asked her. "If it was going to be you, or them?"

"Yes," she said, though Derek heard the uncertainty in her voice.

"They are already dead," he reminded her. "They don't breathe. They're not the people they were before they died. Some crawled up from the grave. Some of them were bitten and drained dry on streets not unlike this one and didn't know what hit them. They are animated corpses bent on destruction. Ghouls. Ghosts. Parasites feeding off the life force of the living."

Riley's beautiful face couldn't have been whiter. She was shivering in the damn shirt, mostly because she was afraid, not because she wasn't wearing a coat.

"You're trying to prepare me for the fact that one of them is coming," she said.

Derek turned around when he heard footsteps. Since vampires didn't make any sounds when they traveled, he expected to see people strolling down the boulevard.

It was a couple. A woman and a man were walking arm in arm, talking among themselves and enjoying a Sunday night. But Derek wasn't relieved by the sight. His pulse had revved. His inner wolf whined and struggled to get out, as if it would make an appearance whether or not there was a full moon to lure it into existence.

He didn't—couldn't—let out the wolf in front of Riley.

In what felt like slow motion, a shadow spread across the sidewalk half a block down from where he and Riley stood. That's all the warning those two humans would have gotten, had they known about the monsters in their midst. But they didn't know. No one had warned them.

One second the young couple was visible, and the next second they were gone...and Derek was running toward the spot where they had last been seen with Riley's hand in his.

Chapter 28

Riley didn't have time to swear. She had seen the couple vanish and realized what it meant, as well as who had to have orchestrated their abduction. Derek wasn't merely going to show her a vampire this time, he was going to try to save that couple from becoming like them.

They ran down the block, located a small space between buildings that she hadn't noticed before and went through in single file with Derek in the lead. His tension, transferred to her through his hand, made her nerves spark with the fight-or-flight instinct that had first started with cavemen. She and Derek weren't fleeing the monsters in this case. They were going to fight them.

She followed Derek into an area she never would have guessed existed. Leaving the modern brick building facades behind, they stumbled across pieces of a much older foundation. Beyond the low concrete barriers stood one emaining wall of an ancient two-story building that had ong since fallen to ruin.

Part of one wall leaned against the side of the building behind it, with enough space between the two for a nice, dark hidey-hole.

Her stomach churned at the sight of that hole.

The alley carried an odor of death. Piles of small bones littered the ground like bleached ivory confetti. Dead dogs and cats maybe, Riley thought. Dead mice, rats and God only knew what other kind of vermin had been caught here. The foulness of the odor was so strong she covered her nose to keep from choking.

Her mind told her to stop the madness and to get out of there as quickly as possible, but Derek's grip on her hand and her own sense of mystery wouldn't have allowed that. And besides, there was no way she'd abandon Derek in a place that reeked of danger, no matter how strong and experienced he was in situations like this one, or how useless she might turn out to be.

Beyond his desire to help the people of Seattle, Derek was also doing this for her.

There was a shoe among the detritus on the ground. A light blue high-heel shoe. Only one of them, and out of place in the filth. The sight of that discarded shoe threatened to make Riley throw up.

Where was its owner? Were Riley and Derek in time to help those poor people? Could they actually help? The space appeared to be deserted. She saw no one at all.

Derek flew to the opening and she stumbled after him, now seeing the need for all the hours Derek and his pack put in hunting down evil in this city.

There was a war going on in Seattle, a secret war that pitted a few good werewolves against hordes of vampires.

Werewolves were the good guys here, so how did that happen? What kind of evolution had taken place to produce justice-minded males like Derek and his friends, who looked like everyone else most of the time and fought to protect humans?

"Here," Derek said, letting go of her hand. "Wait."

"No way. I'm not staying here alone," Riley argued. "I'd rather face a pair of fangs than watch you disappear."

It was too damn dark inside the opening in the wall. On closer inspection, the hole was actually the entrance to a long corridor that was unforgivingly dark, where the severity of the foul odors increased by a factor of ten.

Riley wished she had that damn stake now. If anything jumped out at her, she was going to scream.

She moved along by trailing one hand along the interior wall, thankful it wasn't slimy. The brief flashes of moonlight from behind the rain clouds outside were gone. The floor in the corridor was dry, and she didn't dare think about the small mushy things that now and then tripped her up.

Derek was silent. Could he hear how loudly and frantically her heart was beating? It boomed in her ears like cannons going off.

When Derek suddenly stopped, she ran into him and let out a surprised squeak.

"Listen," he whispered to her.

She thought she heard a woman moaning.

Derek's arm around her waist kept Riley from backing up. He placed something in her hand and closed her fingers around it. It was the wooden stake. The weapon that for whatever reason killed vampires.

"Use it if you have to," he said. "Don't think. Don't delay. You've seen how fast they move and how they operate."

After that warning he released her and was on the move again, walking so fast she had to trot to keep up. The crude weapon she clutched seemed like such an insignificant thing in the dark when human lives were in limbo.

There were sounds behind her now, too. More footsteps. Somebody was moving equally as quickly. It couldn't be a vampire. Hadn't Derek mentioned that vampires made no sound…or had she invented that fact out of sheer desperation?

Derek had to have heard those footsteps, though he didn't slow down. Afraid to speak again in case doing so might alert the vampires in this corridor, Riley walked on with the wooden stake held in front of her with both hands, thinking that actually meeting a vampire would be better than waiting for the unknown to jump out at her from the dark.

A scream echoed through the corridor. As if it had been the gunshot that started a race, Derek was suddenly all legs and speed. And it was a speed Riley couldn't hope to match.

Something solid pushed past her as she ran forward, also moving fast, and scared her even more. But there was no option for giving up, and there was no going back. She had asked for this. Her request had brought them here.

There were more footsteps behind her, then next to her as another body pushed past. This one had a scent she recognized, and her heart leaped. Derek's packmates were here. Dale had come. Jared was here.

Although the situation remained desperate, Riley wanted to cheer.

Derek pulled out the small flashlight holstered on his belt with one hand and his revolver with the other, glad he had reloaded with silver bullets. With Dale and Jared on board, finding whatever lay ahead of them would be easier. He wouldn't have to worry about Riley quite so much

In the tight space of the corridor, and with darkness all around, he read Riley's emotional upheaval as if she was telling him about it. With her lineage in question, that unspoken link of communication was a point in favor of Riley being a werewolf.

Another scream, originating from somewhere ahead of him, ripped through the darkness, which would have been absolute if it wasn't for his flashlight beam. That scream might have been a good thing and mean that the woman the vamps had snatched wasn't dead yet. It also meant that she had the use of a throat that hadn't yet been rendered silent by razor-sharp fangs.

"Right behind you," Dale said. "How many are involved?"

"Two people were taken," Derek replied.

He considered whether the vampires could be making her watch the death of her partner as an added form of torture. Maybe they were taunting that poor soul, like cats playing with a mouse for a while before they went in for the kill.

"Damn leeches," he growled.

The corridor they raced along grew narrower for several feet and then opened up to a larger space. Derek barreled into a cavernlike room with Dale on his heels, following the beam of his flashlight. But there was light here. Two lanterns illuminated a twenty-by-twenty-foot area occupied by five shadowy figures. Three were vampires.

Sliding to a stop on a slick floor without caring to think about what might have caused that slickness, Derek took aim at the pasty-faced bloodsucker that was leaning over the body of a man on the ground. Though blood dappled the vamp's white face, Derek sensed the downed man's heartbeat. They had made it here in time to save a life. Hopefully two of them.

He fired the gun without speaking. The woman, pressed to a wall by one of the ugliest suckers Derek had ever seen, screamed again. The vampire trying to drink from the prone man's veins flew backward as the silver bullet struck its chest. Derek fired again, anyway. As the vampire exploded into ash, the other two came at him with their fangs exposed.

"I'll take the cute one," Dale quipped as the vamps came on. He got his gun out in time to take care of one of them right away.

The third vampire didn't attack. It stopped in its tracks and stared at Derek with flat black unreadable eyes. Derek experienced a moment of complete stillness as their gazes connected. With that stare, Derek suddenly understood why the sucker had stopped, and what was going on.

The rail-thin vampire lifted its arms and spread them wide, offering itself to the future impact of Derek's silver bullets, providing the way for a direct shot to its defunct, functionless heart.

"Why?" Derek asked.

Speaking in a deep voice that showed no emotion, the vampire answered. "Would you want to be me? Be this? Become like them?"

"No," Derek said. "Most assuredly not."

"Neither do I," the vampire confessed.

"You could tell us a lot before I pull this trigger."

"I'd tell you nothing you don't already know."

"Where to find *her* would be a good start."

"She is everywhere and nowhere, wolf. Only the old ones have the privilege of meeting the Prime face-to-face, and they would rather not."

"She wants something from us," Derek said.

"I have no knowledge of that."

"You're different, though."

"Which explains my desire to end this dreary existence."

Derek waved the gun. "Can you change? Be trusted? Is that possible?"

"Not possible for me. The thirst is all-consuming. If you don't kill me, I will kill this woman before you can change your mind."

"Even when you don't want to?"

"Even then," the vampire replied.

"Then I'm sorry," Derek said.

"And I'll go back to being at peace."

Sensing Derek's hesitancy, the vampire advanced, showing fang and producing strange guttural sounds in its throat. Derek didn't have to turn around to figure out that Riley had entered the room, and that the vampire had seen her.

The creature moved toward her with the fluidity of running water. Jared shoved Riley aside the second the vampire reached her and looked the creature in the face.

Pale hands went for Jared's throat as Derek rallied. Dale was there, too. The vampire lunged, spun and caught Riley by the arm. Derek watched her wrench it away. The fabric of her shirt tore, stuck in the vamp's long fingernails, and exposed one of her shoulders and part of her bruised neck.

The vampire could have slid its fangs into her right then, before Derek got enough of a hold to yank the bloodsucker back. But it didn't take that bite. As the creature glanced to Derek with a look that said, "You have to kill me. You know you do," Riley slammed the stake into its back, high enough to have punctured its chest if she had been strong enough to get it through. Derek finished the fight by helping that blow find its mark.

Gray ash swirled in the air and then rained down like the weather outside. Riley stood there as it fell and shivered, staring at her empty hand that was now missing the wooden stake.

Dale, having taken down the vampire he'd been fighting, rushed to help the woman who had been captured and who, though untouched, had sunk to the floor. They were going to have to find a way to convince the woman that she had not seen who had abducted her and what had taken place in this cavern. It was going to be a tricky business. Maybe Riley, with her training in psychology, could help with that. Forgetting was essential, so they would have to try.

Jared went to help the man on the floor, who was still alive and very lucky. Derek observed the end result of a fight that was like so many others in his experience, other than the fact that a vampire had purposefully choreographed its own final death.

That creature might not have harmed Riley, but who was to say? It appeared to have wanted to push Derek and his packmates into sending its soulless body back to wherever it belonged. This was something Derek had never encountered before. Something he had to consider in the days ahead, if there were to be more vampires like that one.

For now, two people were alive to see another day. Riley was safe and she was in his arms...though he couldn't remember how she had gotten there.

Chapter 29

Shock had the power to change a person's chemistry at the cellular level. Riley actually felt it change hers.

As she stood with her back against Derek's chest, stress hormones weaved through her system. Though the chaos and danger she had faced were over, the effects were going to last for some time.

She had helped to destroy a vampire. She had wielded the weapon that had dealt him the blow. They weren't considered living things, Derek had explained, since they were dead already and existed according to somebody else's plan. Therefore, she hadn't actually killed anyone at all.

Yet she had felt the jarring sensation of piercing something solid as the stake went into the vampire's back. She had felt the pointed stake veer off the bones of the creature's spine with an impact that shuddered through her arm and shoulder.

Riley was both horrified and elated to have helped to

save herself from such a cruel fate as the one that had twisted the vampire species into being. Yet she had stepped up. Lucky for her, she had also been surrounded by a few good Weres each time a vampire came around.

The scene in front of her was like another aspect of the nightmare that clung to the outer recesses of her mind. Dale was attending to the woman who had nearly met her death. He had lifted her up in his capable arms. The fact that she still wore one blue shoe was a heartbreaking detail.

Jared had hoisted the woman's male companion over his shoulder, and walked with an unburdened pace toward the corridor they had all used to gain entry to this terrible place. *Two lives* was the phrase Riley kept silently repeating. *Two lives saved out of how many others that might have needed help tonight?*

These people had also been extremely lucky to have Weres watching their backs.

Speech remained an impossibility as Riley watched the Weres clear out with their human treasures. When only she and Derek remained, he broke the silence. "Are you okay?" Before she could reply he asked, "Can you use those long legs to carry yourself out of here?"

Riley nodded twice—one nod for each of question. She was thankful that Derek was encouraging her to move on her own volition.

"It will wear off," he explained as he turned her toward the dark opening in the wall. "The shock will be assimilated once you view what happened here in perspective. You're probably already aware of that, I suppose."

Riley found herself back in the tunnel-like corridor, in the dark. The vampire gymnastics were over for now. She and the Weres were headed for fresh air and a cloudy night sky. Like a benediction of sorts, she would welcome the rain on her face.

Preceding Derek in the dark hallway, she heard Dale and Jared conversing in the distance. Some of the shock she had suffered was already easing, and it felt good to move on legs that didn't falter.

Jared and Dale were waiting in the narrow space outside. Although the rain had stopped, the ground was wet.

"Boss?" Dale asked.

"Hospital," Derek said, reaching for his cell phone. Into it, he barked two words. "Code wolf."

Riley wasn't the only one looking at him now and trying to imagine what the hospital staff was going to say when these two victims showed up. Or when they spoke up.

"There's no time to correct this," Derek explained. "The guy will need a transfusion. And she…" He glanced to the woman in Dale's arms who seemed to be in a catatonic state. "She won't dare to repeat what happened here, will she, Riley? For fear of reprisals."

"No," Riley agreed. "She won't tell."

If the woman with the one blue shoe so much as mentioned the word *vampire*, she, too, might be locked away in an institution. *Like my mother was. And like I might be someday if I believe I'm a werewolf.*

Derek was getting all that. He was reading her again, picking up on her thoughts with his special Were antennae. If he was expecting her to speak, he was going to be disappointed. Really, what else was there to say? *Good job, boys? Bravo on the rescue of two innocent people, and now make me one of the pack?*

No amount of accolades could put a dent in what these three Weres were due for their bravery and their sense of justice. Derek had championed a series of good deeds tonight. And damn it, in spite of her sickness over what she had done with that wooden stake, Riley was in awe of Derek and his friends, as well as how tonight had played out.

"Dinner, Riley?"

She wasn't sure she had heard Derek correctly. She'd been concentrating on the sound of the cruiser now idling at the curb beyond the narrow passage to hell between her and the street. Jared and Dale were already squeezing through that passageway with their human bundles. More cops had arrived to help.

Derek caught hold of her arm when she moved to follow the others. "Dinner," he repeated a bit louder, as if she'd been deaf the first time.

"You and me," he added. "Some small place nearby where we can unwind and talk."

The thought of sitting down in a restaurant was alien at the moment. Unsuspecting people would be dining. Glasses would clink. Food would be served. No one would be aware of what was happening in the dark spaces all over the city and how close some of them might come to a gruesome death if they crossed paths with a monster.

There was no way she could face Derek across a dinner table. Her pulse still thundered. After she'd seen so much blood, it would be a miracle if she'd ever be able to eat again.

"You will," Derek said way too astutely, since she hadn't voiced those thoughts. "You will be able to eat and sleep, and now is a good time to start the process of getting back to normal."

"Normal?" Her voice was pitched dangerously low.

"We might as well enjoy the downtime while we can," he said.

Downtime... He probably meant they'd take advantage of a brief lull before having to fight off more vampires in the near future. It was going to be an endless cycle of vampires on the rampage.

"I have just the place," Derek went on, ignoring the

signs of her uncontrollable tenseness, and acting as if nothing out of the ordinary had occurred here.

He again took her hand in his...

The pleasure Riley got from the warmth of his skin and the support of that hand was a complete surprise compared to the grit and grime of a supernatural crime scene.

She closed her eyes to absorb the sensation of connecting to Derek. Little licks of flame flowed up her arm and into her shoulder, leading her to believe she might be crazy—insane, even—for reacting this way, at this time.

Because what she wanted right this minute—more than food, more than facing a werewolf in a crowded little restaurant without announcing to the world that everyone in it was in real trouble—was the sudden, unquenchable, totally flammable desire to have Derek inside her. To wrap her arms and legs around him and never let go until she became like him. Until she became one of *them*.

A werewolf.

A synonym for strong and fierce...

And just like my mother.

In honor of a moment that was both rich and terrible, Riley looked up at Derek's exquisitely chiseled face, and frowned.

Derek's wolfishness surged beneath the surface of his skin. His chest constricted. Phantom claws that were mere ghosts of the real things made him tighten his grip on Riley's hand.

How he felt about Riley was the impetus for his wolf struggling to get free from where it sat curled up until he called upon it to appear. Though his wolf wasn't actually a separate entity and was as much a part of him as his heart and his breath, Derek felt his inner beast stir as if it actually was distinct.

Riley now knew some of his secrets, but not all of them. Very few people knew the reality of what he kept inside, and what actually made him the alpha of this pack. *Lycan* wasn't a word most Weres understood properly or fully, and yet that was the word that best defined him and the talents he possessed but didn't often show off.

Being near to Riley was like being flooded in moonlight.

He wanted to devour her. Save her. Be with her.

"You're right. A restaurant is a bad idea," he agreed, voice tight, body tighter.

The eyes staring back at him were dilated, so that most of the blue was gone. Riley's body gave off the kind of seductive female pheromones that his body readily translated. She didn't move or try to explain what was happening to her. She didn't have to. He knew what this moment was and how it had to end.

Riley was caught up in the hype that followed a fight, and that hype registered as being sexual. She had staked a vampire, nearly been scared to death, and had survived. Her nerves were hot-wired. She was high on a cocktail of fear, thrills and adrenaline, and her body needed to release all that energy and emotion somehow. Like his did. Like every other Were in a similar situation did.

Riley Price, with her fair hair, big eyes and trembling lips, was exhibiting telltale signs. She was proving to him and to herself that she was no longer the human being she thought she was, and never had been.

"Wolf to wolf," he whispered to her as he backed her toward the street. "This is what it is. This is what we do."

Her eyes darted away and then came back.

"Go ahead, Riley. Try to ignore what we both want."

Her left shoulder grazed the brick in the narrow space. She winced but kept backing up. They were ten steps from the street. The cruiser was gone. Dale and Jared were gone. And like the damn vampires he fought on a weekly basis, Derek wanted to take Riley's soft ivory skin between his teeth tenderly enough to hear her shout his name.

They reached the street far too soon and found the sidewalk mostly empty. When Derek stopped, Riley did, too. He wasn't touching her now, and again felt the ghostly claws she seemed to be luring from him by eyeing him so fiercely.

Riley's face whitened further as he felt his own emotions modify the expression on his face. It was too late for her to bypass the charges running through her. The charges he felt as if they were his own. Her eyes flashed with need. Her body swayed slightly.

Instead of stepping back, Riley stepped forward to meet him.

Chapter 30

Riley couldn't slow the reaction that drove her toward Derek. Activity on the street around her faded into the background as soon as her chest bumped against his. They were in the middle of nowhere, on a public street, and she wanted him right then as badly as she had ever wanted anything.

"Riley." His tone was low, his voice hoarse. "I can explain this, and about what you're feeling."

"Don't you dare try," she said.

Derek's acutely handsome face lost some of its seriousness as her rebuttal sank in. Right then she wanted to find a safe, private place where they could go at each other like the animals they were supposed to be. Like the animal *she* was supposed to be. The animal she felt like right then.

Her quick remark was all it took to get them moving. Although they couldn't actually sprint down the street, the pace they kept up was invigorating.

A light rain fell as they rounded the corner where Derek had left his car. Raindrops clung to her hair and eyelashes. The updo she had pinned to the top of her head was long gone, and her shirt was plastered to her torso.

As they approached the SUV, Derek swung her around, his arm gripping her waist. Pressing her damp hair back from her face, he leaned into her. Their bodies couldn't have been closer. There was hardly room to take a breath, and yet Riley knew this was only a teasing taste of what would take place once she got into the vehicle.

Her stomach was on fire. So was her throat. Derek's heat was similar to being up against a wall furnace, and left her even more breathless.

His mouth hovered above hers, taunting, teasing. Accepting the challenge, Riley closed the distance and bit his lower lip…but not too hard. Enough to tell this wolf she was game.

*Crazy…*her mind warned with really poor timing. *This is so freaking crazy.*

Derek got the door open somehow and backed her inside. His mouth returned for a kiss that was deep, molten, obsessive and much too short. Then he slammed her door, circled the SUV and got in. After starting the engine, he stopped long enough to look at her, his demeanor revealing the preternatural predator that he was.

Excitement flared inside her. "Turn it off," Riley whispered. "Turn off the damn engine."

Although Derek had to know exactly what she was suggesting, he said, "Not here. Not like this." He shook his head and added, "I can't believe I just said that."

They stared at each other for a long time, each daring the other to cave on the idea of fulfilling their fantasies in the back seat of Derek's SUV. That might have been someone else's dream date, Riley supposed. It remained hers for about ten more seconds before she nodded and sat back.

Derek was right, maybe not for the reason he intended, but because there wasn't enough room to contain their sudden need for each other.

He drove like a madman, but didn't resort to using the police light he could have tossed onto the roof of the car. His apartment was closer than her house by several minutes of driving time, so he headed there.

Riley anticipated the moment when she'd come to her senses and remember what they had done tonight in the cavern behind those buildings, and what she had seen that had made her so sick. But both the tingle centered between her thighs and the buzz of electricity that spanned the length of the seat separating her from Derek, refused to dissipate.

He parked on the street. Riley didn't wait for him to open her door. They didn't touch when they raced up the stairs, when he unlocked his front door and while they both tore off their wet shirts inside his place.

They didn't make it to the bedroom or the bed.

Derek, with his bare, bronzed arms and strong hands, simply pulled her to the floor.

The hours passed by in a blur. Finally spent, though he was quickly regaining his strength and up for another round of mind-blowing sex and seduction, Derek listened to the rain hitting the window and the sound of Riley's breath as she was lying in his arms.

She was awake. Patches of her bare skin glowed with a light shimmer of perspiration. Their lovemaking had been feral in intensity. It had taken them to a place he'd never really known could exist for a male and a female.

"I will never get enough of that, and you." He didn't

look at Riley when he spoke, sure he'd start all over again if they made eye contact. But he needed to give her respite. Her entire backside had to be aching already from the hardwood floor.

They had made love several times and on varied surfaces, from the floor to the sofa and the dining table, and had ended up right back where they'd started, which gave them more room to spread out. Riley had to understand at this point that no mere woman could have kept up or walked away from the past couple of hours on her own two feet.

He toyed with the idea of bringing the subject up.

"What can I expect?" Riley asked, beating him to it. It was the first time she had spoken since he'd brought her here tonight.

"How will the wolf part of me show up?" was her second question.

"Your wolf has already made an appearance," Derek replied.

She took some time to think about that. "Am I supposed to feel different?"

"It will take a while for you to mesh with your new senses, and then we'll find out how things are to go. I'm guessing you're already using some of those special senses without realizing it."

"Like my ability to read people fairly easily at work?" she asked, having remembered that from their conversation in her office.

"Yes. Like that."

"Will I be able to shape-shift?"

"I honestly don't know. Some half-breeds can. Others never do."

"Half-breed." She repeated the word.

"She-wolf," Derek said.

Another minute passed before she asked, "How many people do you think I meet, either at work or in my personal life, who are werewolves?"

"Probably more than you might think. Weres don't outnumber the people in Seattle. We're just a small sect trying to blend in."

She had more questions. "What will happen to me now?"

"Nothing, unless you want it to. But you'll have to wait for the next time a full moon comes around to be sure."

He quickly added, "Some people who share their DNA with humans remain human, as you have for most of your life."

"So I can choose for things to stay the same?"

"Possibly."

Rolling onto her side, Riley looked at him now. She said, "And possibly not?"

"What has developed between us has a name. It's called *imprinting*. When that happens and when both Were parties feel the bond that forms, latent Were abilities are often exposed as if they've been tugged out of hiding."

"I can choose not to accept that part of me," Riley repeated.

"The best you can do after this—" Derek gestured to the floor "—is to learn to control whatever shows up. I can help with that. So can the rest of the pack. Everyone will be willing."

"Imprinting is the driving force behind what we just did?"

"Yes."

"It's a real thing?"

"It has ruled Were behavior since the beginning of time and has kept our kind from extinction," Derek explained.

She sat up, whispered, "Our kind," and said louder, "This now makes us inseparable? You and me?"

Derek nodded and wondered what she thought about that. He couldn't read her face at the moment. Riley's father, also a cop, would have been the poster boy for teaching his daughter the art of the good cop face.

"I can't tell him," Riley said, as if she had heard his thoughts. "I can never tell my father about this. Never let on about Weres or vampires. He wouldn't understand."

Her eyes, Derek noticed, were again a bright sky-blue in the sliver of light coming through the open window shutters.

"We keep our secrets," Derek said. "We keep them for reasons like the way your mother was treated, and for so much more."

Now that Riley's wolf had retreated, content to have sampled what a Were male could do to activate and satisfy that part of her, Riley would have time to think. Without the pressure of her wolf battering at her insides, she was again free to be the psychologist who dissected the problems and issues in front of her.

She was almost painfully beautiful. With her blond hair in tangles and her soft lips daring him to kiss them again, Riley was the epitome of a bona fide she-wolf. Naked, wild-eyed and willful. Intelligent, streamlined and strong. He had never seen anything quite like her.

"I'm sorry if this isn't what you want," Derek lied. He was excited about the prospect of keeping Riley with him and getting to introduce her to his world.

"I'm sorry this complicates things with your family," he added earnestly, wondering if Riley had siblings, or if she was an only child. "There will be more time to talk. This, I hope, is only the beginning of a new trust between us."

He watched Riley get to her knees, then to her feet. She

stood up, showing no sign of being self-conscious about her current state of undress. Tall and sleek, with her ivory skin gleaming, she faced the window for a while before walking away from him.

She'd want a shower, time in the bathroom, a drink or some food, Derek thought. So he stayed on the floor, hoping she wouldn't be long.

The sound of a door closing jerked him to attention. Heartbeats bounced off his ribs as he sat up with the sudden realization that it was the front door.

Riley walked down the stairs and onto the sidewalk in front of Derek's apartment house while pulling on her damp shirt and zipping up her jeans. Her shoes dangled from her hand. Chills cooled her flushed skin.

She had to get away, needed time to think about things without Derek gumming up the process. How could anyone just accept the fact that they were part werewolf when it could be a toss-up between truth and hearsay, and with a mother who had fought against the system and died believing she was one?

Justice for all? Innocent until proven guilty? Didn't those same things apply to everyone, in any circumstance? Didn't doctors have a way of knowing truth from falsehood?

She had toyed with the idea of werewolf existence early on, half-heartedly wanting to believe. Her father had never known about that. After his wife had been committed, her dad's time away, on the job, had increased exponentially.

When Jessica Price died in that institution, most of the communication between father and daughter had died with her. But Riley loved her dad, and he loved her. He was proud of how she had turned out. Or had been...though now, when the werewolf theme had returned to bite them all in the backside, she wasn't sure how he'd feel. She'd never know, because she couldn't tell him her secret.

You have no idea what it's like to finally find out the truth, she wanted to shout to Derek. Life was painful sometimes. It could be bleak and heartless. But the fact remained that no one had helped her mother prove she was right, and that was the pain that made Riley grimace as she strode away from Derek in her bare feet.

Werewolves existed. They were real, and here. Not just that, but they said she was one of them.

"Damn it. I am one of them," Riley whispered.

Derek would come after her. He'd be worried and would want to help with the dilemma she now faced about her future. Her lover was perfect and everything she could want in a mate. Yet his presence was too powerful and too overwhelming for her to be around at the moment. With him, she had let out the wildness she had kept buried inside. Being near him at a time like this might influence the decisions she'd have to make.

Had that inner wildness always been a sign of her real heritage?

Riley said over her shoulder, with a brief glance at the apartment house, "Don't follow me. Please let me go."

Derek stood on his front step in all his shirtless splendor, looking every bit the sexy wolf detective. How could she not love him for the brilliant combination of all those things?

Love...

"Don't," she repeated, loud enough for him to hear her warning.

She began to walk faster, listening for the sound of footsteps without hearing any. Half of her wanted to turn back, but that was the part of her that had fallen hard for Derek. The part that made her howl at the moon and fantasize after-hours about a supernatural world. That, and the blood her mother had given her.

The other part of Riley Price had been trained to analyze those things unfavorably. Unfortunately, that part of her was shrinking. She felt it beginning to go.

Don't turn back...

At the corner, she paused to look behind her. Derek was still there, watching her, observing her departure and giving her some space. He was worried, though. Something glittered in his hand. His cell phone. He would probably call for help.

It was dangerous for her to be alone. She had seen what could happen. Though vampires were after her, Riley could not make herself turn back. "Not yet. I need time," she muttered. "Give me that time. A minute to breathe."

She walked past more apartment buildings, determined to reach her office, reasoning that after one vampire had died trying to reach her there, no others would try, at least for a while.

She might even have been right about that, but wasn't, her senses told her. Half a block from the warmth and safety of Derek's apartment, one of those monsters was waiting for her.

Perched on the rim of a bench on somebody's front lawn, crouched there like a bird or a goddamn bat, a white-faced apparition in a long black coat blinked its ghastly red-rimmed eyes and smiled.

Chapter 31

Danger rode the breeze.

If anyone assumed he'd let Riley walk off into the night alone after everything that had happened in the past few days, Derek would have called them mad.

He knew exactly what to expect. Letting Riley learn her lesson the hard way, over and over, would eventually change her mind about alone time for the foreseeable future. For now, she was too vulnerable to see that, and was thinking with the human side of her brain.

He didn't place a call for backup. Sensing what was waiting for Riley, he was already moving, following her at a discreet distance.

With some luck, chasing off the one vampire he sensed without wolfing up would be a piece of cake for him. Fists clenched, lungs filled with the odor that threatened to overpower Riley's sweeter fragrance, he sent a message to her over Were channels, hoping enough of her wolf had risen tonight for her to hear him.

"Don't engage or do anything stupid. I'm on my way."

The back of his neck iced over when he caught up to her. Recognition struck when he saw that the creature that was nose-to-nose with Riley was the same bloodsucker he had chased off her property. Pasty face. Long black coat. The damn thing really wasn't going to give up.

It didn't turn to look at him when Derek approached. It was searching Riley's face the way he once had, as if the fanged bastard also wanted to see for itself what might have been hidden behind all that beauty. If the abomination had discovered her secret that she was half wolf, why would it and so many other vampires be interested in her?

That question remained on the table.

Derek needed to focus on those fangs, and how close they were to Riley's skin. The question of why it hadn't already tried to bite her in the seconds preceding his approach nagged at Derek's mind, but he shoved it into the background for now, out of necessity.

"Back away," Derek directed as he came up behind Riley. "Do it now."

The creature ignored him. Its dark eyes were locked on Riley.

"She's one of us," Derek said. "One of my kind, and not very tasty."

"She is more than you think," the vampire remarked.

"If you're trying to get at me, I'm right here. Harming Riley will do nothing," Derek said.

"This pretty morsel is like you, you say?"

"You can sense her wolf if you're any good at sensing anything other than how to find your next meal."

"I wonder," the vamp said slowly, with great precision and without looking at Derek, "if you've looked very deeply into the thing you also covet."

"I'm right here, and I'm not deaf," Riley said with a shaky voice. "What is it you want?"

"I want to find out why my Prime wants you so much," the vampire replied.

"I don't know anything about that, nor can I conceive of a reason for being harassed by her or by you," Riley said bravely.

The vampire cocked its head. "Her? You know about the Prime?"

"I do," Derek said in Riley's place. "We've met, or nearly did."

The creature turned dark eyes to him. "Then you'll understand why I must take your new pet to her, wolf or no wolf."

Derek said, "If that's the case, I'm wondering why you haven't taken her already, and why you're standing here speaking to us."

He also couldn't figure out why the damn vampire was again showing off the fact that its wits were intact.

"I have learned to bide my time, since I have an endless supply of it," the vampire said.

"What do you want?" Riley repeated.

She hadn't moved. Derek sensed the quaking Riley was trying to hide. There was the slightest flutter in the tousled strands of golden hair that draped over her shoulders, and her hands were fisted.

"Back off," Derek warned. "Riley is not going anywhere with you. Not tonight. Not ever. You can tell Damaris I said so."

His remark immediately captured the vampire's attention. Again, the dark eyes found Derek's. "Damaris?"

Derek took in the way the creature repeated its Prime's name.

"I'm guessing I've just provided you with information

you didn't have," Derek said. "Perhaps we can call it a trade."

With an incredible show of speed, the vampire had Riley by the throat with both of its hands. With nearly equal speed, fueled by his anticipation of the creature's next move, Derek had his own hands on the vampire's bony arms, restraining it.

The curious thing was that Riley didn't struggle. She didn't duck, strike out, scream or try to fight the monster in front of her. She continued to stand there quietly. Now that he was by her side, Derek witnessed the fiery flash of anger in her eyes.

The vampire put its face closer to hers, but Derek had a firm grip that would have stopped those sharp fangs from reaching Riley's artery if that's what the vamp had in mind.

"Damaris," it repeated, studying her.

"Go to hell," Riley said.

"Hell is my middle name," the vampire replied. But it backed off, dropped its hands, stepped away from Riley and turned to Derek. "She will never stop coming for this one. She knows, you see."

With a flip of its coattails, the vampire turned away with a last word. "And now, unfortunately, I also see."

The dark-eyed beast was gone before Derek could yank the vampire back to ask for clarification. What had it gotten from this little meeting? Names had power, sure, but wouldn't a vampire as old as this one have found out Damaris's by now?

Riley was motionless. Now that the immediate threat had been removed, the shaking overtook her. Her shirt and her pants were still damp from the earlier rain. She stood on bare feet and was as white as the vampire she had just faced.

"I think that thing found what it was searching for," she said, her teeth starting to chatter.

For the life of him, though, Derek had no real idea what that discovery could have been. Between keeping his wolf from making an unscheduled appearance in front of Riley and prying those fangs away from Riley's throat, he was sure he had to have missed something crucial.

Fear and shock kept Riley motionless. The vampire had gotten too close. She had been foolish again to have so blatantly ignored Derek's warnings, and he had come to her aid when she already owed him more than she could ever have repaid.

So much for taking time for herself to think things through. She was tired of being the center of attention for both sides of this ongoing war. The only way to get out of this stranglehold on her freedom was to dig deeper and try harder to figure things out. Get down and dirty. Think outside the box.

"What did it feel like when that creature got close?" Derek asked, gently rubbing her chilled arms with his warm hands.

"It was like being sheathed in ice."

"You had no sense of what it was thinking?"

"When that freak looked at me, I guessed that it saw something, but not until you mentioned the name of its Prime," Riley said. "After that, every breath I took seemed to be tied to that vampire somehow. I can't explain it, Derek, other than to tell you that some part of me responded to that creature's hands on my throat as though I had experienced a moment like that before."

"You have been close to them before," Derek pointed out.

"It was like that one touch produced a memory I couldn't

quite reach—information hidden so deep inside me, there'd be no way to access it without cutting me open."

That brief explanation seemed to worry Derek even more, Riley noted. Damn it, it also worried her. Derek had said she was half wolf. She had tasted that kind of wildness when they made love, and was now ready to believe it. She wanted to believe it. On the other hand, being close to that vampire had left her with a strangely similar feeling.

The urge to be sick returned with a flourish. Riley covered her stomach with both hands in a futile attempt to settle it. It was the incredible warmth of Derek's body that she melted into now, grateful to have his support, sorry she had left him without a word about what she was feeling.

If she had just told him she loved him, despite the short duration of their unusual relationship and the fact that they weren't actually human, things might have gone better.

The mix of feelings stirring her insides was causing a riot. Thoughts about digging into what had happened here with that vampire were starting to fade, the way extraneous thoughts usually did when Derek was around. The alpha wolf's presence was dominant. The suddenness of her need to be like him, and with him, took precedence over everything else each time he looked her way.

Wolf to wolf, he had said. That was the way things happened for the Were breed. How else was such an intense relationship to be explained?

Her burning desire to be with him was her animal side coming to the forefront: her wolf making its first appearance. Nevertheless, in order to get a grip on what faced her, she had to find a way to put aside those feelings. She had to delay her wolf's arrival and allow her intellect and psychological training to take the lead.

"Could I have something else inside me?" she asked

without expecting Derek to understand the question, let alone answer it.

His handsome face creased. Fine lines edged his eyes as Derek struggled to comprehend what she meant.

"Not just a wolf I never knew about. Would there be room for anything else? Anything more?" she asked.

His tone was serious enough to make her wince. "Like what, Riley? What are you suggesting?"

"Is there any way I could also be a vampire?"

Derek shook his head. "No way in hell."

When she fell silent, he said, "Had you ever met a vampire before?"

She shook her head. "Before a few days ago? No. Who could forget something like that?"

"Do you have a craving for blood?"

Her stomach reacted to his ludicrous question with a whirl. Riley closed her eyes to ride the feeling out.

"You aren't a vampire, Riley. No one can be half vampire, or even part vampire. They are the walking dead. Every one of them has died sometime in the past and been reanimated by an ingestion of the blood of their maker. That's the only way it happens."

She didn't miss how the last few words of his argument had been offered in a different tone, as though something Derek had said keyed a thought that hadn't previously occurred to him. She opened her eyes when he stopped rubbing her arms. His eyes met hers, and Riley saw pain in them. She watched him catch and hold a breath. The bronzed features of the face she loved lost some color.

Fright was already making a comeback when he said, "Oh, hell no. Christ, Riley…it can't be happening again."

Chapter 32

"It can't be happening again."

The realization sat heavily on Derek's heart. He blinked, and then blinked again so that Riley wouldn't see his anger rising.

He wasn't sure about the idea that had hit him like a runaway train, and yet it made sense in a perverted sort of way. That vampire's temperament had changed when it heard Damaris's name spoken, though anyone would have imagined the creep had to have already heard it in the long years spent in her service. No, this new insight had more to do with connecting that name to Riley.

There was only one reason for that. One reason that, if proved true, would seem like a curse had been laid on him, and that curse had found a way to include Riley.

"You're scaring me, Derek."

He was leaving her in the dark, yes, but there was no way to explain the horror of what he was thinking. How could he tell Riley there was a chance, a possibility, that she could be housing the stray soul of a monster? That the essence of what had once been Seattle's vampire queen when she was still a human being resided in Riley's body?

Out of all the people in Seattle, a city with a huge population of humans, a stray soul might have landed inside Riley as an unwelcome guest? A freeloading parasite? That same floating soul had also chosen to reside within his former lover, McKenna, and because of that, had kicked off the last big battle with Damaris's vampire hordes.

Because Damaris, now a soulless vampire queen, could no longer possess a soul, the black-hearted diva had somehow managed to set her old soul free at the time of her death. The story he'd heard from the immortal who had taken McKenna away from Seattle was that Damaris followed that stray soul around from human host to human host as though she hoped to get it back someday.

The odds of this kind of soul transference happening to two women Derek had fallen for had to be astronomical. And yet it seemed to be a very real possibility here, with Riley. What other reason would make vampires single her out?

Agitated, Derek turned around in a circle to check for the sound of vampires laughing, as if the joke was on him. He avoided Riley's beseeching stare, not willing to face the fear he'd seen in her face, or let her see his.

"Tell me what this means," Riley demanded. "I have a right to hear what you're thinking."

"Inside," he replied. "Let's go inside. You're shivering again."

"And you're procrastinating."

"Inside, please," Derek repeated, adding silently, *And I hope I'm wrong about this.*

Riley went with him without further argument. Back

n his apartment, he handed her dry clothes that were four times too big for her and made her look even younger and more vulnerable.

She curled up on his bed with her back to the headboard and peered at him from beneath lowered lashes. "Talk," she said.

Derek paced back and forth beside the bed, needing to burn up his excess agitation. "We're talking about the past," he began, finding this hard to verbalize.

"Her name was McKenna. We were an item for a couple of years while she was a cop on the force. McKenna was shot on the job. She became a nurse after the department put her out to pasture, due to that injury."

Riley interrupted him with a question. "An item? You loved her?"

Derek reluctantly nodded. "Just not enough for it to go anywhere."

Riley was watching him. "Was she human?"

"She was human, yes. But it turned out that she also housed a soul that didn't belong to her. A secret soul that had no right to be hiding inside her."

He paused there to decide how much of the story Riley needed to hear to understand the reason for his new round of fear. His mind buzzed with thoughts that merged the past with the present.

What if this was a replay of those times with McKenna Randall? What if Riley did host a second soul that didn't belong to her?

He had no idea how soul transference could actually happen.

He swallowed and went on. "Someone new came to town and fell for McKenna, and that's when the real trouble began. The soul that had been hidden inside her was tied to that new guy without anyone realizing it."

"What soul?" Riley asked in frustration.

He stopped pacing again to look at Riley, wondering if he might see the truth of this new theory if he looked real hard…and if there could be evidence of what he now suspected in Riley's expression, or her eyes.

Would talking about it bring that hidden soul to attention? He didn't dare wake something that was so dangerous before Riley had a chance to protect herself from it.

"Go on," she encouraged, unaware of the degree of danger they'd face if his idea turned out to be true.

"After that stranger arrived, McKenna was hunted," he continued. "Things got messy real fast."

"She was hunted by vampires?"

Derek nodded. "They were after her because hers was the body a vampire's former soul had chosen to be housed in, and it just so happened that the stranger McKenna had hooked up with was both the best and the worst thing that could have happened to her because that stranger was also an immortal, and had, in a century long past, been that vampire's lover."

"What vampire?" Riley demanded, her voice rough, almost raw.

"The other soul inside McKenna once belonged to Damaris," Derek said.

Riley skipped ahead. "Did McKenna die?"

"No. And yes," Derek replied.

"Explain."

"She became an immortal in the end, like that stranger who helped her to survive the ordeal with…"

After a brief hesitation, Derek again spoke the name that had been elevated to the forefront of so many minds tonight. "Damaris."

Riley had slid to the edge of the bed after hearing that name. Her shaking rustled the edge of the blanket she sat on. She had to recognize the wariness in his tone each time he mentioned the vampire queen.

Derek fought the urge to take Riley in his arms, afraid that if he did, he would never get the rest of this story out.

"Damaris had given up her soul in exchange for the gift of immortality, but stayed close to the humans it found a home in through the centuries. The only thing you need to know is that the soul couldn't be returned to Damaris. That wasn't possible. Vampires have no souls. The souls of the people they were before being reanimated leave when they die."

He took another break for a breath. "Damaris couldn't have hers back but for some reason wanted to be near to it. However, the soul could no longer continue to attach itself to my ex, McKenna, after she became immortal. So it must have fled again, and…"

"It found me?" Riley's voice wavered. "You believe that soul might have migrated to me, over everyone else around here? You're serious about considering the possibility?"

She had more to say before he could answer her question. "I haven't been in Seattle for very long. Where would it have been before I came along?"

"I don't know. Maybe it's been through a couple of others before finding you."

He saw her disgust over that idea.

"If what you say is true, what would make me so special, so worthy of housing such a thing?" she asked.

"That's where I get tripped up, Riley. You're part wolf, and as such you're an enemy of the vamp nest Damaris lords over. It seems impossible that two of the women I've known could have been in line for such a thing, or that anyone with an ounce of wolf blood in their veins could be involved."

Derek waved at the air with a gesture of hopelessness

and went on. "Nevertheless, I can't help thinking this might be the case, since you haven't been injured in any of these vampire sightings and that vampire tonight seemed to get a kick out of something he saw in you."

He paused to think that over. "It's inconceivable to think that souls have minds or powers that direct them, and that this one could be tired of Damaris chasing after it. Who would believe such a thing? But if any of this is true, having that soul end up inside a werewolf would be a final joke on Damaris."

Riley stood up. She didn't sway. Her voice wasn't panicky. "I'm not sure there even is such a thing as a soul. And this is getting more absurd by the minute. First, I find out I'm part wolf. Now you're proposing that I'm a wolf housing the soul of a vampire?"

Derek ran a hand through his hair. "Not the soul of a vampire. The soul of the human that vampire once was."

"You're serious?"

"I saw the vampire's reaction when it touched you. I heard the way it repeated its queen's name. Then what happened, Riley? It left. No argument. No fight. I can't tell you how rare that is."

Riley moved to the shuttered window as if she could see past the shades. Her long hair was tangled enough for him to see evidence of chills rising near the graceful curve at the base of her neck—the spot male Weres loved second best in their mates. Derek longed to place his lips there and ask Riley to forget all the rest.

But he couldn't forget any of this.

"How do we find out if this is true? If it is, how would I get that extra soul out of me?" she asked.

Riley was again showing her trust in him by asking that question. She was considering his theory and weighing her options in case it actually was the truth.

Derek hated to say what else he was thinking. If he were proved right and Damaris didn't like having her old soul harbored in the body of a Were, their future would be bleak in the hours and days ahead. It meant Damaris might want to cut that soul out of Riley, or cause Riley enough damage for that soul to flee elsewhere.

The only being on the planet that was strong enough to take on Damaris was the immortal that had faced her the last time such a thing happened. Unfortunately, that immortal was long gone, and McKenna with him.

There was no way Derek was going to allow that same thing to happen a second time, not to Riley Price, the first female he had ever loved enough to kick off the imprint sequence. The female with whom he already wanted to spend the rest of his life. The woman who was wolf enough to carry Were secrets and become part of the pack.

Riley said, "It's just a theory."

He nodded. "Only that." Nevertheless, Derek believed it was the only explanation for Riley being hunted by Damaris so specifically, while not being harmed by the vamp queen's minions.

Riley was thoughtful. "That could explain the feeling I had of being like that creature, couldn't it? Something inside me recognized what a vampire is?"

Derek didn't respond to the question. He couldn't utter a damn word.

"Is your ex, McKenna, here in Seattle?" she asked.

"No."

"Then we're on our own with this theory?"

"We are."

"I'm half wolf?" Riley said.

He nodded. "According to what we know of your history, that's what we believe."

"If Damaris can't have the soul back, why would she

bother with me or anyone else who had it? Why send her vampires after me?"

When Riley turned around, she again met Derek's eyes. "Maybe you're right, and she doesn't like the idea of her soul being housed in the body of someone associated with werewolves and surrounded by a werewolf pack. She can't get close to Weres, can she?"

Riley's words meant she'd been listening to him with an open mind. She'd started to believe—or already knew—that down deep she was a Were.

"So," she said carefully, "it was a mistake? Since I didn't realize I had wolf in me, and neither did you when we first met, could Damaris's floating soul have accidentally gotten lost in the body of an enemy it didn't recognize as such? Could that be right, Derek? Would she try to take my life in order to rectify the matter?"

Derek was out of ideas. They were going to need help in sorting this out, and he could only think of two places to get it. The first would mean finding McKenna Randall and her immortal lover, and asking them for backup, which would take time they might not have.

The second path would be to find the vampire that had been nosing around Riley and try to get some answers out of it…which was a dicey idea, at best, because what would it have to gain by giving information to the enemy?

"It's only a theory," Riley repeated half-heartedly.

"Only that," Derek again agreed.

Riley was silent for a long time. Finally, she spoke. "If all this is true, I might be in need of a wolf to get out of this in one piece."

"I'm here, and going nowhere," Derek promised.

She shook her head. "I meant that I might need mine," she said in a low, tight voice.

Chapter 33

Riley was right about the necessity of getting her wolf on, Derek thought. Even as a half-breed, she'd be stronger and more aware of her surroundings once she accepted the surprise coded into her bloodline. Her senses would be fine-tuned. She'd be better able to see trouble coming.

The wolf nestled inside her was ready to spring. They had succeeded in rousing it from dormancy during both of their sexual encounters, only to have Riley's refusal to believe in such things send it back.

He would protect her with his life if it came to that, but Riley wasn't helpless. She was tough when necessary and had proven that with a wooden stake. When she became one with her wolf, she'd see the world in new ways. He could see her weighing thoughts about that now.

He just didn't understand how Riley could have housed that runaway soul before he had met her. Had the transplant been more recent? Without figuring it out, he didn't see a way to help Riley in any meaningful way.

She was looking at him expectantly, so he nodded for her to say what she was thinking.

"You told me that being near other Weres would tug my wolf free from its bonds. Was that right?"

"Yes," Derek replied.

"Would finding my wolf rid me of that stray soul, if I had one?"

"Maybe. So we'll go to the pack and give that wolf of yours a little push," he said.

"We can do it now?"

"Now would be a good time if you're ready."

Derek wanted there to be a better way to initiate Riley into the clan. To get her in tune with her wolf nature. Another lovemaking session might have done that if they'd had more time, and if vampires weren't a continued threat.

Unlike humans and Weres, those damn vampires had too much time on their side. "An endless supply of it" was how the one they'd met tonight had put it. They could keep coming.

Together, he and Riley started for the door. But then they stopped outside, on the front steps, surprised to find a car already idling at the curb with the passenger door open.

Seeing Dale in the driver's seat of the dark SUV comforted Riley as she climbed into the car. Derek jumped in after her.

"Got the message loud and clear," Dale said as he stepped on the gas.

Riley didn't recall Derek making a phone call.

"Were channels allow us to communicate telepathically," Derek explained, as if she had voiced that concern aloud.

Of course, Riley thought. *That's why Derek can read my mind.*

"We need to get to the pack," Derek said to Dale. "We'll have to gather whoever is around."

Riley was sure she saw sympathy in Dale's eyes when he glanced at her, though she wasn't going to ask questions. She didn't want to find out what was in store, and what "giving a little push" to her wolf meant.

Dale drove expertly through the city, careful to keep an eye out for potential problems. Derek split his attention between watching what was going on outside the window and looking at her. Sandwiched between both big males, being entrenched in the heat their bodies exuded, made Riley feel truly safe for the first time since her encounter with the vampire that had stalked her.

"Do they like being vampires?" she asked.

Neither Were tackled that question. Riley couldn't imagine how anyone would want to end up like one of those creatures that lived off the life force of other living beings and couldn't set foot in the daylight.

The city lights eventually dimmed and Riley recognized the route Dale was taking to the Were community. They reached the gates and passed through.

Dale didn't take them to his house this time and instead parked near a small building that stood in the center of a neighborhood park. It was late, though who the hell actually knew the exact time? There were no children playing. No one milled round.

The absence of activity was in itself scary. Riley didn't ask any more questions, though, preferring to trust Derek with her welfare, counting on him to help her out of the jam she found herself in and hoping no blood-sucking vampires would decide to try their luck here tonight.

Derek opened the door. He led her toward the building, where flickering candlelight shone from behind the windows.

She hesitated on the walkway, unsure.

"It's okay," Derek said. "This will help. You'll see."

Riley took a firmer grip on Derek's arm as they entered the building, where there had to be forty people—make that forty werewolves—waiting to meet her.

It was called The Ceremony, an event that had been cultivated so far back in the past that only a few Weres understood its origins.

The original purpose of such a gathering was to save the Were species that had been hunted nearly out of existence. By breeding Weres with humans and accepting those half-breeds into the community, Weres could perpetuate the species as a whole in one form or another.

It was believed that this was how some werewolves had evolved to appear more like men than wolves when the moon was full. It was extremely rare these days for Weres to become real wolves, though it wasn't unheard of. Those special Weres were revered as throwbacks to the old days. Their bloodlines were coveted. They, like Derek, were known as Lycans.

Derek's secret nature fell within that definition. Although he didn't take on full wolf form, his unique coding allowed him to shape-shift with or without a full moon overhead, and anytime he wanted to.

The Seattle Were community included no other Lycans of his caliber and bloodline. Though human-Were bonds were no longer necessary or frequent, there was no prejudice here regarding the human race and the part they had played in werewolf evolution…except where Lycan blood-lines were concerned. In order to protect Lycan skills and traits and keep the lines undiluted, Lycans only mated with other Lycans.

He had fallen hard for Riley Price, though, and wasn't sorry.

Tonight, if all went well, Riley would begin to feel the wolf essence nestled up inside her. Nothing more than that. It would be enough for her to deal with and would show Riley that she was one of many.

"Will it hurt?" Riley asked as the faces of his friends appeared, accentuated by the light of a room full of candles.

"No one will touch you," Derek explained. "You just have to be here, among us."

Her eyes were again wide. "What if I'm not what you think I am?"

"I don't think there's a chance of that, but shouldn't we find out? Walk with me. Keep hold of my hand."

She did as he asked with her head held high and her blue eyes curious. *"I'm proud of you,"* he messaged to her. *"You just need to be able to hear me."*

"All you have to do," he said to her aloud, "is breathe and look around. Look at the faces of the Weres who have come to welcome you. Inhale their scent and internalize it. See if your body recognizes what that scent represents. Can you do that?"

She squared her shoulders and briefly closed her eyes. When he stopped walking, she stood silently beside him—a worthy she-wolf if she accepted that part of herself.

Derek waited for her to reach inside and find the part he had seen glimpses of. Through her hand, he felt every thunderous beat of her pulse as she looked around and took it all in—the faces of the pack that had supported him since he inherited the title of alpha.

This was where he had been raised. Where his family had lived for a while when they were alive, and before they had been taken down by vampires overseas. He knew every one of the Weres gathered here. They were his family now, as well as his friends.

"These are our allies, Riley. Can you feel their welcome, my brave and lovely wolf?"

She was quiet. Still. Maybe she was in shock. Derek perceived a trace of doubt in her expression as Riley did as he asked. He wondered if she was hearing him already on Were channels.

After several minutes of inactivity had passed, he began to sense something stirring inside her. It wasn't panic. He would have recognized those signs. There was a subtle change in the way she stood, a new straightness and a stiffness in her limbs. The fingers that slid from his curled into a fist.

Her shoulders quaked. She slowly turned her head. The circle of Weres around her began to close in. Everyone here expected her to speak, but she didn't. Instead, Riley groaned like she was in pain and doubled over.

When her legs buckled, Derek swore out loud. He had promised her there would be no pain, so what was this?

He reached for her as she sank toward the floor, catching her under her arms. She was breathing heavily and was unable to regain control of her legs.

Murmurings rustled through the crowd, sounding like wind in the trees. He had to ignore that. He had to help Riley.

He swore again as he lifted her into his arms. The stiffness left her as soon as he held her close. She rested with her head against his chest and her eyes closed.

For about twenty seconds.

And then she began to change.

Shape.

The sound of her bones cracking pierced the silence. Her muscles began to dance. She shuddered, moaned, convulsed as if an alien entity had taken her over. As if something was twisting her body from the inside out.

Her head snapped back. Her chest rose and fell laboriously. She acted as if she was being squeezed, crushed… Why, when this meeting should have been so simple?

She began to tear at her clothes as if the confinement they provided was an added source of agony. The supernatural striptease left her without her shirt. Still in his arms, she wriggled out of the jeans, and he moved with her, struggling to keep her close.

Half-naked now, she opened her eyes. He saw their color had moved closer to gold on the spectrum. Riley looked him in the face, pleading with him to help her. He didn't know what to do in circumstances so far from the norm.

Dale was there beside him, and Jared. The other Weres backed away slowly to give Riley some space. In the end, though, there was nothing Derek or anyone else could do to help her. With an ear-shattering sound that contained all of Riley's fear and pain and uncertainly, she twisted so violently Derek lost his hold on her, and she dropped to the floor.

He stood back in utter disbelief as Riley's golden eyes again met his seconds before she turned and headed for the door.

On all fours.

In the form of a wolf.

A real one.

Chapter 34

A collective gasp went up from the room. From behind him, Dale loudly echoed Derek's curses. Everyone was as stunned as Derek was, and that was an understatement, since no one knew for sure what had just happened.

Riley was supposed to be half wolf only, and up to now that half had never been acknowledged. There was no full moon in the sky and hardly any light inside the room, and yet she had shape-shifted into the real deal.

The truth hit Derek like a battering ram. Riley's mother had to have been more than just a misdiagnosed Were. Hell, that woman had to have been a full-blown Lycan in order to produce a Lycan. Even then, Riley couldn't have managed a shape-shift like this one unless... Unless her father also was a Lycan.

And if that was true, her family had kept that incredible secret from everyone, including Riley.

Seconds after that thought, Derek was on the move with

Dale and Jared on his heels, his mind moving as swiftly as his legs did.

Not only did the Prices have to be Lycans, they also had to be the rarest form of the breed—the rarest of the rare. They became wolves. Maybe, like Riley, they could shape-shift with or without the moon's influence. And they would have to have been so in control of what they were that they had been able to hide their true identities from everyone, including other Weres.

So, how had Riley's mother been caught?

That question rang like a bell in Derek's mind as he raced across the park at full speed. He had to find her. Christ, this rude awakening to the truth of her family tree was his fault, in spite of the fact that he was elated. Riley was a Lycan, like him, and also so much more. That's why the bond between them had formed so quickly. That's why he couldn't help loving her.

"Riley, stop!" he shouted. "Wait. Pease wait."

She wasn't fast. Not yet. And that was in his favor. Shape-shifting took time to get used to. She'd have to learn to coordinate all four legs and breathe with a new set of lungs. Her surroundings would be pressing in, one scent after another, to bombard her with information. He remembered his first shape-shift and had hoped to guide Riley through hers.

"Riley!"

He saw her on the street, where she had stopped to look back at him.

"Good," he said as he stopped several feet away from where she stood. "It's going to be okay, I swear. How could anyone have predicted this?"

Riley had paused near a streetlight, which gave him a full view of what she had become. Derek didn't have time to process anything more.

"You're light-years beyond merely being special," he continued. "I'm sorry we didn't see it. You might be in shock. Anyone would be. If you'll come with me now, I'll help. This shift probably won't last long and is only a hint of what lies in our future."

He'd said *our* future, when it was possible she'd never trust him again after tonight.

"I can explain. Try to, at least," he said. "This new shape is a gift from your parents. Both of them, it would seem, and not just from your mother. That's one of the puzzles solved. We'll work on the rest."

Riley looked to have been carved in stone. The only thing to counter that impression was the way her soft brown fur, as shiny and silky as Riley's blond hair, rippled in the light.

"Riley?" he said as softly as he could, to get his point across. "Please let me help. Don't run away. You'll change back any minute. I'm here and will always be here. You can count on that. I'm swearing it to you now."

There was no way he could even think to utter the word *trust*.

"Come this way slowly. Do it, Riley. Let me help you."

When she turned her head, Riley's golden eyes caught the light.

"We can call your father and ask him to explain," Derek said as a last resort to get her to move. "In the meantime, you have all of us here to lean on." He gestured to the darkness beyond the lights, in the direction of the city. "Out of everyone out there, we're the ones who understand."

She took one step, paused and then took another. Riley was still unsure how to maneuver her new body. Derek had to go to her. He willed her to allow his approach, as he also silently asked Dale and Jared to remain on the curb.

"It's okay," Derek repeated. "In either shape, you are beautiful, and you can handle this."

She let him get closer. As he reached out to touch her, he saw that the strength of Riley's wolf was already starting to fade.

Her reverse shift was fast and accompanied by snapping sounds similar to those of her initial transformation. Bones, ligaments and muscles all moved like liquid in a process that was ageless. Shoulders, hips, legs and arms morphed in rapid succession. The fur disappeared last, and the process left her panting.

What stood in the wolf's place was the pale, naked female he had grown to love and had vowed to protect. Derek loved her so much in this moment he was sure his heart would break if Riley rejected his help.

He caught her when she swayed, and again lifted her into his arms. He had carted several new Weres home in his time as alpha, but none like this. *"None like you, Riley."*

She was too weak to wrap her arm around his neck, and seismic shakes rocked her. He cradled her in his arms, inhaled her sweet scent, stared at the long blond hair that hung like golden streamers across her face.

"This might be the last time you allow me to be the strong one," he said to her. As a full-blooded Lycan, Riley would eventually be stronger than any of the Weres in Seattle because Lycans were genetically coded that way.

"Amid all the chaos, we've managed to find each other," he said to her. "All the events have lined up, it now seems. Hell, Riley, maybe there is such a thing as fate."

Riley's insides continued to churn as though her body hadn't finished sorting out the multitude of shocks to her system. She still couldn't speak, but was thankful to have regained her shape. Like this, she could breathe. She didn't have to be so afraid or at a loss as to what to do or where to go.

She was a wolf, and nothing remotely like a half-breed. She had fur, a long face, all of it, and wasn't sure how that had occurred.

A new kind of sickness clenched her stomach. Her hands and feet still felt strange. She wanted to touch her face, make sure it was her face, but couldn't lift her arms. It was as if the wolf had sucked the life out of her, the way vampires would have if they had caught up with her.

She gave little thought to the fact that she didn't have any clothes on, and couldn't recall taking them off. It didn't matter to her who might have been looking on. The only thing she sought was the warmth she found within the circle of this man's arms, as she remembered the promises he had made. As independent as she was, Riley didn't relish the thought of facing the future on her own...like this.

She thanked Derek with her eyes, the only part of her that wasn't aching, and silently pleaded with him to take her home.

"All right," he said with relief. "Let's get you warm."

He began to walk, and his packmates followed. Riley found it odd how she heard every sound so clearly after her body had betrayed her and her pulse continued to pound in her ears. Footsteps, wind in the trees, cars in the distance and doors opening and closing were abnormally loud. The heartbeat inside Derek's wide chest drummed in her ears, alongside hers.

She thought she heard Derek's voice, though he hadn't spoken to her again. Like with his previous midnight assurances, he was urging her to be okay. If it wasn't for the way Derek's face had set and the tautness of his body, Riley might have gone so far as to wonder if she had made this whole thing up, too.

"Only the beginning," Derek said.

There were others in the periphery, hugging the darker areas of her vision. Derek's friends had seen what happened to her and were curious. Surely they had seen a naked woman before? And a wolf?

"*Woman* is no longer the correct term for you, my lovely she-wolf," Derek said, having again read her mind.

The term *she-wolf* sounded as strange as everything else. Did it actually suit her? Define her?

Was she going to shape-shift again?

Her mother had done this to her, Derek had said. Her mother had been special, too. Not mad or crazy. Truly special. So was her dad, for her to be able to shape-shift like that.

As they took the walkway leading to the house where she'd spent the previous night, Riley directed what was left of her flagging energy toward speech.

"No room," she said to her sober-faced lover.

He glanced down at her.

"No room inside me for both things, wolf and an extra soul. The wolf takes up all the space."

A look of surprise rearranged his features, which led Riley to believe Derek had forgotten all about that part of the puzzle they had been attempting to solve—the part about Damaris's traveling soul. For Derek, seeing her shape-shift tonight had been the revelation of the century.

And hell, that's what it had been for her.

Derek set Riley down in the bedroom, on the bed, and leaned forward with his face inches from hers. "This is a game changer, Riley."

She continued to stare back. He saw that her eyes were again a bright, summer blue, though the golden hints he'd seen in her wolf eyes remained as small flecks of light.

Derek pulled the blanket around her shoulders. The shock of what he had witnessed hadn't worn off yet, so he could only imagine what she must be feeling.

"You might be right about your wolf taking up space," he concurred. "In the meantime, and until we find out, Damaris doesn't know anything about what took place here tonight. Chances are good that she's still looking for you and the rest of us."

Her voice was rocky. "I was a wolf."

Derek nodded. "You certainly were."

"That's not normal?"

"Not in this community, though they all have heard the stories, like I have," he said.

"The wolf takes over everything, but leaves our minds? I was me, and not me. I had thoughts and recognition, except that my body wasn't my body." Her eyes keyed him to the alarm running through her.

"We don't go mad when we shift," he explained. "We stay us, with a different outline. Only rogue Weres, who were bad to begin with, get worse when a big moon comes around and like to use their moon-induced strengths for no good."

"Will it happen to me again?"

Derek tucked the blanket tighter around Riley, hoping to stop the shakes that made her teeth chatter. "It's highly possible."

"Could my wolf combat the soul you believe is inside me?" she asked. "Force it out?"

"I don't know. I doubt if anyone does."

"Then I need to test it out. I need to change again and kick that vampire's old soul out of me if it's there. Maybe the monsters will leave us alone if it's gone. Maybe Damaris will go elsewhere to look for it."

Derek wrapped a strand of Riley's hair around his finger and let it slide off before tackling what she had said. His muscles were nearly as jumpy as hers were. Beneath his skin, his nerves felt like strings of fire.

"That doesn't sound like a healthy prospect for anyone, especially if the soul finds an unsuspecting human next," he pointed out.

"How many others has she chased down?" Riley asked. "Is Damaris content if her soul is inside a more normal human being? Does she merely keep an eye on it from afar, or does she interfere with everyone who houses what's left of her humanity?"

Riley didn't give him time to respond. Her words rushed out of bloodless lips. "The unknowns will continue to plague us. You and your pack might look at every death in this city as being something she had a hand in."

Derek said, "You're right about that, too."

"Then there's only one way to find out if that soul is what she's after," Riley asserted. "How can I ever be free of the curse until that soul is gone? How can we move forward if we believe it's there?"

Derek didn't care to hear the proposal that had to be coming. He was already building up to a hearty "No!" when Riley overruled his as yet silent protest.

"We can bait that vampire into coming into the open," Riley said. "Let Damaris come to us, on our terms, and we can deal with her once and for all. I'll shape-shift, if I can, and if you teach me how to do it. If I don't pass out with the effort, I can shove that soul out of me in front of Damaris."

Derek held up a hand to protest all of what Riley was proposing. But she had more to say.

"Will you teach me, Derek? I will try again despite how scared I am if it means only one soul stays with me. Mine."

"I can try to teach you," Derek replied.

She was waiting for him to go on.

"Maybe not until the next full moon. Maybe sooner. I told you you're rare. I can't predict what kind of instincts rule your system. To be honest, I've never seen anything like what you did tonight."

She continued to wait for more of an explanation, so he gave it to her.

"Only a few Weres can shape-shift without a full moon present," Derek said. "No one here becomes a full-on wolf, like you just did."

"Is my ability a good thing?" she asked.

"Yes. And highly unusual."

"Then you will teach me about it and help me adjust to a new identity? Will you do that?"

"And then what?" Derek said. "We dangle you like a carrot and hope Damaris takes the bait without cutting you down? You don't imagine that she's been around for centuries for a reason, and can probably handle herself better than any creature on the planet?"

Derek shook his head. "What you're suggesting is too damn dangerous and comes close to being suicidal."

"Yet it's the only option for getting what we all want, isn't it?" Riley insisted. "What I want and what you want. A little bit of peace."

Derek closed his eyes. His plan for Riley had worked too well. She had become aware of her wolf, all right. But he hated it when the most dangerous path forward from here was the only one with the slightest hint of promise.

Chapter 35

Derek had been reluctant about climbing into bed with her after her recent ordeal, but Riley needed him there on a nightly basis now, ever since her first shape-shift.

He satisfied every craving she had in the most delicious ways, and the rapidly growing strength of Riley's wolf learned from his, though she hadn't shifted again after that first time.

She was saving the next shape-shift for later.

They both went to work each day, and at night returned to Dale's house, where they were safely tucked away in the community of werewolves Riley had quickly become part of.

There had been no vampire sightings near her home or office in the past ten days. Riley spent no time in the city after dark to give them access to her whereabouts. She returned to her house only for fresh clothes in the morning, accompanied by Dale, Jared or Marshall, who, thank goodness, was okay after that bite he'd taken.

If Damaris had spies, they either hadn't been able to track her to the Weres behind their closed valley gate, or were afraid to test their skills against a whole community of werewolves.

Riley was one of the pack now, and held two honors as the alpha's mate and a full-blooded Lycan. Her strength increased day by day once she had accepted those things, and her mind had followed suit. Her energy had returned, as Derek had predicted. She was no longer so afraid of being something other than human.

The discolored bruises on her neck miraculously disappeared after that first shape-shift. Now that she knew what she was, she healed superfast. She was leaner, fitter, and worked to have better control of her muscles in preparation for the fight that lay ahead.

Together, she and Derek ran, talked, researched and explored her new status. They made wild, passionate love, and never stopped thinking about each other. And though she had not placed that call to her father about the secrets he'd kept from her, Riley finally adapted to what she had been destined to become.

It was all right. Being even remotely like Derek was what she desired most. Who wouldn't have considered added strength and finding a mate like Derek anything less than a dream come true, despite the discovery of her weirdly wired DNA? Then again, she supposedly housed someone else's soul, and that remained a burden.

It was on the eleventh day after her indoctrination into the Were clan that events took a turn. It was then, and for the second time, that Riley felt something other than her wolf stir inside her.

An inexplicable fluttering sensation came, centered way

down deep. She thought about mentioning this to the others, but waited to see what those unusual stirrings might mean as she sat between Dale and Jared on the front seat of the black SUV that was idling at a red light.

There was a sudden and unexpected thud on the roof that was loud enough to make Dale jerk the wheel to the right. The SUV swerved toward the curb, where other cars were parked, narrowly missing one of them. Slamming on the brakes, Dale reached for the door handle, intending to find out what had happened, but Riley put a warning hand on his arm to stop Dale from opening the door.

"They're here," she said. "They've found us."

Dale muttered an expletive that Jared echoed. The two Weres looked at each other for a split second before both of them leaped from the car.

Riley whispered a curse of her own. They had been expecting this to happen eventually, but she had hoped it wouldn't be this soon.

The time for a showdown with the vampires had arrived.

Derek lifted his head and turned. With a glance to the window above his desk at the precinct, he growled low in his throat and tossed the file he'd been holding to the detective stationed next to him. "Emergency. Have to go."

"Backup?" the detective called after him, and Derek nodded to the Were.

He ran faster than he had ever run before, and without a thought for the pedestrians on the sidewalk. His car was too far away to reach when his deep connection to Riley told him she was in trouble.

The route Dale took to get Riley out of the city was planned in advance and changed daily. Vampires and their spies must have staked out each street that led out of town, waiting for the chance to score points with their Prime. Their damnably elusive queen.

It wasn't yet dark. The sky was a dusky shade of navy blue mixed with the purple haze of a cloudy sunset, so if vampires were out already, something had changed. *What?*

A cruiser turned the corner at 5th Street. The cop driving it must have seen him running. Derek waved as if to say "I've got this, thanks anyway," and hustled to the next light, where a second police unit trailed the path he was taking. This cop was okay, and knew what to expect as much as any of the Weres on the force did.

Calling Dale would have taken up time he didn't have. Streets here were in the open and in full view of anyone and everyone that might have been out at this hour. The plan had been to purposely avoid the darker places and potentially troublesome alleys that had become vamp dens and playgrounds, hoping to avoid this kind of attack.

When Derek saw the SUV, his heart skidded. Two vamps, wearing hoods and clothing that fully covered them up so they wouldn't burn to a crisp in what was left of the lingering daylight, were jumping on and off the hood of the car. Dale and Jared were fist-fighting with the bastards each time they hit the ground.

He couldn't see Riley, but she had to be in the car.

Derek's pulse amped up in seconds. He had made it here in time to help. His pack mates were fighting maniacally, as fiercely as if they had some devil in them. That same devilishness overtook Derek as he joined the fray.

Without a full moon overhead, and minus the claws and extra bulk these guys would otherwise have had, Dale and Jared were holding their own. Derek channeled his inner wolf without shape-shifting on the street, and fed off its extra strength. Fueled by adrenaline, his muscles geared up to do some damage to the suckers that would dare to confront either his friends or his mate in the open like this.

He hurled himself at one of the attackers, swinging his right fist while drawing his gun from his belt with his other hand. The chambers held two silver rounds, one for each of these monsters if there was a clear shot.

Luckily for everybody, the street was relatively quiet at the moment, though it wouldn't be for long. He didn't dare shape-shift here, though, where he might be seen. To any onlookers, this fight would look more like a tussle between the police and a street gang than a species war.

He yanked a bloodsucker off Jared and tossed the bag of bones sideways. The vampire hit the side of the SUV and bounded back as if its body was made of rubber. Dale had swung the other vampire away from the car so it wouldn't get a glimpse or a whiff of Riley.

Derek moved in to help without pausing to look through the window at the female he'd come to love more than life itself, hoping Riley would stay in the car.

He managed to get the hood off one vampire as Jared gave it a shove. Though there wasn't much light to speak of, the creature whined and scratched at its face with long, yellow-tipped fingernails. Then it slipped from Derek's hold and faded away from the scene like a ghostly specter.

Dale wasn't faring quite so well. Since chasing after the other vampire wasn't in the cards at the moment, Derek and Jared rushed in to provide him with backup.

Derek managed to get the stake from his boot as his packmates bent the vampire over the warm hood of the SUV. Red-rimmed eyes stared blankly at all three Weres. The creature was surrounded by beings hyped up with adrenaline-pumped testosterone. Werewolves with a grudge.

Unable to extricate itself from their grip, the vampire

snarled, writhed and kicked out with booted feet. But it was going nowhere, and had realized that. In an attempt to take one last bite, the vampire snapped its sharp fangs and hissed like a cornered snake.

"She's not yours to mess with," Derek snarled as Jared took the stake from his hand, looked to make sure the sidewalk was clear of pedestrians and drove the sharp end into the bloodsucker's chest.

Dark eyes looked directly at Derek in surprise before the vampire's body exploded. But by then, Derek had sensed a new problem. His neck chilled up as he pressed his face to the glass of the SUV's window. His heart, which had beat so strongly and so surely seconds before, seemed to stop when he saw that sometime during the fight with the two vampires, Riley had escaped from the car.

Riley had long since realized that the monsters would never stop attacking and never stop trying to harm the Weres she owed so much to for making her see the light. She owed them for giving her mother back to her, not as a madwoman, but as a caged Lycan with no hope of escape from the cell that had held her prisoner. And she owed them for helping to explain why her father had never remarried or spent much time at home. It was all about secrets, she now understood.

She felt her mother's spirit with her now, as well as that other, more parasitic thing that might be clinging to her like a black internal fog. There was only one way to solve this problem, one way to end this ongoing struggle for the dominance of Seattle's supernatural underworld. She was the key and had to be brave now, no matter what came next.

She walked swiftly down the street without bothering to use the sidewalk. People were coming out of their businesses to see what was going on, and that was okay, since the Were cops would take care of the mess before anyone got close enough to see what was really taking place.

Where there was one vampire, there were always more, Derek had warned, and the dusky sky was rapidly disappearing. Minutes from now, darkness would fall. If waylaying the SUV had been meant as a trap, she could expect to see more bloodsuckers anytime now.

Riley didn't feel so brave after she had left the Weres behind. She slowed her pace to look back. The SUV was parked at the curb and there were no longer any Weres in sight.

She sent her senses outward to locate the place she sought and the vampires that would be occupying it, chanting to herself over and over, *There's no stopping now, and no room for tripping up.*

Mistakes meant death. And yet Derek had also told her that no werewolf could share the kind of afterlife vampires inflicted on human beings, so there was a possibility she would survive this ordeal.

Too many nasty fang bites could eventually kill a werewolf, Derek had also told her, but since no Were could return as one of the opposing side, that much was in her favor, Riley supposed.

She reached the first block, where narrow alleyways were tucked between buildings. Her pulse sped. Her throat went dry. Two blocks from here was where she had been attacked by that drunken creep. Derek and his pack knew about this area and had been avoiding it when she rode along with them to and from the city proper.

This is where I met you, Derek...

And this is where I was kissed by fate.

An awareness of an Other slowed her pace. The air was tainted by a new scent that was more than smelly garbage cans and discarded detritus. She felt a squeezing sensation in her chest that wasn't a sign of a heart attack, but was her new detection system at work. Newly developed senses were warning her of danger, and that's exactly what Riley had been waiting for.

She stopped to allow people to pass her by, remembering what had happened the last time she visited the area. Vampires had been waiting to snatch unsuspecting souls, and she had made her first and only kill, with Derek's carved wooden stake. Tonight, all she had were her wits, her inner wolf and a parasitic soul that had once belonged to someone else.

Exterior lights were coming on to illuminate the sidewalk beside her. Riley fine-tuned her sight by staring into the darker spaces and allowing her eyes to adjust. But it was the smell, the directness of the odor that hit her, that brought the first wave of chills. Trussed up in that odor was a hint of vampire. Besides that awareness, there was another surprising addition. Wolf.

The blackness in the alley across from Riley started to fill with supernatural beings. She sucked in a breath in an attempt to sense the shape and the species of the creatures, processing the input her body was giving her with a shudder.

There couldn't be Weres here. She had left them behind. So why did the place smell as if there were more of them? The area reeked with the scent of over-the-top wolf pheromones that she was now used to, only this odor was stronger. It was an angry scent. An animal scent.

Something moved in the shadows.

Riley stayed motionless. When nothing emerged from that alley after a minute had passed, she called out, "Come out and face me. Isn't that what you wanted?"

She heard the sound of moving feet and something

sharp scraping the brick. Her heart twisted as she waited to see what would answer her taunt.

When that creature showed up, Riley leaned a shoulder against the wall to keep from falling down.

Chapter 36

Derek was hot on Riley's trail five heartbeats after discovering her missing. He had an idea where she might be headed, and the dread that filled him was gut-wrenching.

His packmates fell in behind him, leaving the cop in the cruiser to placate the neighbors and pick up the slack from the street fight. Derek had a notion that Dale and Jared might have felt as sick as he did if they'd known what Riley was up to. If Damaris actually was to show up when Riley was alone, the situation would become dire.

He didn't want to face that vampire. This was the one thing he had tried to dissuade Riley from doing, obviously with no success. More time was needed to acquaint Riley with her wolf side.

They sprinted after Riley, able to smell the darkness gathering ahead. No one spoke. Their energy was concentrated, focused. Derek didn't want to believe the two vamps that had attacked the SUV had been a setup, and yet he couldn't rule that out. He had to consider that if the vamp queen was so damn good at predicting outcomes, she might have fostered this one by luring Riley to her with a game of bait and switch.

He wanted to kill Damaris with his bare hands, though that couldn't happen. She had died so long ago Damaris might not recall her real death, only what had happened afterward. The sad part, if there was one, was how she still sought that old, abandoned soul of hers to this day.

As he turned the corner, Derek saw Riley push off the alley wall. He watched her take a step forward with both of her arms and hands outstretched, as if to keep whatever she was looking at from reaching the street.

"Don't," he shouted to her. "Do not go in there."

But it was too late to stop her, so the best he could do was to fly into that darkness with her, with his eyes wide open and both his gun and the wooden stake clenched in his fists.

Shock rippled through Riley as she entered a darkness that siphoned the rest of the air from her lungs. Her senses hadn't played tricks. There were werewolves here, the likes of which she hadn't yet seen in Derek's pack. One step toward the big Were that had come to greet her was all it took for her courage to flounder.

He was the biggest Were she had seen: well over six foot five. Long brown hair draped over his bare shoulders. His pants were tight enough for her to view his outrageous musculature. He wore a black T-shirt and short black gloves with metal spikes attached to each fingertip that mimicked the claws he couldn't possess without the moon. Riley thanked her lucky stars there was no full moon tonight to make this Were even more terrifying.

When Derek and his packmates slid in behind her,

she felt the surprise that rippled through them as well. *"Rogue,"* Riley thought she heard Derek say, so this had to be an example of one of the bad guys Derek had mentioned—a rogue werewolf with a mean streak who had chosen the wrong side to champion and ignored the laws governing his kind. However, his scent didn't quite mask the other, far more potent odor that pervaded the space.

"Vampire," she muttered.

That wasn't the worst part, Riley soon discovered as two more unsavory Weres like the one in front of her strode into view.

Derek pulled Riley back and addressed the three giants coming toward them. "You'd help an enemy? A vampire?"

Their closeness brought a new revelation that shut him up after that. None of these rogues could have answered him. Their lips had been sewn shut with black leather laces that left them looking like wolfish versions of Frankenstein's monster.

Menacing growls rumbled in their throats, unable to escape. Their metal-tipped gloves clacked lethally as they opened and closed their hands. Derek didn't see any way to get out of this, and inwardly vowed to fight to the death any of these guys that laid a hand on Riley.

He widened his stance, stuffed the stake in his belt and waved the gun. Dale was already aiming his weapon at the rogue wolves that had crossed over to the dark side. Jared growled, but carried no loaded weapon. Jared wasn't a cop, though he should have been one.

It was going to be three males against three in another minute. The air was already charged with anxiety and trepidation, but a sudden shift in the atmosphere made the rogues hesitant to move.

Derek felt this new presence before he saw what it was.

The sensation that flooded his system was icy. Wave after wave of chills cascaded over him as he kept the gun aimed at one of the rogues.

Shadows parted as if this new presence controlled them. And perhaps she did. Seattle's vampire queen had arrived, gliding into the meager pools of light from the street like a phantom.

Black-haired, black-eyed and terrifyingly beautiful in her agelessness, with skin like white velvet and a rail-thin body draped in black silk, Damaris at last showed her face.

Her intelligent, curious, treacherous, dark-eyed gaze landed on Riley. She had a voice that was like listening to someone speak from the bottom of a well. "I believe you have something that belongs to me, wolf."

That voice alone could have scared off half of Seattle's population. Derek remembered hearing it before, many days ago, in an alley like this one.

Damaris's image wavered in and out of focus as if she also controlled how corporeal she could become. The harder Derek looked, the filmier she appeared, until he had to watch this abomination only through the corner of his left eye to be able to see her.

In Riley's place, he said, "That soul is no longer yours to command."

Riley also had found her voice. "I'll give it up gladly if you can tell me how to do that."

Damaris's gaze intensified. Derek couldn't take his attention off her in order to look at Riley. He didn't dare lose track of a vampire that had mastered the art of speed well enough to have evaded them all for so long, and for whom one move of her little finger could bring a horde of vampires to her side.

Damaris shook her head when her Were henchmen took

a few steps toward Riley, and they stopped advancing, as if she had hit them with a spell.

"There is only one way I know of to take that soul from you, little wolf," Damaris said to Riley.

"Would that be to kill me?" Riley asked with steel in her tone.

"How else can a soul take flight?" Damaris replied.

"Yes, well, the problem with that is that I'm not ready to die," Riley said.

"I suppose we can't all get our way," Damaris returned.

"Exactly. So unless you have an alternative, I guess that soul you lost and now want back so badly will have to remain in the body of a werewolf."

Damaris's eyes flashed a demonic shade of red, but she modulated her verbal response to sound as calm as the exterior she presented. Her form was more solid now. Her black silk dress rustled as if the wind had given her a caressing stroke. But there was no breeze in the alley.

Derek didn't know much about Damaris's background or history. He hadn't been told how she became a vampire, and what she could possibly get out of remaining near the soul she had lost in the days that could well have been when knights lived in castles.

That's how he imagined her now—climbing the stone staircase of a castle in her black silk dress, with her ebony hair trailing behind her and fanged monsters bowing at her feet.

Hell...

Derek shook his head to dislodge that image. He was sure Damaris had slipped it into his mind as a further distraction. It might even have been her version of a way to solicit sympathy.

He refocused.

"Why do you want it so badly?" Riley asked the vamp queen.

Derek took Damaris's silence as a warning sign that the calm was about to end. He slowly moved the aim of his gun from the big Were's chest to Damaris's.

Riley went on. "If you can't have that soul back, why bother chasing after it? What good does it do you?"

She was asking the questions they all wanted answers to. But the rustling sound was back, though Damaris hadn't moved.

The odd thing about this meeting was that Derek sensed no other vampires in the area. Maybe their black-hearted queen didn't trust her nestlings to let her take her time toying with the enemy. It also could have been possible that Damaris didn't need help of any kind to get what she wanted, and was confident about the power she possessed.

That thought, out of all the others, made Derek's blood run cold. He could easily sense the power Damaris projected, and didn't like it one bit.

"I should keep the soul until you can give me a better option for passing it along to someone else," Riley said, as the rustling sounds grew louder. "Humans are so easy to kill, though, if you don't care for the person who gets it."

"Perhaps I'll take it from you now," Damaris returned with mounting venom in her tone.

"You can try," Riley said. "But I'm warning you, vampire, that I've been told I'm no ordinary werewolf so often that I'm starting to believe it."

Derek hadn't seen Damaris move and yet she now stood close enough to Riley to breathe in Riley's face. He inched toward them, proud that Riley was standing her ground instead of retreating from the seriousness of the threat in front of her...though he wanted her to run. He wanted her to survive this meeting and to be free of the burden she carried. He had to see to that outcome in spite of the odds.

So he fired at the black mass, guessing the bullet would miss its mark and daring Damaris to turn her attention his way.

Suddenly, she was in front of him with her hand on the barrel of his weapon and an expression of anger on her thin face. Derek wrenched the gun away, but by then, Damaris, living up to her reputation, had moved again.

The rogue Weres crowded in to protect a creature that needed no protection, expressing their displeasure with grunts and groans. Dale lunged forward and fired a shot that struck one of the rogue Weres in the chest. He back-pedaled and hit the wall. No one took the time to see how much damage had been done, because all eyes were on Riley.

Damaris was floating through the shadows like a nasty dark cloud to hover in front of Riley in a second confrontation that again brought them nearly nose-to-nose. Wolf and vampire. The new Lycan versus a centuries-old queen of the undead.

Derek couldn't see any good outcome in this. Leaving the remaining rogues to his partners, he rushed forward, slowing only when Riley raised a hand.

"I don't want your leftovers," Riley said to Damaris. "Neither do I want any other innocent person to die by your hand for harboring something they don't even know about."

"You think I kill them?" Damaris countered. "And that I'd have reason to do that?"

Derek felt Riley's new strength begin to waver, and tried to bolster her by slipping closer.

"The rumors aren't true?" Riley asked. "You think I'd believe that lie?"

"So many of them aren't true," Damaris replied. "Including that one."

"And yet you're willing to kill me," Riley said.

"No part of me can belong to my old enemies. My soul cannot exist in the body of a wolf."

Derek supposed she could just as easily have been lying as telling the truth. Still, he began to have more insight into the problem.

He had been right in thinking that Damaris couldn't stay close to that soul if it resided in one of her enemies. She wanted to be near to it, watch over it, for reasons only Damaris knew. Maybe she longed for it, missed it. Maybe she regretted having given it up to become what she was today. As intelligent as she seemed to be, Damaris couldn't possibly imagine that she could ever have that soul back, so what was the next best thing?

What did that soul she no longer had the option to possess give her in return for her vigilance?

Another shot was fired behind him. Derek heard something heavy hit the ground, and he didn't turn around. He was entranced by the conversation between the two females in this alley, as well as the fact that Damaris had not yet gone in for the kill when Riley was less than six inches away.

"Tell me how to give it up," Riley said. "Make us a deal we can't refuse."

Damn it. No... Derek wanted to shout. This was a monster, and monsters didn't make deals. This was, in fact, the greatest monster of them all. No kind of deal existed that could justify her bloodsuckers being allowed to run amok in this city, or for her to have Riley.

When Damaris leaned closer to Riley, Derek managed to wedge his body between them. Damaris's anger was like an ice bath. Her dark eyes glared. But she did not go for his throat. She merely turned her head, as if to acknowledge the presence of a newcomer.

Derek heard a familiar voice cut through the dappled light.

"I'll take that soul, wolf, on my queen's behalf."

Chapter 37

Riley pressed herself to Derek as Damaris reacted to the voice that filled the alley with a swift turn that again left Seattle's vampire queen as misty and ill-defined as if the rawness of her anger had vaporized her.

Two more shots were fired. Riley heard Dale shout something, but for her, the moment seemed to stretch out in a kind of slow motion.

She heard Derek ask, "You again?" which led Riley to believe he had met this newcomer before. All she could concentrate on now was the fact that Damaris's talent for manipulating senses had robbed the good guys of a true target.

The new presence also carried the foul odor of a vampire. Riley tried to find it among the shadows as Damaris, moving like a black mist, cut through the alley to confront the vampire that had spoken in her stead.

The black-clothed, black-haired Prime now hovered beside a white-faced vampire in a black coat. If Derek had been right about vampires crawling up from the grave, this one had died in his fifties, with stringy hair and a lined face.

It was the vampire that had been watching her home.

The creature didn't cringe when Damaris faced it. Nor did it turn away. It didn't seem to be afraid of anyone in the alley, including the powerful Prime.

Something new was going on, overshadowing Damaris's mission to extract an old and unusable soul from the she-wolf she'd been stalking. Riley knew it, and so did Derek.

Sensing movement from behind her, Riley jumped to her left and was joined by Derek. The rogues were on the move, only they weren't heading for her, Derek or his packmates. The two big Weres were barreling toward Damaris as if protecting her hadn't been their goal, and they had come to fight her.

Derek muttered under his breath as he again placed himself in front of Riley like a human shield. However, no one was coming after her. Everyone's focus had shifted to Damaris.

"It's a coup," Derek said, and she tried to follow that thought to a logical conclusion.

"This was planned," Derek added.

Riley struggled harder to understand what Derek was suggesting. The rogue Weres had been brought here to help take down Damaris, and not anyone else who showed up? That's why they hadn't attacked?

If that was true, then the old vampire now facing Damaris might have been part of that plan.

The moonlight winked out, as if someone had hit a switch, and the alley was thrown into darkness. Riley felt the roughness of the wall behind her and expelled a breath when Derek jumped back.

She heard scuffling noises and a series of grunts before becoming aware of more heavy breathing beside her. The familiar scents of both Dale and Jared filled her with an odd kind of hope. She was alive. Derek was alive, and so were their friends. So far.

A harrowing, keening cry went up that sent her pulse soaring. Something wet splashed her face. Derek swore again and handed her the wooden stake. Then he, too, was gone, and Dale and Jared after him.

She was alone in the midst of a fight scene that was going on without her. She was supposed to be the grand prize. Maybe the white-faced vampire had lured Damaris here by dangling her old soul in front of her.

Derek had said this was a coup …

Sudden insight struck Riley as the events began to take shape in her mind. The white-faced vampire wanted to be Seattle's next Prime and was attempting to wrestle the title from the most powerful vampire Derek had ever heard of.

It seemed to Riley, as she stood there gripping the wooden stake, that Damaris must have won all of her battles in the past, because the vamp queen was lethally formidable.

More shots were fired. The growls Riley heard were exaggerated. Moonlight reappeared for a few seconds before the darkness returned again. Still, there had been enough light for Riley to view the scene.

Dale was crouched on one knee, taking aim at the last rogue Were standing. The two other rogues were lumps on the ground.

"So much for the muscle," Riley whispered as she pushed herself off the wall.

She didn't get far before her attention was drawn to Derek's voice, echoing from near the end of the alley. Though she could barely make him out, her eyes were beginning to adjust to the dark.

He was fighting the old vampire. Derek had taken on the black-coated bloodsucker by himself. So where the hell was Damaris, and why would Derek help her by ridding this alley of the vampire that was attempting to take her place?

Anger flared inside her as Riley left the temporary safety of the wall. Something flew past her that nearly knocked her back. Though it might have been a stray bullet, she was determined to get this over with, once and for all.

A strong hand stopped her from executing her plan. The icy grip on her arm instantly chilled her to the bone. A cold breath whispered in her ear, "They are fools to imagine I can't see what motivates them, and plan for that."

Shit...

The fox hadn't been outfoxed at all. And all of this, every last move, had been predicted by the one vampire able to do it.

Everything fell into place in Riley's mind. The old vampire had expected to lure Damaris here for the sake of the soul she coveted. That vampire had instigated a coup. Had tried to. And Damaris, queen for more reasons than merely being older and wiser, had seen it all, and had been prepared.

"Congratulations," Riley said as those icy fingers scraped the hair away from the back of her neck. "You deserve the crown."

Numbness followed each touch of Damaris's chilled fingers. Riley shook, wondering when the bite would come to kill the wolf and steal the soul that had been hidden inside her.

Her grip on the weapon in her hand made her hand quake. Instead of speeding up, her pulse slowed down as she anticipated Damaris's final move. But this wasn't over yet, Riley's body told her. A tiny spark had ignited inside her, and that spark became a flare, then a heated lick of flame that seeped outward through her pores to counteract the numbness and the cold Damaris had caused.

The next whisper she heard was a combination of anger and surprise. In those few seconds of reprieve from the cold that had been about to overtake her, Riley whirled, raised the stake Derek had tucked into her hand, and brought it down hard.

It was no surprise that Damaris had anticipated that, too, and dodged the blow that could have, and should have, put an end to her.

Seattle's vampire queen reappeared by Riley's side—a ghostly apparition wearing a cruel smile, caught in another sudden ribbon of moonlight. Black eyes found Riley's. Pale fingers wiped away the wetness on Riley's face with a gesture that was obscenely intimate.

With another flare of heat-backed courage, Riley spoke. "I told the truth. I don't want that soul, even if keeping it would mean you'd lose the closeness to it."

Moonlight reappeared long enough for Riley to see the black eyes flash with an emotion that was unreadable. She went on as if she still had time for conversation.

"You told me you don't kill the people who house it. Is that true?"

"Why would I lie?" the voice of darkness replied.

The swish of Damaris's silk sleeve seemed out of place amid the chaos. The sounds of fighting hadn't ceased, though Riley had the sensation of being far removed from the battle, and in another space altogether.

"Then why am I still alive?" she asked, withholding another shiver as the vampire touched her hair. "I've been in Seattle for a while without realizing my heritage. You've had plenty of time to confront me."

Getting Damaris to answer that question would be a long shot. But she did.

"It was when you came into your heritage that things got tripped up," the vampire said. "Until then, I merely kept watch."

"It was you who placed that heritage in my lap by sending your vampires after me. Your vampires drove me into the arms of a Were."

"Not my plan," Damaris said. "His."

Riley didn't turn her head to look for the old vampire Derek had been fighting. "So, what now?"

"You must give it up. You are a wolf, an enemy, and can no longer sustain that soul. Nor can any usurper be allowed to control me through it."

Cold lips rested on Riley's face, next to her right ear. *This is it. The bite will come now*, her mind warned.

"It was a beautiful thing once," Damaris said. "Never pure, you understand, and yet it was mine to keep or share as I saw fit."

The bite had to come.

Damaris was toying with her.

"Nevertheless, I gave it up for love," the vampire continued.

Riley felt the tiny scratch of Damaris's fangs across her ear, and was determined not to faint.

"Which is what you must do, wolf," the vampire said. "Give it up for love."

The sting of those fangs sliding toward her neck made Riley's fingers curl. That's when she remembered the stake that was still clutched in her hand.

"If you believe that other vampire would be better in my

place, you know nothing," Damaris said. "Blood will run on every street if I lose control. Rivers of it. There will be no reprieve from the horror those vampires will inflict."

"Yes, well, we can't see anyone getting the better of you, can we?" Riley dared to say. "So I doubt if that will happen. And I didn't have to give up my soul for the man I love. I only had to be willing to share it."

She didn't know how she could have moved when faced with such terror, but Riley pressed the sharp edge of the stake against Damaris's side without using it.

Something the vampire had said rang true, and that was about the threat this other vampire posed to Seattle and its inhabitants. Damaris could have lied about that, of course, but Riley had a feeling this vampire queen had been telling the truth…though the thought of Damaris, who everyone believed was evil incarnate, actually being the lesser of two evils here was beyond the realm of imagination.

"I refuse to die," Riley said, straining to hear what was happening outside of her little chat with Damaris. "I've only recently started to live, you see."

She continued in a rush. "The deal is this—you and I both live. The wolf in me will push your old soul out once I'm fully indoctrinated into the clan, and someone else will have it. I can feel it trying to get out. I don't want to keep it from you, and have no ulterior motive to do so. Until then, there has to be a way to end this. A truce."

A breath was necessary to get out the rest. "Take care of your bloodsucker problem and we can see this through. See if I'm right. Otherwise…"

Her voice faltered. She didn't have any threat that could top the closeness of Damaris's razor-sharp fangs.

Riley started over. "Call off your dogs. Help my pack here, and in return, I'll help you."

She pressed the stake into the black silk without causing

a tear in the fabric, hoping that if Damaris was as smart as Derek said she was, the vampire would see the promise in the deal Riley had offered.

There was always the future, another alley and lots of dark, moonless nights if things didn't work out as planned. The vampires would keep killing. And Damaris wasn't really losing anything in postponing the use of those damn fangs.

The fangs moved again. Riley felt another brief sting as Damaris said, "You will owe me, wolf, if I agree."

"If I die here, that soul might die with me. My wolf might see that it never gets loose again."

As Riley saw it, time was up for negotiating with a vampire that actually had nothing to lose. She closed her eyes, willed herself to stillness and searched for the spark she knew was waiting for her.

That spark burst into bright flame that spread through her before Riley's next breath. She tore at her clothes, had a sensation of falling through space. Every part of her, from the roots of her hair to her toes, hurt with excruciating pain as her body convulsed.

The wooden stake made a hollow sound as it hit the ground. She no longer had the hands with which to wield it.

As Riley looked out from her new wolf eyes, and up at the vampire queen from her position on four legs, the thing she saw standing behind Damaris was what stole her next breath.

Chapter 38

Derek roared with anger over Damaris's closeness to Riley. He spun away from the cunning old vampire that had helped to set all of this in motion, and left the bloodsucker to his packmates.

He changed shape midstride as he sprinted toward Riley, letting his wolf out without worrying what Riley might think of this neat trick he hadn't shared with her. There was no moon to speak of, certainly no full moon, but it was going to take a fully wolfed-up Lycan to get that damn vampire queen away from the love of his life. And he was that wolf.

Riley shape-shifted as he closed in. Her gold eyes glowed in the thin beam of moonlight that swept over the alley. She had crouched, as if getting ready to spring at the vampire that had taunted her, and he couldn't allow her to make contact. Her crouch deepened when she saw him like this, and she issued a bark of surprise.

Damaris wheeled when his claws caught in her skirt, her dark eyes alight with anger. Derek didn't wait for the vampire to react. Before she could fade, disintegrate, or whatever the hell she was capable of doing to rapidly move from one place to another, he wound his claws into her hair and yanked her head back so that he could growl in her ear.

"Never touch what's mine."

Damaris's fangs were slender and needle-sharp as she turned to snap at him. In his current form, his canines also were lethal. With his tight grip on her hair, not even a vampire queen like this one could escape his wrath.

In seconds, his teeth were on Damaris's neck in what Derek assumed had to be a complete turnaround from her usual routine. Still, she was rumored to be the strongest of her kind for a reason, and she managed to slip from his grasp, leaving him with nothing but a fistful of her long black hair.

Oh, no you don't...

Again, he caught her silk skirt as she moved toward Riley, and he reeled Damaris back. Without a gun or a wooden stake, his hands and jaws would have to strike the necessary blow.

Damaris spun around fast and went for his throat, fangs gleaming. He held her off with the brute strength inherent in most full-blooded Lycans. She might have been angry, but his was the greater need to protect his own.

When Damaris began to fade away, Derek shook her hard enough to bring her back. She might have planned for that, too. Her fangs grazed his shoulder, cutting deep without doing any real damage. Lycans were far more resilient than most Weres. The wound had already begun to mend when he roared again, letting out more of his anger.

Her fangs skidded across his right cheek as she flexed her jaw. Even angrier now, he shoved Damaris to the wall behind them. As she righted herself, Derek pressed in for that last bite, thinking how ironic it was that a pair of sharp teeth was going to end this vampire's long existence.

He didn't take that bite, however, hesitating when a fresh streak of pain tore through the skin of his left thigh. Hell…had another vampire shown up?

Not a vampire…

Riley.

He hadn't hesitated long, and yet it was long enough for Damaris to move. She didn't go for him or retaliate for the rough and almost fatal treatment he had showed her. Instead, Damaris flew across the alley, pushed Dale and Jared from their battle with her pasty-faced adversary, as if both big Weres weighed nothing…and in less than five seconds, snapped the old vampire's neck.

The explosion followed. Gray ash rained down. And every Were in this damn alley, including Derek, stood there, gaping.

Riley wasn't sure if she had just doomed Seattle to an even darker fate or not. She remembered what Damaris had said.

If you believe that other vampire would be better in my place, you know nothing. Blood will run on every street if I lose control. Rivers of it. There will be no reprieve from the horror vampires will inflict.

Had that been a lie? Was it true that Damaris as queen kept vampire activity to a minimum?

She supposed they were going to find out.

A gloriously scary werewolf stood between her and the vampire queen that had effortlessly sent the traitor in her midst to a more appropriate afterlife. With that show of superior skill, strength and speed, every being here realized Damaris could have just as easily killed them all if she had wanted to…except maybe for Derek, who remained in his frightening new shape.

Gathering her courage while steadying herself on her four legs, Riley stood at Derek's side. After one brief glance up at him, she waited for Damaris's next move, hoping it wouldn't be to lunge toward the two Were males nearby.

When Damaris spoke, Riley held her breath.

"You can do it?" Damaris asked with her dark eyes on Riley. "Set the soul free? Use the wolf to do so?"

Riley hadn't exactly expected a thank-you for possibly saving Damaris from Derek, but these questions were unexpected, too. There was no way to answer, though, without human vocal cords, and Riley wasn't sure of anything, other than having just completed her second shape-shift.

She hadn't known that vampires and werewolves existed, and that she was part of the breed. She hadn't realized her mother and father had possessed so many secrets of their own that they hadn't shared, or that Derek did, too. Would foreknowledge of those things have changed this moment? Would it have sent her in another direction that might have kept her from meeting Derek and his pack?

She had nipped at Derek to stop him from killing Damaris, taking a chance that Damaris was right. She waited to find out if the vampire queen would accept the offer she'd been given.

Derek's claws stroked her fur. He was wary and ready to spring at the vampire facing them. He had faced vampires regularly and probably recognized an ill-gotten lull in the fighting that had taken place tonight.

Damaris, cunning, intelligent, might see Riley's hesitancy now in Riley not immediately responding to her questions.

Weres used telepathic channels to communicate, Derek

had told her, but Derek's voice was also out of commission at the moment. So Riley spoke to Dale. *"Tell her I can't be sure. I can only promise that I will try to stand by what I said I would do. I want this as much as she does. Maybe more."*

Dale, with his eyes on Damaris and his finger on the trigger of the gun in his hand, repeated her message, out loud.

Damaris's dark eyes seemed to penetrate Riley's new disguise and see into the mind of the woman beneath the fur. Then, without another word, the vampire faded into her filmier form and wafted away on a nonexistent breeze.

Derek took hold of Riley's fur. He pulled her around to look into her wolfish face and sent a message of his own. *"What did you do?"*

"I made a deal with the devil," Riley messaged back.

"About that damn soul of hers?"

"That, and to keep more humans from being harmed."

Derek paused to consider what Riley had said. He couldn't really argue with her approach, seeing how Damaris had not only rid the streets of one bad actor belonging to her nest, but had also left every Were here alive and without major injuries.

Riley had stopped the fight, maybe only for tonight, and yet who was to say? The damn Blood Knight that had faced Damaris in the past had also let her go. Either everyone had gone insane, had been bewitched by that vamp queen, or they saw something in Damaris that he didn't.

Eventually he'd find out the truth. But tonight his sole focus was on Riley.

Dale broke the tense silence. Covered in ash, he wiped off his shoulders and pointed to the ground where the shredded remains of Derek's clothes sat in a pile.

"We'll have to do something about that, boss," Dale said, taking in the extent of Derek's physical changes and how Riley was standing on her hind legs with her front paws carving fine red lines on Derek's chest.

"Unless you also can fly, looking like this will scare the pants off everyone on the street," Dale continued. "Because hell, you're scaring me."

Derek glanced down at himself, then into Riley's golden eyes. He saw no fear in those eyes. Riley Price had always been adventurous. She was the daughter of a Lycan cop and his Lycan wife. Could she accept his new semblance, the one that few had known about?

"It's all about secrets," he messaged to her, repeating a former sentiment. *"Too damn many of them."*

He added, alluding to the grooves she was accidentally making on his chest, *"And just so you know, that hurts."*

Riley growled and failed to move. Derek growled back with a force that ruffled her fur. Acceptance was a rare side effect of love. That whole love-is-blind thing was going on here, big-time.

He loved Riley with every patch of fur and every over-stretched muscle currently covering his bones. And he planned to love her forever. Lycan love. Unrelenting and unstoppable.

What a pair they were. Two werewolves coded with different genetics, but Lycans all the same. The merging of their bloodlines would carry their rareness forward. Their offspring, if they were blessed to have some, would protect Seattle, just as their parents did, and his parents had done before him. Derek couldn't wait to get to that part.

Damaris was still out there, and real trouble had merely been postponed. Yet everyone here would live to fight another day. That was something. For now, it had to be enough.

As a wolf, Riley wasn't as delicate as she was as a human. She was actually quite menacing. Lucky for him, she didn't get that yet, and was relatively tame at the moment.

Now that those after-fight impulses were on him, Derek wanted her more than he ever had. The brightness of Riley's golden eyes told him she felt the same. They just had to get to a place where they could safely downsize and get on with more of the physical culmination of their love. Doubly seal the deal. Become as one. Forge another link in the chains that already bound them together.

"Yes," she messaged to him, as if she had heard every word of those thoughts and seconded them. *"Let's get to that."*

"Derek," Dale said from the periphery. "Time to go. I'll grab some clothes for you and…"

Derek wasn't listening, didn't hear the rest of Dale's sensible remarks. Riley was on the move. People or no people out there beyond the alley, she was heading for the street like a streak of lightning, leaving a trail of lush, fragrant wolf pheromones in her wake and growling come-hithers to him every few strides.

"Hurry, werewolf. Catch me."

Swear to God, he had never been as happy as he was in this moment…

Give or take the next moment, when he'd catch up with her and get a start on that future.

* * * * *